"Now, Tom, do not be mad. You agreed I could speak with him in the garden. You even brought me Meredith's old dress from the attic."

Tom shook his head and leaned back against the stone facing away from the Keep. He had made his excuses to leave Aidan and Lady Elizabeth and make his way back to the garden as soon as polite to do so.

He bristled. "What I saw was no' talkin'. There were a lot more goin' on there than a few simple words."

Alyssa raised her chin and set her jaw. "Now you listen here, Tom Jeffreys." Her fists clenched and unclenched in her white linen shift. "It may not be what you wanted to see, but I have waited two hundred years for that man to return to me. If I want him to touch my face, touch my hair, or touch any other part of me, you will not be stopping him. Your family has been good to me, keeping my secret all these years. But can you not understand? This is the closest I have felt to really living since Gedrych burned me. Although I know what I feel for Aidan de Morgan is as doomed as my love for Cai, I will have what little happiness I can grasp, until he learns my identity and spurns me. I do not want to hurt you, Tom," she finished gently. "But I am more than capable, and you know it."

Praise

"It is always hard for an author to find a creative way to involve a ghost with the limitations of a spirit's body in the tantalizing, heated love scenes of a romance. Julie Darcy's method is smooth, superb, and original. I found myself so attached to the intriguing, fully fleshed-out characters of Alyssa and Aidan that I know they will haunt me for some time to come. *Whispers of Yesterday* is a page-turner from a familiar Gothic beginning, when an American Scientist braves a blinding thunderstorm on Halloween to reach a castle he unexpectedly inherited, to a surprising, thrilling, and joyful twist at the end. *Whispers of Yesterday* is an enchanting read that should not be missed. This one's a keeper.

Cornelia Amiri
~ Author and Reviewer

Whispers of Yesterday

by

Julie A. D'Arcy

This is a work of fiction. Names, characters, places, and incidents are either the product of the author's imagination or are used fictitiously, and any resemblance to actual persons living or dead, business establishments, events, or locales, is entirely coincidental.

Whispers of Yesterday

Contact Information: info@thewildrosepress.com

Cover Art by *Debbie Taylor*

The Wild Rose Press, Inc.
PO Box 708
Adams Basin, NY 14410-0708
Visit us at www.thewildrosepress.com

Publishing History
First Edition, 2024
Trade Paperback ISBN 978-1-5092-5285-5
Digital ISBN 978-1-5092-5286-2

Previously Published 2015 as A Whisper of Yesterday
Published in the United States of America

Dedication

This book is in memory of my beautiful mother,
Dorothy Joan Brauman who was a loving inspiration to all those who knew her.
Thanks, Mum for all your support through the years.
You will always live in my heart.

She is far from the land where her young hero sleeps,
And lovers around her are sighing:
But coldly she turns from their gaze, and weeps,
For her heart in his grave is lying.

—Thomas Moore

Chapter One

Death could not part them—

Rain slapped at the car like fingers of the dead as the old rental crept along a road not much more than a dirt track. The continuous thumping and crashing of the wipers pounded rhythmically into Cole's head with repetitious monotony. He could barely see twenty feet in front of him.

A damn idiot to be here in Cornwall in the dead of night. He was thirty-two years old, an American scientist, and not some fool kid hell-bent on a quest for a dream. But when the lawyer had rung him with news that he had inherited a castle in Cornwall, he could think of nothing more than hopping the first plane to England.

He swiped a hand across his tired eyes, struggling to see the dimly lit clock on the rental's dash. A quarter to twelve. He had left St. Agnes at ten thirty. It had taken him more than an hour to drive twenty-five miles. Old Fergus Dane, who owned the rental service and doubled as the owner of the local pub, had argued that the moors were no place for—how did he put it? A body at night. Especially on All Hallows Eve. The hair on his nape prickled, and he grimaced as he glanced out the window into stark blackness.

All Hallows Eve meant little to him, just a night when weirdoes gathered to celebrate a bygone folktale steeped in superstition. However, he believed nobody, living or dead, deserved to be out in *this*.

Two signposts loomed before him, and he stopped the car and switched off the engine, but still allowed the headlights to flood the signs. A crossroad. Two signs. One guiding him to Thornwood Castle, two miles, the other pointing to the next town, fifteen miles away. He'd met with several crossroads in his life of late. His decision to split with Janna, his ex- fiancée, had been the first. It was over anyway. Quitting his job had been the second. But hell, he'd wanted a clean break. Then the phone call had come, and he'd leapt at the chance to travel to England. Not that he intended to keep the castle. His home would always be in America. He hadn't even known he had relations on the other side of the ocean. Family history had never been one of his interests.

He twisted the key in the ignition and brought the engine to life, keeping to the road. He had come this far. He might as well go the rest of the way and see what fate held in store. Not that he believed in fate. A man's destiny lay in his own hands.

He could see no trees on the moors. No landmarks to break the repetitious blackness. No moon and no sound but the slashing of the wipers. He had long tired of the battle between himself and the ancient car radio with its continuous white noise static.

The old vehicle labored as it chugged up a steep hill, and again he strained to see the dashboard clock. Almost midnight and the weather not improved one iota.

Then, in the glow of the headlights, a pair of iron gates loomed. He slammed down his foot and brought the car to a screeching halt.

The barred gates supported by two gray stone

columns of at least six feet dominated the view only inches from the car grill. On the top of each column rested a stone statue of a crouched lion clutching a rose between its jaws.

His gaze shifted as a slight movement caught his eye, and there she stood. Deep emerald eyes stared into his. Her hands clutched tight to the bars of the gate, and dark red hair lay wet and bedraggled around her pale face and frail shoulders. Caught in the beam of the headlights, she was the loveliest creature he had ever seen.

Her long white shift, rendered almost transparent by the rain, accented the fine line of her body, and his heartbeat accelerated, causing his blood to race. He stared wide-eyed through the windscreen and slashing wipers. His mouth dried, and he tried to swallow, his head filled with a strange humming, and his vision blurred.

Time had no essence…

Alone on the moors, the sun shining, she smiled up at him, and he lowered her to the heather and came down over her. Their lips met, and her skin smelled of jasmine and roses. Her mouth tasted of pure honey, and his hand found her breast, firm yet soft, her nipple hardening beneath his thumb…

His eyes flew open. He hadn't known he'd closed them. He was back in his car. She was gone. He fumbled with the door, scrambled from the car into the pelting rain, and raced for the gates. "Hey, come back!" He grasped the wet bars and peered into the darkness. "Come back. Who are you? I won't—"

His words met with silence.

He called several more times. Then, realizing there would be no answer, struggled to open the gates. This proved a hindrance in itself, due to the thick weeds twisting around the bottom of the bars.

Eventually, tired and soaked to the skin, he managed to drag the gates wide enough for his car to enter. The old rental lurched forward. Its thick tires crunching on the white crushed stone of the ornamental drive. He didn’t know why he’d felt transported when he’d seen the girl, or why he thought he’d met her before. The very idea now seemed preposterous. Still, he was curious. Why had she appeared to be calling his name?

The rain eased, and he glimpsed patches of manicured lawn stretching away into the murky distance. The overgrown rose bushes clawed at the sides of the vehicle as it traveled the last part of the drive, and he passed through a stone archway beneath the gatehouse into a round courtyard. The blue stone castle appeared grander than he expected, and while it was hard to see plainly through the drizzling rain, he detected two turrets, one at each corner.

In the headlights, he noted five steps leading up to the keep. Ivy clung to the walls and half-covered a crumbling griffin perched at each corner of the lintel above the door. Such creatures were common in fourteenthcentury castles to ward off evil. He remembered that bit of trivia from his high school studies.

Dragging his coat from the back seat, although already soaked, he killed the headlights and, for an instant, until his eyes adjusted, darkness surrounded him. He stepped from the car, slammed the door, and picked his way carefully up the lichen-covered steps. Finding and using the steel doorknocker, he hammered three times and waited.

A shutter slammed above him, and he peered up through the rain at the closest turret. Suspecting the wind, he then realized none blew and jammed his hands into his trench coat pockets to cover his agitation, the rain finding every accessible opening in his jacket.

Suddenly a shiver washed down his back, which had nothing to do with the rain, and a strange mist rose up around him. It dissolved, and the rain stopped. In the doorway stood a man. Cole…but not Cole, dressed as a medieval gentleman, from wet, bedraggled plumed hat to waterlogged buckled shoes. The man smiled down into the eyes of a red-haired girl. Deep red curls spiraled down from her coiffure, and she wore a creation of gray satin and pearls. A torch set into the blue stone above the door hissed and spat, casting an eerie veil over the laughing couple. Then the vision cleared, and he stood alone as the door of Thornwood flew open.

Before him stood the most unlikely butler. A woman no more than five feet tall with blue dyed hair, a mauve cashmere sweater, and a long gray skirt smiled up at him with a curious glint in her dancing blue eyes. She held a four-pronged candelabrum with three spluttering candles, which she protected with the curve of her fingers. For several long moments, her gaze caught and held his, then her eyes widened, and she stepped back into the shadowy hallway. She ushered him inside. "Cole de Morgan, I presume?"

He nodded. "Sorry to arrive so late. I would have called, but—"

"We have no telephone," she finished. She studied his face in the candlelight, then gave a small smile. "Forgive me. I am Jeannie Jeffreys, guardian of this monolith." She offered her hand. "Sorry to keep you standing in the rain. Mary called me from the west wing. I wanted to open the door myself." She glanced away. "For all that I'd been told, I did not expect you to look so much like *him*, despite the newspaper photograph."

He frowned. "I don't understand." He wasn't sure what the old woman apologized for, and he didn't really care. He was wet, hungry, and tired and only wanted to rid himself of his saturated coat, fill his stomach, and see a comfortable bed. However, as he took a step along the hallway, he was struck by a great gush of warmth, and for the first time in many years, he had the uncanny feeling he was coming home.

He shook off the feeling as foolish and followed the woman as she ushered him down the slate hallway into a large foyer, then a room, which appeared to have once been a parlor. She switched on a brass lamp on the mantel above the burning fire, placed the candelabrum next to it, and blew out the candles, then she turned. "Come, young man. Sit by the fire and warm yourself. I'll have Mary fetch a plate and a cup of tea, or would you prefer coffee, being an American?"

He smiled as he shrugged off his coat and dropped it beside the hearth. "Tea is fine."

Jeannie tugged on a bell pull, and several minutes later, a young girl popped her head around the edge of the door. The older woman ordered the tea and a plate of sandwiches, and the girl disappeared back the way she had come.

Cole studied his surroundings. A large oriental rug in shades of blue and gold dominated a room decorated almost entirely in early nineteenth-century furniture. Dark oak paneling lined the walls, the same color as the polished floorboards. Everything about the room appeared familiar, as if he had seen it before. He put a hand to his aching temples, and again that feathery tingling trickled down his spine.

He moved to the carved marble fireplace and stood warming his hands. A large portrait covered with a blue velvet curtain hung on the wall above his head. He lifted his hand to take a peek when Jeannie spoke from behind him.

"I think you best sit down, young man." Jeannie's voice held no anger but brooked no argument.

His hand dropped to his side, and he spun to glance at the overstuffed pink-and-white-striped sofa and delicate Louis XIV chairs. "I'm soaked to the bone. I'll ruin your furniture."

"*Your* furniture, you mean. That is, if you meet the stipulation of the last owner's will."

He shrugged and took the chair nearest to the fire. "I thought I already had—met the stipulation, that is."

Jeannie remained expressionless. "Not entirely. What did Mr. Hardwright tell you?"

"I only spoke to him by phone. He said he would send me a copy of the will. There was no need to meet. He told me it was more important that I get here. That I had inherited a fourteenth-century castle in Cornwall from a distant relative, and to gain my inheritance, I must arrive on All Hallows Eve and spend the night."

Jeannie settled into the opposite chair. "Almost right, but you must spend one entire month, not only All Hallows Eve. Fool man, I knew I should have contacted you myself. Lawyers. My father always said they could not be trusted."

He laughed shortly. "He was right on that one." Janna and her lawyer had certainly done a number on him. He changed the subject. "I saw a girl tonight at the gate."

Jeannie paled. A shutter came down over her features. A soft knock broke the heavy silence that followed. Mary entered with sandwiches and tea, which she placed on a small wooden table inlaid with mother-of-pearl between the two chairs.

"That will be all tonight. Thank you, Mary."

"Goodnight, ma'am." Mary gave them a small bob and exited the room, and Jeannie leaned forward to pour the tea from a silver teapot.

"Milk and sugar?"

He nodded. "Both. Does she live far? It's a dirty night."

"Thank you for your concern, but she has a room in the North wing." She handed the fine bone china cup primly to Cole, and as she did so, she caught his eye. "Ah, this…girl you saw at the gate. What did she look like? The groundskeeper has a young daughter around ten. Perhaps it was her."

"I saw her for only a moment, however, this girl was definitely no ten-year-old. I would put her age at around nineteen to twenty. She had the deepest red hair, and the greenest eyes even in the dim headlights. She wore a long white shift, like an old-fashioned nightgown."

The color drained from Jeannie's face.

He leaned forward, about to touch her hand, but caught himself. "Do you know her?"

The old woman's hands shook, and her saucer rattled as she set down her cup. She hid her clenched hands in her skirt. "I know her, though I have not seen her for quite some years—forty-five, to be precise." She shook her head.

"I never thought she would come. She said she would, but..." Jeannie rose, walked to the mantel, and pulled the cord at the side of the painting. The blue velvet curtain rolled slowly to the side. "Is this the woman you saw?"

He came to his feet with a hitch in his breath. It was his mystery girl, but she was dressed as a lady from the eighteen hundreds and sat on a stone bench surrounded by red and white rose blossoms. "Who...what?" He frowned and flopped back into his chair, shaking his head. "What the hell is going on here? Who is she and why is she dressed like that?" But even as he spoke, he felt a deep foreboding that he wouldn't like the answer.

"The woman you are looking at, the woman you saw tonight, is Alyssa Llewellyn, born 1624 and burned as a witch in the year 1644 by Gedrych de Morgan."

His gaze locked with hers. "What are you saying? She is a ghost?"

She returned his stare. "You might say that, yes. But to me, she is the mistress of this house."

His jaw tightened. "I am a man of science. You expect me to believe this...this fantasy?" He rose and began to pace, then stopped. "I don't know what you are playing at—"

Jeannie slid him a stern look. "Sit down, Cole. May I call you Cole?"

He nodded and sank into his chair, running a hand through his hair.

"At my age, I am not in the habit of playing games. The matter is this castle has not had a proper owner for almost two centuries. In the late eighteen hundreds, it was left in the guardianship of the Jeffreys family with a small fortune to see it cared for. My father knew something about the stock market and invested wisely, transforming a small fortune into a large one. Should you agree to the terms of the will, you will be the beneficiary of almost three million pounds."

Cole, who had just taken a bite of a meat sandwich, coughed, almost losing it. "Sorry, can you repeat that?"

"A tenth of the money is to go to the caretaker of the house, which is myself, as is stated in the will. You are to inherit the rest. You can view a copy of the will if you wish."

Cole held up his hand. "No. I'm certain you deserve it. If I decide to remain, I will wish you to stay on. That is, *if* I remain."

Jeannie shook her head. "No. I am tired. And as much as I love the moors and this castle, I have a longing to see something of the world before I pass on. However, I promised I would stay until someone found you. And it was only through sheer luck you were found, that is. As the Jeffreys line is almost at an end. I am the last. If it were not for that article in the newspaper about you accepting some science award, and my old friend Josh Hardwright, I doubt you would be here now."

"Found me?" He leaned back in his chair. "I think there is a story here, and you better tell me what this is about. Are there no de Morgans this side of the ocean?"

"Other de Morgans, yes, but none that had a likeness to Cai de Morgan. And that was a stipulation of Aidan de Morgan's will."

Cole released a deep breath. "Aidan de Morgan? I don't understand any of this."

Jeannie sighed and shook her head. "Young people, they are so impatient." She rose and moved to a cabinet at the side of the room and picked up a small gilt-edged frame. Returning to her seat, she passed the painting across to him, and all the pieces fell into place, with him unfortunately as the key pawn in the game.

The frame held a miniature of a man with short dark hair and deep blue eyes that could well have been him in another lifetime. No wonder he'd been filled with *déjà vu.* Why he thought he knew the woman. Why the house seemed so familiar. Sweat broke out on his forehead, and he loosened the top button of his shirt to run his finger around his collar. If he had ever believed in reincarnation, it would probably be now. "So, who was Alyssa to Cai de Morgan? A wife, a sister, a mistress? And where exactly does Aidan de Morgan fit into this?"

Jeannie gave a soft laugh and raised her hand. "Perhaps this should wait until morning. It's after midnight. You must be exhausted."

"No." Cole leaned forward, and his voice held an edge. "I have never been so awake. And"—he glanced up at Alyssa's portrait— "I feel I have a right to know." He reached for another sandwich and munched on corned beef and relish as he moved to a more comfortable chair. "We have all night if you are up to the telling?"

The old woman eyed him with a glint in her sky-blue eyes. "Then tell you I shall, all of it. The story of Alyssa Llewellyn as she told it to me in the rose garden in the summer of fifty-five, with one stipulation."

"That being?"

"That you stay for the one month."

He nodded. "Done."

"Good." She picked up the teapot, poured them another cup, and leaned back with an air of satisfaction. "No older than you are now, I was on a visit to my father, the castle's caretaker, when I first met her. She appeared out of nowhere and sat down beside me. I knew who she was, of course, for my father had spoken of her often, but it did not stop me from being afraid. However, my fear soon turned to pleasure, for she had a way of putting one at ease with no more than a softly spoken word—a way of making you feel at peace with yourself." Jeannie smiled in gentle remembrance. "She was the truest lady I ever met."

"She wore a white dress." Jeannie cupped her tea in her hands and leaned forward. "And a bonnet tied beneath her chin with a blue ribbon. She wished for me to write down her story. But I had no reason to write it down, as it is as fresh in my memory now as it was then."

For a moment, she sat staring into her cup, and Cole coughed quietly to break the silence.

"Sorry." She smiled up at him. "Where was I? Ah yes…Thornwood Castle." Her voice deepened.

"June 1644, Cornwall."

****

"Burn her. Burn the heretic! Burn the witch!"

With a sense of unreality, Alyssa heard Gedrych's shout cut through the voices of the eight soldiers guarding the inner courtyard. This could not be happening. This could not be real. She had not thought he would go so far. She could feel the tiny bag of black powder hanging around her neck beneath her gown that her friend William de Bracey had given her. It weighed keenly now.

At least she would not die slowly.

Controlling her fear, she watched the earl's men step in to light the pyre, heard the crackle of kindling, and smelled the smoke. Flames leapt high around her. A small scream escaped her lips as fire nibbled at her toes. She drew back against the stake, attempting to make herself smaller, and stared up into the dark eyes of Gedrych de Morgan as he peered down at her from his balcony. His face reeked of pure evil. His black eyes glittered like those of a bird of prey. His wavy black hair and a small, pointed beard gave him the air of Lucifer.

A pox on the day she had first seen Gedrych de Morgan outside her father's castle. A pox on the day he had brought her to Thornwood. For that day had been her undoing.

The yellow and blue flames rose higher, burning hotter now, licking hungrily at the sticks that made up her pyre. "Curse you, Gedrych de Morgan," she cried, as the billowing white smoke brought tears to her eyes. "Curse you for the murder of your son, the murder of my child, and the murder of me. May your line be cast from Thornwood Castle until Cai walks its halls again!"

Sweat ran down Alyssa's back. Flames caught at her linen shift. She turned her head and gritted her teeth. The bite of a thousand scalding needles ate at her feet. She heard a scream—her own.

Through the smoke, she saw Jane, her maid, race across the dimly lit courtyard. Hope leapt in her breast, and a plea burst from her throat. "Jane, help me. For the love of God, help me!" But Gedrych's men captured Jane and wrenched her back from the fire, kicking and screaming, as Alyssa watched through a sea of pain.

Tears rained upon her cheeks and disjointed screams spewed from her lips. "My God. My God, Cai! Why did you leave me?"

Her last coherent thought—a man with black curling hair and eyes as blue as a summer sky. The face of her love, her only love. A face she would take with her into eternity—the face of Cai de Morgan.

The fire engulfed her, and the bag of black powder caught and exploded.

Her soul flew free.

****

Never usually one to feel fear, for some uncanny reason, Gedrych crossed himself and turned from the balcony into his chambers. The fear of God touched his soul. He stood perfectly still, staring down at his hands. They shook. Alyssa's screams rose from the courtyard, and he blocked the sound from his ears with his hands. The witch called the name of his son! "Curse her to hell!" But even as the words left his lips, he could not forget her cry.

"May your line be cast from Thornwood until Cai walks its halls again!"

What a ridiculous curse. What had she meant by those words? Were they merely words hastily spoken by a delusional woman in the throes of death, or something more sinister? How could Cai possibly stride the halls of Thornwood when everyone knew his son died in battle? That he had been laid in Thornwood's own crypt five months ago after being brought home from Marston Moor. He peered into the shadows at the end of the room. Nothing moved, and all was silent. Even Alyssa's cries had ceased. But a cold hand of fear ran down his spine, and a lone bead of sweat trickled down his cheek. He tore off his fur cloak, tossed it onto a high-backed chair, and dragged an arm across his brow.

The girl could not get the better of him in life. She would not get the better of him in death.

He spun on his heel, marched to the door, and flung

it open. "de Bracey!"

The guard peered at him in confusion.

"Don't just stand there, man. Get de Bracey. Now!"

The soldier fled down the dimly lit corridor.

Gedrych swung back into the room and strode to the fireplace. Grasping the fire iron, he poked moodily at the coals, trying to stir life into the low-burning fire. Then tossing the poker aside, again he peered into the dark corners of his chamber. Thunder boomed overhead, and he rounded to see a flash of sheet lightning pass across his window, lending light to the gloomy morning sky. Once more he strode to the door and shouted into the corridor, "More candles. I will have more candles in this room! And more wood," he added, about to slam the door, when a young man with long golden-blond hair strode down the corridor toward him.

"My lord wishes to see me?" He dragged off his plumed hat and swept Gedrych a bow.

"William, good, you are here." The earl stepped back and allowed de Bracey to push past him. "You heard that Protestant bitch curse my name?" He paced to the fire, drew his dagger, and stabbed it into the mantelpiece.

de Bracey hesitated. "I did, my lord, but I do not think—"

Gedrych drew his dagger from the mantel and spun to hold the tip to de Bracey's throat. "I did not ask you to think!"

William froze.

Gedrych lowered the knife and expelled a heavy breath. "Forgive me." He dropped into the chair by the fire and leaned his head back, closing his eyes. "You know you are as a son to me, and with Cai gone—" He left the sentence hanging and pressed his hands to his temples. "This is so unsettling. If the wench had not been so stubborn…" He glanced up and met William's gaze. "You must gather what is left of the men." He leapt from his chair and paced. "The standing stones outside the castle? I want them dragged into the courtyard." He stopped. "Yes. That is it. Surround her pyre. Take particular care of how the stones stand. They will be arranged in the exact same manner."

William frowned. "But, my lord, that could take—"

"I do not care how long it takes," Gedrych cut in, his face flushed, his fists clenched. "Do you know what those stones are, William?" He did not wait for an answer. "They are Druid stones. Said to be thousands of years old. Said to harness the magic of the first Celtic priests. If I am to protect myself from the witch's heretical curses, I must have those stones in that courtyard."

"But my lord, you never really believed her a witch?"

"I do not know what to believe anymore." He ran a hand over the back of his neck, and it came away damp. "All I know is that when she stared up at me and cursed my name, I felt a coldness pass through me."

"But the stones." de Bracey shook his head. "To what end?"

"To harness her spirit." He paced again. "To keep it bound." He stopped. "She has not finished burning. I still hear her scream." He put his hands to his ears. "You must hurry."

Gedrych watched de Bracey open and close his mouth as if to say something but knew he wouldn't for all knew, that to defy him, met with harsh punishment.

As William's father had met with harsh punishment after Gedrych found out about his dalliance with his wife. The boy never suspected that his father's best friend had anything to do with his death and never would. Yet still, he watched William for any sense of betrayal. He had befriended Alyssa, and someone had slipped her a bag of black powder to hasten her end.

"And her ladyship's body. What shall we do with that?" William asked. "Should we send for a priest?"

"No. The priest has done his part. And do not call her lady. She does not deserve that title. A witch, a heretic, a whore, but no lady." He spat into the fire. "She will have no priest, and none will touch her body. When the fire dies, dig a pit within the circle and sweep her ashes therein. Cover it over with earth, and no man shall tread upon it. To venture within the circle is death by my hand. Let this be a lesson to anyone else who defies Gedrych de Morgan, Earl of Thornwood."

"And what of her father, Lord Llewellyn? What shall he be told?"

"She caught a fever and died. Swear those few who watched here today to secrecy. Those you cannot trust, deal with. The last thing I need is trouble from Herbert Llewellyn and his sons."

William's expression darkened. "And her maid, Jane?"

"The wench will never leave this castle." Gedrych held his gaze. "Is my meaning clear?"

William's lips thinned. "It is, my lord."

"Good." Gedrych spun to warm his hands by the fire. "Now go. Enough time has passed."

"But, my lord, you must see reason."

"The only thing I want to see is this deed done

before another sun sets, or yours will be the next body to grace the pyre."

William's expression hardened, but he bowed low, and without further word, strode stiffly from the room, just as a servant entered with an armful of wood.

He gave a heartfelt sigh and sank into a chair, watching dully as the man stacked the fire to a roaring blaze and lit several more tallow candles.

However, as much as he tried, he could not rid the chill from his body or dismiss the feeling of being watched.

Chapter Two

London
April 1821

Lord Aidan Tristan Wyndemere de Morgan, new Earl of Dunmore, entered White's gentlemen's club with an air of unalterable boredom. His cousin Freddie had insisted on his company, even though he had pleaded off. He had no liking for such establishments with their superficial air of splendor and inhabitants of not much better caliber.

On entering, Freddie headed straight for the gaming tables, leaving Aidan to his brandy and cigars and the unfortunate ramblings of Colonel Hodgkins, a squat little man in a pinstripe waistcoat and a thin moustache that curled at the edges. The colonel had accosted Aidan the moment he saw him alone and insisted on bemoaning the fact that he'd lost three thousand at the tables and had no knowledge of how he would make it up to his family. A fact that Aidan cared not one fig about.

Only half listening, he stared around the opulent room at the heavy crimson curtains, deep leather armchairs, lavish Oriental carpets, and mammoth white marble fireplace. His lips thinned as he reckoned that the wealth of the place could have fed the poor for at least five years.

He had seen many establishments of this ilk in

Europe and France—all very respectable on the surface, but underneath a seething hotbed of gossip and intrigue. He wished he could relax. However, too many years in reconnaissance had trained him to take in his surroundings and the particulars of those around him.

He noted the rakes, Corinthians, and Whigs who made up this select assembly and wished he'd stayed back in Ford Street with his grandmother. At least there he had the satisfaction of that fine woman's dry wit. He'd had enough excitement on his assignment to Ireland last month, barely escaping with his life after being betrayed. The wound to his leg ached, and as he leaned back against the doorjamb to give it relief, his fist tightened at his side. On the far side of the room, Count Landan Denero, a tall dark-haired man of Italian descent, stood observing him—the man Aidan blamed for his misfortune.

Although he could not prove it, since Denero covered his tracks well and the people they worked for defended Denero to the hilt, Aidan believed him to be a double agent. However, he was not sure for whom he was working. Only that he knew what he had seen that night in Belfast. Denero scurrying away like a weasel after the bomb explosion in the Irish parliament.

The Count acknowledged him with the slightest tilt of his head, and Aidan glanced away. He'd be dashed if he would grant a man who almost caused his demise even the smallest courtesy. He straightened away from the door and, with a polite if weary bow, made his excuses to the colonel and moved toward the no less sumptuous gaming room. There he stopped within the doorway.

He found no pleasure in viewing the wasteful habits

of the rich and bored, though his lips twitched at the thought that he, too, could have been counted among that illustrious crowd.

The stench of cigars and heat from the open fires was overpowering, but his discomfort was lost as his attention flew to the loud expostulations of a young man of around twenty years. The man's carefully brushed windswept hair, the most difficult style of all to achieve, blue velvet frock coat, and buff skin-tight breeches announced him somewhat of a rake. Indeed, he might have stepped straight out of an advertisement for the Man of Fashion, but it was not his fine figure that drew Aidan, but the note the man was waving about and the name of Thornwood Castle.

Aidan watched as the man took another sip of brandy from his snifter and gestured to his companions. He could tell the fellow was well into his cups and wondered at his connection to Thornwood.

Several generations ago, the property had belonged to the de Morgan family. Aidan had known this from the age of fifteen, when he had overheard his father speaking of the castle with such an air of passion he had never forgotten. There had been mention of an uncle who should have inherited after the death of his brother but been denied the property by the Crown for some misdeed of the former owner.

However, when he had begged to learn of the circumstances of the loss, his father became closemouthed and sent him on an errand, which took him almost a day and a half to achieve. He returned to find his parents out to dinner, and the subject had not been broached again. Not long afterward, his parents had set sail for Egypt and Napoleon's fleet had sunk their ship.

Aidan still missed them dearly.

"Aidan, there you are." Freddie stopped before him, seeming all out of breath. His fair hair appeared not so artfully arranged as it had earlier, almost as if he had run his hands through it numerous times. His elegantly tied cravat, slightly askew, and his brown-spotted silk frock coat sported more than one crease. "I must insist on leaving this place at once. I'm reluctant to say, I have lost all that I brought and have not a penny more, unless—"

"Not now, Freddie." Aidan pushed past his cousin, leaving him open-mouthed as he strode toward the young man with the loud voice. He stopped slightly behind the man's chair. The young gent, sensing Aidan behind him, spun about, pushing his chair to one side, and came to his feet.

On closer inspection, the chap looked not so finely attired. One edge of his waterfall cravat appeared frayed, and one lapel of his fine velvet coat sported a slight shine. His face on closer inspection seemed jaded and his pale blue eyes bloodshot, but the look he turned on Aidan tended jovial enough.

"You have interest in my wager, Lord de Morgan. Come join us." He gestured to the seat beside him. "I must admit I am down on my luck, but I do have one trump up my sleeve." He waved a piece of paper before him. "A deed to a castle." He gave a handsome grin. "Moreover, no ordinary castle. A haunted castle, no less. A murdered countess, they say—late sixteenth century."

Aidan gazed upon the young man with studied nonchalance and raised a brow. "You know my name, sir. You have me at a disadvantage."

The man swayed on his feet and bent in an exaggerated bow. "Not at all, my lordship. My name is

Wyndham," he slurred. "Charles Saas Wyndham, late of Brussels. It is pleased I am to make your acquaintance." He straightened. "And as to *your* name, I had the pleasure of playing several hands with your delightful cousin, Freddie, not one-half hour before my luck changed. On seeing you through the doorway, I had interest to know the name of the chap who could arrange a cravat almost as fine as my own." He smiled charmingly.

Aidan's lips curved ever so slightly. Flicking his coat tails out behind him, he took the proffered seat, nodding to the three other occupants as they were introduced.

Studying the three, all of whom he knew either by sight or through his cousin's continual gossip, he listed their attributes and disadvantages in his head. Sir Richard Bingham, a bloated man filled with a sense of his own self-importance, yet still no fool when it came to a wager. Beau Lavenham, a young man of high fashion who carried a quizzing glass, had his snuff box in readiness before him and held out a pale, limp hand to Aidan. No stamina there, he mused. Finally, Doctor Ludovic, a grand enough chap and very good physician, but one who already lived a life of credit. Too rich a game would see him gone.

Aidan was not one to throw away his own fortune either, not when so hard gained by his ancestors and entrusted to him by his grandfather. However, this wager he could not walk away from. The thought of Thornwood drew him as nothing else could.

"So what game is afoot?" asked Wyndham, a little too exuberantly. "Whist?"

The other men readily agreed, but Aidan stayed

them with a shake of his dark head. He leaned back in his chair, his gaze resting pensively on Wyndham. "Let us make this interesting, shall we?" He reached inside his jacket, drew a wad of notes, and placed them in the center of the table. "Ten thousand on the turn of a card. Just you and I, Wyndham." He looked at the others. "Unless any would care to wager more?"

"By Jove, this game is too rich for me." Dr. Ludovic pushed from his seat and made haste for the door. The others remained seated.

"I had a fancy to own a castle," said Beau with a sigh, "especially one with a fair lady ghost, but I feel I must decline. He took a dainty sniff from his snuffbox. As the good doctor said, too rich for my blood, but I shall watch."

Aidan glanced at Sir Richard, and the older man shook his head.

"Very well," he said, striving to keep a satisfied inflection from his voice. "That leaves you and I, Wyndham. My ten thousand against Thornwood." He raised a brow. "You do own the castle outright, do you not?"

Wyndham's face flushed a faint shade of puce. "Of course, I own the castle. What do you take me for, sir? I own Thornwood and five thousand acres surrounding it with fifteen tenants making a good living. My late Uncle Percy Llewellyn, bequeathed to me the property on his deathbed. Here is my note. Examine it if you will." He picked up the paper and placed it before Aidan.

But instead of looking at it, Aidan pushed it to the center of the table, then counted out three thousand pounds more and placed it beside the ten thousand and the note. "The turn of a card for the whole estate," he said in a bored tone, meeting the young man's gaze. "How much to clear your debts?" He heard murmurs from the crowd forming around the table but did not move a muscle.

Wyndham swallowed and loosened his cravat. "I must insist on knowing how you came by knowledge of my affairs, sir."

"I guessed."

Wyndham gulped and licked his lips. "If I should lose Thornwood, it will ruin me."

"Perhaps you should have thought of that before making the wager," Aidan stated dryly.

Wyndham ran a hand through his windswept hair. "Damn you to hell, de Morgan. I don't know why you should wish for the fool castle so?"

Aidan ignored the question. "How much?" he repeated, knowing Wyndham could not back down or he could never show his face in polite society again.

The young man snatched a brandy from a hovering butler and quaffed it in one swallow. "Twenty thousand."

"Twenty thousand pounds," Freddie expostulated from behind. "Twenty thousand is more than any dullard would pay for a castle unseen. It could be in ruin."

Aidan glanced over his shoulder. He hadn't known of his cousin's hovering. He faced Wyndham again and raised a brow.

"Thornwood is no ruin," countered Wyndham, but he refused to lift his gaze from his empty brandy glass.

"See reason," Freddie begged. "This is not at all like you, Aidan. You hate gambling. Take back your money, and no one will see you in any less light." He peered around the crowd to acknowledge a number of nodding heads. "There," he said with a satisfied air.

Aidan tensed his jaw, and the gaze he threw at Freddie could have frozen him to the carpet. Freddie had gone through his own inheritance of thirty thousand pounds in less than five years. The young man relied mostly now on the generosity of his grandmother, Lady Elizabeth, Aidan, and a small annual stipend his grandfather had provided in his will. His own father had gambled away his inheritance when Freddie was sixteen, then fought a duel with the man he had lost to and lost that also. His mother, unable to live with the shame, drank herself into an early grave a year later. Freddie had wandered aimlessly through life since, going from one rich widow to another.

Many times, Lady Elizabeth had remarked to Aidan that as much as she loved her second grandchild, she was glad it was he who had inherited Dunmore, or she would now be residing in the poorhouse.

The space of only two weeks had seen Freddie miss out on inheriting the title and Dunmore Castle, but he had never shown the slightest hint of grievance. In fact, he was prone to laugh and say, "If there was one thing you could not control, it was the timing of your own begetting." Dear, wasteful, handsome Freddie, society's favorite beau. It was hard to deny his cousin anything, but this was something Aidan was determined to do. "I would thank you, Mr. Fitzwilliam, to stay out of my affairs."

Freddie flushed and refrained from saying more and disappeared back into the gathering crowd.

"Done," said Wyndham with more conviction than Aidan would have given him credence. He grinned at the crowd with a new burst of confidence. "By Jove, I will do it. I will take the wager. See if I don't."

A tall man standing to their left placed a deck of cards in the middle of the table. Aidan frowned as he glanced up and noted Landan Denero, but quickly regained his composure. So deep in concentration, he had not seen the wily cur slither toward his table. With a hard set to his jaw, he swung back to Wyndham and nodded.

The young man's newfound bravado seeped away as quickly as it had arisen, and he appeared almost like a lad of twelve, fumbling and unsure of himself. His hand trembled as he reached for the deck. His fingers lingering momentarily over the cards, then he snatched up a card and brought it close to his face. His eyes focused on the card facing him, and he could not contain his smile. The King of Spades was laid with a flourish on the table, and silence befell the room.

Aidan's stomach clenched, but he made sure not the flutter of an eyelid proclaimed his unease. No less than an ace could win him Thornwood now. He drew a deep breath and reached with a steady hand, lifted the next card, flipped it over, and laid it face upward on the table.

The Ace of Hearts smiled up at him.

****

It took three days by horse and coach for Aidan and his grandmother, Lady Elizabeth, his valet, Bevan, and his grandmother's companion, Dora, to reach St. Agnes in Cornwall. As the castle lay only three miles farther along the coast from the town, they decided to continue on.

Aidan glanced across at his grandmother in her new lilac bonnet, fur-trimmed coat, and ermine muff and gave her a smile of genuine fondness. She smiled back and arched a dark brow the replica of his own. It was said his grandmother had been a handsome woman in her prime. He could well believe it. There was still a gracefulness in her trim figure and her fine patrician features with barely a wrinkle belying her seventy years.

He suggested Lady Elizabeth return to the Dunmore estate in Northern England, but she insisted she accompany him and declared herself well since visiting the restorative waters in Bath. In fact, the waters had done his own injury wonders, but the bullet wound still ached when he stood too long in one place. He shifted now in his seat to relieve the niggling pain just above his knee. The doctors said it would take many months to heal correctly. It was uncanny how he survived three grueling years in the navy and a year undercover in Paris during the Napoleonic war without so much as a scratch, and now he should be wounded during a simple assignment which entailed no more than the collection of a package. His mind wandered to the man he held accountable.

"What do you know of a Count Landan Denero?" he asked his grandmother.

The lady in question rested back in her seat. "Old money. His mother was the Duke of Wellington's niece, and his father was an impoverished Italian count. Both are deceased. I believe they died of smallpox in Venice, around the time of Waterloo. Landan inherited the title from his father and a small fortune from his mother."

Aidan nodded and remained silent. He could always rely on his grandmother to keep up with the who's who in society.

Lady Elizabeth watched him closely. "Why the sudden interest in the Italian?"

"Curiosity, I suppose. Saw him last night at Whites. Piqued my interest, that's all. Seems a bit of an odd chap, really. Doesn't say much, never lays a bet, and never partakes in so much as a brandy. One would wonder why he would even belong to a club."

"Perhaps he is associated with one of those quaint new religions, which forbids them to wager or imbibe."

Aidan nodded but doubted that was the reason. He would lay a fair wager that the Count was up to something more sinister.

The coach struck a rut and threw his grandmother forward. He caught her and helped her back into her seat. During their long journey, he had questioned her on the history of the de Morgan family and their relationship with the castle, but she had pleaded ignorance, saying her father had been of the old code and never held with teaching history to females.

He had let the subject go but decided now to try again. He had learned all his grandmother knew about Denero. It was time he pressed her on a subject dearer to his heart—his newly acquired castle.

"So," he asked as his valet sat reading quietly beside him and Dora perched primly on the opposite seat, crocheting her doily despite the bouncing of the coach. "You say you know nothing of our family history connected to the castle. What of the countess who is professed to haunt it?"

Lady Elizabeth gave him a steady look and dabbed a lace handkerchief to her nose. She gestured to Dora to turn the warming brick at her feet. "The only countess I know of whose spirit might inhabit the castle would be Meredith Llewellyn, an uncommon beauty with red hair, green eyes, and too much charm by far."

She shifted in her seat, pulling her lap rug tighter about her knees. "Her husband, fearing her unfaithfulness, hid her away in the country. To no avail, I am afraid. It is told that the count arrived home from London one eve unexpectedly and caught her with her lover. Her husband was reported to have shot the pair, gone down to the library, drunk several brandies, and turned the pistol on himself.

"Blew out his brains. But it was not the fifteen hundreds, as young Wyndham said, but late last century, no more than thirty years ago. And as to why the woman would haunt the castle while the men rested peacefully…" She gave an unladylike shrug and sniffed. "To that, I have no answer."

Dora, who had dropped her hook to stare open-mouthed at Lady Elizabeth, gave a small scream as a boom of thunder exploded overhead, and Aidan's lips twitched as his grandmother gave her companion a gentle pat on the hand. He turned to draw the red velvet curtain aside so he might view the countryside.

The same tedious low rolling hills, hedgerows, and sunken lanes that last filled his vision persisted. Though the weather had grown more inclement.

Evening pressed, rain lashed at the coach, and the north howled increasingly, tossing their vehicle to and fro. Still, what caught his attention was not the moors or the foul weather, but the tall dark sentinel on the hill ahead, whispering to him of tragedies past, yet more so, of a sense of coming home.

His grandmother spoke, and he shook his head, turning back to her with a frown.

"What is it Aidan? Are we nearly there? Do you see the castle?"

He rested back in his seat and indulged her. "I do believe we have arrived, madam."

Ten minutes later saw them stop before a pair of iron gates supported by two stone columns at least six feet in height. On the top of each rested the carving of a crouched lion bearing a rose between its jaws.

The footmen alighted and rushed to push open the gates, and the carriage lurched forward, its ironbound wheels crunching on the white crushed stone of the ornamental drive. Both the drive and surrounding park had the William Kent look about them and would have had to be later additions, neither being common to castles of the fourteenth century.

They passed through a stone archway beneath the gatehouse into a small courtyard to come to a halt before the keep. The castle, built of blue stone, appeared grander than Aidan had expected, though it was hard to see plainly through the drizzling rain and diminishing light. He thought he detected two turrets, one at each corner; there would most likely be a matching two around the back.

The gardens were badly neglected, and thorn bushes scratched at the coach as it traveled the drive. Weeds evident in every crevice of the five stone steps leading up to the keep. Ivy clung to the walls, and a stone griffin perched at each corner of the lintel over the door.

Donning his top hat and triple-layered coat, Aidan stepped down from the carriage and waved the footman away to assist Dora before helping his grandmother to alight. Attempting to shield Lady Elizabeth beneath his raised cloak, he hastened her up the steps as the heavens opened with another deluge of icy rain.

Aidan's valet held the lantern and pounded on the heavy oak door. As they waited for an answer, he wondered what had become of the man he had sent on ahead the day before to make ready for their coming. He could see no trace of him now, nor of any kind of welcome.

The door opened slowly, and a small man with a slash of iron-colored hair on a balding pate peered out at them with weary gray eyes. He held a four-pronged candelabrum with one spluttering candle stump, protected by the curve of his gnarled fingers. His gaze caught and held Aidan's, and his eyes widened; then without word or ceremony, he stepped back into the shadowy hallway and ushered them inside.

As he crossed the threshold, Aidan felt a great gush of warmth wash over him, and again, he experienced an overpowering sense of déjà vu. He was coming home.

****

After the man at the door introduced himself as Tom Jeffreys, Steward of Thornwood, he excused himself to call instructions to the coachman as to where he and the footmen could spend the night and where to take the horses. Then, turning back to Aidan and his party, he led them down a dim, draughty corridor into a gray slate antechamber.

With the Steward's meager candle and only one rush light, smoking and burning fitfully in a bracket on the far wall, very little of the interior could be seen. However, Aidan was able to make out enough to determine a sweeping staircase leading up to the first story landing and several doors branching from the foyer.

Jeffreys pushed open an oak door and ushered them into a room that, at one time, must have been a parlor. Dark oak paneling lined the walls, the same color as the dusty, once polished floorboards. There were no rugs, only one low table, a high-backed chair, and an ancient over-stuffed sofa, the same shade of rose as the faded drapes at the window.

However, the room boasted one fine asset—a roaring fire.

Aidan requested Bevan and Jeffreys help to move the sofa closer to the hearth, so that the ladies could benefit from the warmth. Jeffreys lit the four-pronged candelabrum on the mantelpiece, which harbored three half-burned beeswax candles, then turned to assist.

"Now," said Aidan after the deed was done, standing beside the fireplace. "I see we *were* expected?"

"Your man arrived 'ere last eve. Said you were on your way. Said you'd won the castle from Lord Wyndham."

"I hope our visit has not inconvenienced you," he said dryly, shrugging out of his wet coat and draping it over the back of a chair.

"'Tis your castle," Jeffreys muttered from his place behind the sofa, staring tight-lipped into the hearth.

"Yes, well, I suppose it is," he agreed, "and on that note, you can call a servant to show my grandmother and her companion to their rooms." He looked to his elderly manservant shivering in the high-backed chair beside the sofa. Bevan was exhausted, but Aidan knew he would rather die than admit it. "And my man, Bevan, too."

"Ain't no servants," returned Jeffreys, not meeting his gaze.

Aidan frowned. Already he had noted the Steward of Thornwood to be a surly little fellow and not one in a hurry to be agreeable. Yet, there was something about the old man he found appealing. An air of mystery, as there was a mystery about this castle. Moreover, there was nothing he enjoyed more than a damn fine mystery.

Something that had worked in his favor while undercover during the war.

Perhaps this place would spark his blood. Bring him to life again. He had not felt alive since Paris—as if he had been sleeping, waiting for something, or someone, to awaken him. He had been surviving since Anni's death, but barely, and the fact that he had to keep the secret from his grandmother only compounded matters. But he would not think of Paris now—for to do so would take too much energy, and he needed all that he could muster to get him through each day. A shutter came down on that part of his life, and his thoughts returned to the little man across from him.

Jeffreys' ancient brown frock coat and baggy outdated leggings showed him to be an honest man who spent money somewhat frugally, if his attire and the state of the castle were anything by which to judge. And from the little time he had known him, he had shown himself to be a man who spoke his mind. Yes. He liked Jeffreys very well indeed.

"Is there a reason for this…lack of servants, Mr. Jeffreys?" asked Lady Elizabeth, breaking the silence that had befallen the room. She held her quizzing glass to her eye to view him more closely. "A ghost perhaps? We have heard talk."

The old man remained silent, returning her look with a closed expression.

"Grandmother." He smiled, a gentle reprimand. "I am certain any questions concerning ghosts can wait until morning. Would it not be more enterprising for Mr. Jeffreys to show us where we can sleep?"

A look of relief crossed Jeffreys' face, which Aidan wondered at but did not comment on.

The old man said, "I 'ave prepared a room for Lady Elizabeth and your lordship and 'is man, but not 'er. I didn't know about 'er." He looked pointedly at Dora, and Lady Elizabeth's mousy middle-aged companion flushed and wrung her hands.

"Is there a problem?" asked Aidan.

"Ain't much furniture," Jeffreys grumbled. "Lord Wyndham 'ad the castle stripped, just after 'e in'erited, of what was left. It took me 'alf the day to make up the rooms I 'ave with the bits and pieces I could scrounge."

"That is quite all right, Mr. Jeffreys. Do not concern yourself overmuch. It would not be the first time Dora and I have been put upon to share a bed." Lady Elizabeth smiled graciously and rose, brushing the dust from the back of her skirt. "We were forced to do just that on our first night out of London when there was a mix-up with the coach horses and there were no spare rooms at the inn. Was that not so, Dora?" She stared pointedly at her lady companion. "I am certain we can manage again."

Dora had come to her feet on the moment her mistress had risen. "Yes, my lady."

"Good. Then that is settled." Lady Elizabeth swept toward the door, leaving Dora to pick up the two small bags they had brought from the coach. She stopped as she gained the door and turned. "Well, Mr. Jeffreys, are you coming?"

Jeffreys, who had been relighting his candle, hastened after her to open the door, then followed the women into the hall. A moment later, he popped his head back through the door. "Per'aps, I might show your manservant 'is room while I'm at it?"

Aidan nodded. "When you return, mayhap a short tour of the keep might be in order."

Jeffreys nodded and made to turn, but he swung back when Aidan spoke.

"Also, if this castle boasts a bottle of port, you might fetch it. My blood could do with a bit of warming."

"There might be a bottle or two below." Jeffreys tipped his cap. "I'll see what I can do."

Bevan, who had been waiting patiently at the door, promised he would see him in his room shortly to help Aidan retire for the night, then he followed after Jeffreys, leaving the door ajar. A moment later, it closed of its own accord.

The drafts in an old castle must be many, he decided as the party moved through the foyer and their footsteps turned to silence. He slumped back onto the sofa and released a heavy breath, but as he did so, his hand touched something on the seat beside him. He glanced down to see a red rose the color of blood by firelight. He could have sworn it hadn't been there before. He picked it up. Ice cold, it sent a chill through his hand. He rubbed at a petal and found it waxy, almost slimy to his touch. And as he watched, one by one, each petal dropped away to wither and turn to rust upon the bare wooden floor.

He realized whatever Thornwood held in store, it would not be of the ordinary.

Chapter Three

He was in her room. She watched while his valet helped him off with his topcoat and muddy boots and knelt to add more wood to the dying fire in the black marble fireplace. The man he called Bevan retired, taking his master's boots with him.

She shivered as the kindling burst into flame and the fire danced higher in the grate. How she hated fire. Although she felt none of its heat, she still remembered its torturous bite as it stole the life from her body. She crossed her hands over her chest in a protective gesture and moved closer to the man standing by the bed, loosening the buttons of his white linen shirt.

He looked so like her love. If she could have wept, she would have. His blue-black hair the same color as Cai's, but whereas Cai's had fallen in a tangle of waves past his shoulders, this man wore his trimmed short and settled upon his pointed collar.

His features seemed softer, less angular, yet he seemed to carry an aura of deep sadness that she could not explain. He dragged his neck cloth from around his throat and tossed it onto a nearby brocade chair. A cravat, she thought they called it. Fashion had changed much over the last two centuries, but she stayed abreast of it, watching people move in and out over the years, hearing their chatter.

She smiled. None ever stayed long. Though in a

strange sort of way, she missed them.

Many years had passed now since anyone other than herself and Tom had occupied the castle. Since Meredith. She had liked the countess. Meredith had reminded her a lot of herself, with her red flowing hair and green eyes and fun-loving nature. They had held such lively conversations in the garden, and Meredith had been not one whit afraid of her. But as for her foolish little husband—Alyssa wished she had pulled the trigger on him herself, the day he killed her friend.

Then there was Wyndham, who had stopped for less than a day, looked over the castle and stables, and hastened away. She had not even had to appear to get rid of that one. Though Tom had told her he still put his hand out for the money from the tenants these past fifteen months. Not that there had been much. For those who had come before had bled the place dry, selling off anything that would bring a shiny penny.

They had not touched her room, though. She had seen to that. And now he was here, and she knew neither the reason nor rhyme and did not care. For two hundred years, she had waited. Knowing one day he would come. He might have a new name, but to her he would always be Cai de Morgan, her lover, her husband.

Her breath caught as he pulled off his shirt. By all that was holy, were she not already dead, she thought surely, she would die now for the want of him. She stepped closer. His shoulders were wide, his waist trim, his chest so smooth it almost gleamed in the light of the candle on the dresser. As he undid the first button of his buff skin-tight breeches, she could see where the faint line of black hair trailed down to his—she cut off her thoughts as his hand stilled. His midnight-blue eyes stared right through her into the shadowy darkness of the corner.

"Is someone there?"

His deep rich baritone voice was akin to fine velvet, the exact timbre of Cai's. Her heart hurt. Although she knew it beat no more, it was uncanny how she could still feel the emotions of the living. She moved to the window as he continued to undress.

She would not watch. She was no voyeur. She had seen enough to know he was Cai, her Cai. He had come back to her, and she could never touch him again. She swallowed the lump in her throat and stared down into the courtyard. The place she had died. She heard the whisper of cloth as his breeches hit the polished wooden floor, the rustle of bedclothes as he climbed into the four-poster. The bed she had shared with Cai on their wedding night—where they had pledged their love for eternity. And she felt grateful when a moment later the darkness descended, as it always did when she stayed too long in the place of the living.

****

"God. My God. Help me!"

Aidan shot up in bed. Sweat ran down his chest. His heart raced. He opened his eyes. He'd heard a woman's voice as clearly as if it were beside him. The room be filled with dark shadows, but upon the windowpane, he detected the repetitive pattern of burning fire.

He threw back the duvet, crawled from his bed, and hastened across the room, not allowing for the strangeness of his surroundings. He kicked his toe on a carved chest and let out a string of fine curses that would rival the devil himself. Upon reaching the window, he pushed open the mullioned glass shutters and peered down into the courtyard. He could barely believe his eyes and rubbed his arm across them twice to confirm the vision he saw in the tiny courtyard below: eight large standing stones, and within these standing stones, a woman burning at the stake.

As he watched, she lifted her face and screamed, but he could not distinguish her features through the curtain of flame. He could only see her red waist-length hair. She screamed again and called a name. He did not catch it properly, but it sounded like "Sih."

He twisted and fled across the bedroom. He had to get to her. He had to help. He grappled for several slivers of kindling that sat on the mantel and held them shakily to the fire. They caught, and he shielded them with his long fingers until he lit the three half-burned candles in the candelabrum beside his bed. He grabbed up his trousers and shirt, pulled them on, and picked up the candles. Jeffreys had given him a short tour of the rooms on the lower floor before showing him to his bedroom. A small kitchen with an exit leading onto the inner courtyard had concluded the tour.

He hastened down the dark corridor, the wood icy on his bare feet. As he hurried, he shielded his tallow candles the best he could with his hand, trying not to gag on their unpleasant odor. He found the wooden stairs leading into the foyer and raced down another corridor that led out back to the kitchen. Again, the woman's screams echoed in his ears, and he wondered that the whole castle was not in an uproar.

He almost dropped the candles in his haste to open the door and prayed that he would be in time to save the girl from such a wretched fate. Who could have done such a thing? Did a madman live within these walls? He should have snatched up his pistol.

Overpowering the ancient lock, he wrenched open the door and stepped into the courtyard. The hair on his nape prickled.

Naught but gray-green silence, shadows, and swirling mist met his gaze.

He trod down the white stone path, holding the candles aloft. No sign of fire. Running a hand through his hair, he frowned. Could he be dreaming? He had not been inebriated. He had only shared one glass of port with Jeffreys before retiring.

He strode farther along the path, chafing his arm through his shirtsleeve with his free hand, wishing he had donned his coat. The rain had cleared, and cold ate at his body, but he could not let this go. He had seen the fire. He had seen the woman. He knew she was real. Damn it! She had stared straight at him. He thought of Meredith Llewellyn. Could his mysterious woman be a ghost, and if she were, what would he do?

Wyndham had mentioned a ghost. However, Aidan had never put much store in tales of the Otherworld and things that went bump in the night. They were more likely the figment of some wretched soul's overactive imagination.

A shadow loomed. He started, then laughed shortly to himself as he realized the object remained unmoving. He edged closer, his candelabrum out in front of him lighting the way. A large stone, four times his width and at least twice his height, stood wreathed in feathery white mist. He stepped onto the grass, and another stone loomed from the darkness. Standing stones—monoliths.

As a child, he had once visited Stonehenge with his grandfather. The old Earl had explained the stones, thousands of years old, were thought connected with the ancient Celts and their Druid priests and used in religious ceremonies. His grandfather told him the stones harnessed strange mystical properties, but none knew exactly what those properties were.

He passed by the stone, and another appeared, and he found the giant stones to be arranged in a circle. The same circle he had seen from his window. His scalp prickled as he lowered his candle and moved closer. No sign of fire, or that any fire had ever been lit. For within the circle resided an overgrown garden, and a tangle of red and white roses reared up to greet his candle. Lower, amidst choking vines and matted weeds, bluebells and small pink daisies fought for supremacy. He lifted the candles higher, thinking he caught a sound, and could have sworn he saw a movement of white in the tangle of growth on the far side.

"Is someone there?"

Only silence greeted him.

"Come out. I saw you. What is your game?"

More silence

With a disgusted sigh, he turned. His candles burned low, and he had little liking to be stranded in a strange courtyard in the middle of the night with whoever—or whatever—lurked in the darkness. He hastened back along the path, determined to see Jeffreys in the morning and glean an explanation to this mystery. But as he walked, he cast several glances behind him into the darker shadows, for he could not rid himself of the feeling of being watched.

****

Aidan entered the kitchen to find Tom Jeffreys waiting for him. He held out an old woolen blanket, and

Aidan took it appreciatively and draped it around his bare shoulders. He blew out his candles, placed his candlestick on the wooden table next to mugs, a stone flagon, and a single low-burning candle. Then watched Jeffreys slosh a dash of golden liquid into one of the mugs.

He thanked the old man for the drink and took a swallow. It burned all the way to his insides, taking the chill from his bones. French brandy if he knew his spirits right. He did not ask its origin. This being the Cornish coast, it had probably been purchased or traded from a smuggler. He nodded for Jeffreys to pour himself a drink. He knew he should be angry that his steward had taken the liberty of having a second mug in readiness but forgave him his lack of etiquette. The old man had lived so long alone in the castle, he was probably used to being his own master.

"I suppose you wonder what I was about at so early an hour. And so inappropriately dressed?"

"Your business is your own, my lord." Jeffreys threw a meaningful glance toward two green primitive chairs set before the wide kitchen hearth.

Aidan downed the brandy, poured another, took the hint, and settled gratefully in front of the fire. He stretched out his long legs to warm and waited. Already he had learned that Jeffreys was a man of little conversation. If he were to worm any information from his new steward, his words would have to be carefully chosen. Seeing the old man down his drink and about to turn away, he spoke quickly.

"Will you not stay and talk with me, Mr. Jeffreys? We did not have much chance for conversation last night, as we were both eager to see our beds."

Jeffreys hesitated and glanced into the shadows by the window. "If you wish it, my lord." He settled his wiry frame into the other high-backed chair, seeming to all the world as if he would rather be someplace else.

Aidan smiled inwardly, remembering that his father had once told him that a face could tell a thousand stories. He would wager that Jeffreys' craggy face held a whole repertoire if he could only pry them from his tongue. "Did you hear anything unusual this early morning?" He broke the silence that had descended upon the room.

The old man's steel-colored eyes locked on his. "Unusual, my lord?"

"A scream, perhaps?"

Jeffreys rubbed his stubbled jaw and studied him thoughtfully. "What kind of scream?"

"A woman's, I would think."

Jeffreys shook his head. "Can't rightfully say I did."

"Do you know anything of the countess who is reputed to haunt this castle?"

The older man glanced down at his gnarled fingers. "Countess?"

"The Countess Llewellyn."

"Aye. That could 'ave been 'er name."

"You knew her, then?"

Jeffreys looked up and shook his head. "Before me time."

"I see." His shoulders slumped.

"But me father knew 'er."

He leaned forward, pulling his blanket more securely around his shoulders. "Go on."

"Gracious woman," said the old man, rubbing a hand over the back of his neck. "Very 'andsome, so me father said. Bad business, though. ’Er ’usband—mean spirited little man, preferred the company of young men, ’e did.” Jeffreys glanced up. “Know what I mean?”

Aidan nodded. “I believe so.”

Jeffreys scratched behind his ear. “As I said, ’e preferred the company of gentlemen but would not allow his wife a lover. Did not want ’er ’imself but wanted no other to ’ave ’er. Invited a young man up from London, ’e did. Apparently ’e and Lady Meredith struck up quite a friendship. Well, you can see where that led.”

He looked at Aidan but did not wait for a reply. “’Is Lordship, called to London on business, returned to find ’is Lady Countess in bed with whom else but the young gentleman.” He stopped for a moment, seeming distracted, then went on. “’E took his pistol and shot ’em both, then went down to the library, locked ’imself in, and blew ’is brains out, while me poor father ’ammered on the door. What a bloody mess if you don’t mind me a sayin’ so.”

“And the ghost?”

Jeffreys glanced away. “Can’t rightly say. This castle is four centuries old, ’oo can say what tragedies it ’as seen, or tales it ’arbors.”

Aidan stared into the fire, contemplating the old man’s words. Jeffreys had already told him more than he thought he would glean from the old man in one night. Perhaps he shouldn’t push him too far. He had planned to stay at the castle for several weeks and put the estate in order. There would be more time than enough to learn about Thornwood’s reputed ghost. He came to his feet and stood with his back to the fire. “So, do you normally rise so early?”

“No. I came to check on ’er Ladyship.” Jeffreys

rose, took up the candlestick, and trudged into a darkened corner. On an old brown blanket, in an arch under a dresser, reposed a huge liver-colored bitch pointer surrounded by a swarm of newborn puppies.

"She 'ad 'em just before you arrived this eve. Thought I'd fetch 'er some milk." The words came with just a touch of defiance, as if he dared his master to refuse him, but Aidan would not be baited. He could see no harm in a lonely old man fetching his pet a bowl of milk from a cow he had likely milked himself. He dropped the old woolen blanket onto the chair. "Thank you for the blanket and the drink."

Jeffreys nodded.

"Well, I best let you get Her Ladyship her milk and myself back to bed," Aidan said, turning. He relit his candle, thus missing the stoneware mug he had placed on the floor begin to rise into the air.

Jeffreys cursed softly, snatched at the mug, and hid it behind his back before Aidan saw it.

"And Jeffreys?" Aidan swung back. "Rinse those two mugs before you take your leave. We don't want my grandmother seeing them. You know what imaginations women have. She might think you were entertaining a ghost." The young lord chuckled and moved into the corridor.

****

Aidan eased open his bedchamber door. Struck by an icy chill, he chafed his hands, and moved to the fireplace to find it filled with barely a glowing ember. He could have sworn it a roaring healthy blaze when he'd raced from the room. He knelt to build up the fire, then snatched his morning coat from the hook beside the door, slipped it on, and strode to the window.

Pushing open the mullioned shutters, he could spy nothing out of the ordinary. No fire. No woman. He wondered now if he had dreamed the whole darn business. The standing stones still surrounded the overgrown garden, and he could just make out the tangle of greenery through the mist.

Trying to bring some warmth back into his bare feet, he wriggled his toes into the dense oriental rug. The first rays of sun were cresting the far side of the castle, painting the mist pale pink and the blue walls silver, giving it an ancient fairytale splendor. He almost expected to see a princess climbing the thick-veined creeper outside his window. However, with a realistic eye, he could see the castle was more dilapidated than he first anticipated. It saddened him that such a grand old haunt had reached this state of disrepair. He didn't know whether the fact that Thornwood was reputed to have belonged to the de Morgans, or whether the strange sensation on seeing the old citadel standing dark and solitary on the hill in the rain giving him that sense of belonging, he had never felt for his estate in North Hampshire with such passion.

He had inherited Dunmore from his grandfather along with his title of earl, and although he had lived on the property since turning fifteen, he had never truly felt he belonged. Never experienced that pride and sense of home that had overcome him on seeing Thornwood for the first time. For that alone, he yearned to see the old castle restored to its former glory.

In the morning, he would see Jeffreys about hiring people from the village. He'd need a stonemason, a gardener, and he grinned. A whole dashed regiment of maids and a cook.

Jeffreys had informed him over their glass of port that there had not been a real cook at the castle for thirty years. Moreover, the only two clean rooms he had seen were those he and his grandmother occupied. As for furniture—there was hardly a stick, except in his room.

He had no idea where Bevan had slept and felt it would be unfair to drag his poor valet from his slumber just to dress him. They were in the country now, with barely a person about. He had no intentions of restricting himself to formal dress.

Feeling a sudden urge to ride the estate, he turned to seek his riding jacket. Bevan had laid it upon the trunk less than a half hour ago.

After lighting a candle to gain more light, he opened the old trunk. No coat, but a pair of knee-length black boots. A little old-fashioned, but the right size. He placed the candle on the floor and pulled them on.

He would talk to Jeffreys about a horse. Surely the stables would boast at least one old nag. If not, he would take a carriage horse. That would suffice until his stallion arrived, along with his luggage, later that day.

He stood. Now for his coat. Still tired, he could be mistaken where Bevan had placed it. Retrieving his candle, he lit up the length of his bed. The light fell upon his pillow, and his heart slammed into his ribcage. There, lying across the pillow, a single perfect rose, still wet with morning dew. The same color bloom he'd seen in the tangled garden among the stones.

The same color as the rose in the parlor. Blood red.

Chapter Four

Tom waited for the young Earl to exit the kitchen, then tossed the old blanket around his shoulders, donned his cap, and stepped into the courtyard to hasten through the swirling mist along the flagstone path. He had no need of a candle, for he had trod this route many times over his fifty-nine years. Every inch of Thornwood, imprinted in his mind.

Reaching the standing stones, he stepped off the path and made his way through the ankle-length grass to the edge of the overgrown garden. There he cupped his hands to his mouth. "*Psst*. Are you there, your ladyship?" His whisper blended with the silence.

"Here, Tom."

Her voice, music to the morning. He would never grow tired of hearing its sweet, gentle melody.

She stepped from the tangle of vines, red and white roses, and swirling mist just as the sun burst over the far edge of the castle wall. With the face of an angel, deep-red hair hung in a cascade of curls to her waist, she wore a white gossamer gown that floated and clung to her body all in one—even at his vast age, the sight of her made his heart miss a beat.

With his first sighting of her at fourteen, he had given up his heart and any hope he would ever marry a woman for love. Over the years his feelings had dulled with his fading youth and been replaced by the fondness a father would feel for a daughter, and should it ever be asked, he would gladly give up his life for her.

He ducked around one of the standing stones. "Quickly, you best come in around 'ere with me, my lady. 'Is lordship has gone back to 'is room, and 'is window looks down on the courtyard. If we stand this side of the stones, 'e will not see us. You must be careful. You cannot move about so freely now. If I know 'is sort, 'e will soon be 'iring more servants and ground keepers."

She drifted toward him as he bid. "Tom, you must be freezing." She laid a hand on his frail shoulder, towering almost a half a head above him, but never would he fear her. "What brings you here like this on such a cold morning?" She smiled so sweetly it made his heart hurt.

"*Me*?" he growled. "What would *you* be thinkin', showin' yourself like that? And all that wailin' too."

The smile fell from her face, and she looked away. "Do not scold, Tom, please. I had to see him again. I had to be certain it was he. And the darkness came upon me. I could not coalesce in his room. So, there was naught for it but to bring him down. Oh, Tom." She hugged her arms to her chest and did a tiny pirouette. "Did you see him? Is he not beautiful? Did I not tell you he was wondrous as the sun? Did I not tell you he would come?"

"As you told my father and ''is father 'afore 'im," Tom grumbled.

"But, Tom." She gently squeezed his arm. "It *is* him. It really is. You have seen the painting. You cannot deny it. Cai has come home to me."

Tom shook his head. "Oh, 'e has come all right. And there is no denying 'e bears a striking resemblance to your lord 'usband. But…" He laid his hand over hers and gave it a pat. "You must see, 'lyssa, 'e can never be yours. There is no joining of the spirit world with the flesh. Not in the way that you would be wantin'. And you would not want 'im dead, for even if it were so, there is no guaranteein' you would be together."

Alyssa stepped back and raised her chin. "I will meet with him here like I did with Lady Meredith. He will think me a real woman."

Tom spoke gently, as if to a child. "Perhaps, but I think it best you allow 'im time to settle in first, get 'is bearings. That way we can take stock of 'im, for 'e may have your lord 'usband's face, but 'e's not only the descendent of Cai de Morgan, but also Gedrych de Morgan, and you knew well the ilk of that man!"

Alyssa broke a ruby-colored rose from an overhanging vine and plucked at the velvet petals. "Of course, Tom, you are right. I am no young miss to go floating about with her head in the clouds." She sighed and looked over his shoulder into the distance, trying to put on a brave face. "I am a two-hundred-year-old ghost, who momentarily got lost in a dream." Tears glinted in her eyes. She hung her head but nevertheless managed a tremulous smile. "Go back to the house. I shan't be making a nuisance of myself again."

Tom swallowed the lump in his throat, and his heart hurt in a different kind of way than before. He had never seen his lady so sad, nor heard such desolation in her voice. "I think it would not hurt if you should pop up to 'is room on occasion. Considering it is your old room. If you do not make yourself conspicuous by your actions, 'e would never know you were there."

She peered up at him through wet lashes. The light returning to her brilliant green eyes. "Oh, Tom, do you really think so? It would not be the same as speaking to him, but at least I could look upon him.” Her face fell again. “Until the darkness claims me. Why do you suppose it is that I can appear as a real woman within these stones? Yet can hold my spirit form out of the stone circle for a mere few minutes?”

Tom shrugged and leaned back against a tall stone. The cold wall felt real in this place of unreality. Sometimes a man needed groundin’. “I ’ave thought on this many times, my lady, and the only fathomable reason is that these stones ’arness some kind of energy. It is told that on your death, Lord Gedrych ’ad ’em dragged in from yonder ’ill.” He looked north. “’E had your body surrounded. It is said the stones would trap your spirit within the circle.” He gave a soft snort of laughter. “Little had ’e known what ’e’d done.”

She swung away. Her face unreadable. “I would prefer not to think of Gedrych and his betrayal. The man got what he deserved. And may God bless the souls of my dear friends Jane and William de Bracey for their part in this travesty.”

Tom crossed himself. “I’m sure ’e did. Them being my ancestors an’ all.”

She turned back. “Your father told me the story of the stones, but there must be more.”

“To that I ’ave no answer, and I must be gettin’ to me milkin’.” He straightened. “’Is lordship and ’is tribe will be wantin’ their breakfast soon, and ’ere I am with no milk or eggs to show for me time.” He gave a small bow and when he raised his head, she was gone.

A smile touched his lips as he stepped onto the path, but was soon wiped away by the sound of his new master’s voice.

"Here you are, Tom." The young Earl of Dunmore strode down the path toward him. "Did I hear talking?" He peered into the small overgrown garden. "Distinctly thought I heard voices."

He ignored the question, snatched his cap from his head in deference, and kept walking.

The Earl disregarded the slight and fell in beside him. "Would you show me the stables? I supposed I would ride the estate. To get the lay of the land, as they say."

Tom stepped over a garden bed and cut across the grass. Determined to dislike the new owner of Thornwood, he could not help but like him and had yet to see anything bad in the man. Still, it was early days. "Ain't no 'orse," he said, noting the Earl still following.

"My stallion will be here before noon."

"The stables are on the west of the castle," explained Tom, then fell to silence, never much comfortable around the gentry. They made him nervous. You could never tell which way they would jump. One minute nice as pie; next, nasty as a wasp. He hastened along the path to the far side of the castle where he unlatched the postern gate and passed through, the earl close at his heels. A large flagstone courtyard stretched before them, and the barn lay straight ahead against a high wall.

****

Aidan noted the barn had seen little in the way of new additions. Two ramshackle whitewashed doors hung from their hinges at an awkward angle, attempting to keep what animals that might inhabit its nether regions at bay. He helped Jeffreys push open one of the doors, which caught greedily at the flagstones beneath it. The inside of the barn appeared worse than he feared.

Two long rows of barren stalls reminded him of days gone by when Thornwood must have been a grand estate. Several timbers had fallen from the roof, and ancient straw turned partly to dust lay on the hard, dirt-packed floor. The whole building smelled of mold and neglect.

"What happened here?" Wyndham led him to believe that Thornwood had been a paying property.

"If there ain't no money t' be 'ad, there's only one way for a place to go." Jeffreys picked up a tin bucket from among a conglomeration of ancient gardening implements, a hardened leather tackle, and a pair of cracked black riding boots that seemed to have been left over from a bygone era and hurried down the aisle between the stalls.

Aidan trailed behind and turned into the last stall on the right. On entering he found the old man perched neatly on a wooden stool, bucket between his feet, preparing to milk a pale-brown cow. Jeffreys moved the bucket beneath the animal and proceeded to catch the steaming milk as he tugged on the cow's rose-pink udders.

"You say there is no coin? What about the tenants? Lord Wyndham led me to believe there were at least fifteen families working this land before Llewellyn's death. Paying two pounds per annum in rent."

Jeffreys gave a snort of disgust. "Oh yes, there be families all right, but as for two pounds a year—this land 'as not seen that kind of money for at least two generations. The soil is poor, and the farmers will not work it. As many as five families 'ave left to try their fortune in London this past year. Two others have taken lodgin' in St. Agnes, preferrin' to work the tin mines. At least there they make enough to keep food in their children’s mouths. I am not a man to be collecting more rent than those who stayed can afford. I will not be seein’ youngins starve so that a rich man can grow fat.” Jeffreys finished milking and came to his feet. “Not for the likes of Lord Wyndham and not for the likes of you. So, if that sees me with me bags packed and no bed on which to lay me ’ead, then so be it.”

The two men eyed each other, Jeffreys no more than five feet, Aidan towering a head and a half over him, both taking the measure of the other. Finally, he nodded and made to turn away but swung back. “Find my coachman and the two footmen, and the man, Gallagher, who arrived the day before yesterday. Tell them I wish to see them in the kitchen on the hour of ten. Until I find my way around, it will have to suffice as an office. Oh, and when you have finished with breakfast, I would like to see you about hiring more staff.” He turned to leave.

“They’re gone.”

Aidan rounded. “What? Gone where?”

“They took two of the carriage ’orses. The other four are in a paddock out back o’ the stable. The men said they would leave the ’orses in St. Agnes at the inn.”

“Oh, they did, did they? When?”

“’Afore sunup. Except for the man, Gallagher. “’E left the night ’e arrived.”

Aidan stilled. “Why would he leave before speaking with me first? He has been in my employment for eight years, and never have I found him untrustworthy.” Jeffreys refused to look up, and he folded his arms across his chest. “What are you not telling me?”

“They can’t abide ghosts, I guess.”

“So, you admit there is a ghost?”

The old man scratched his head and picked up his

milk pail, giving the cow a gentle slap on the rump. "The castle is old. A few things are liable to go bump in the night." He pushed past Aidan into the long aisle between the stalls.

"I am more interested in what *you* might think, Mr. Jeffreys."

Again, Jeffreys ignored the question. "You won't be gettin' anyone comin' from St. Agnes, you know."

Jeffreys halted and Aidan tried to meet his eyes, but the old man refused to look at him.

"And why would that be?"

"Some people be funny creatures." The old man glanced up. His eyes clear as a rain filled pond. "They be afraid o' what they canno' see."

Aidan raised a brow. "And if they could see her?"

"Then, perhaps they would still be afraid." He dropped his gaze and kept walking, and Aidan let him go, turning to stride back the other way.

The back door led through the high gray stone wall and looked out upon an apple orchard. White fragrant blossom thick on the wind-stunted trees, the carriage horses frolicking in carefree abandonment within a small, enclosed paddock of lush, tall green grass, appeared inviting. Perhaps he'd take that ride after all on one of the carriage horses. He untied his cravat and shoved it into his coat pocket. He hated the strictures of convention. As often as his grandmother pointed out the importance of dress in a gentleman, he had never been a stickler for propriety when he considered it unnecessary.

As he gained the paddock, caught the mane of a large chestnut gelding, and swung up onto its back, he realized he had a lot of information to digest. Not the least his steward's roundabout admission that a ghost did reside at Thornwood, and it was indeed female.

Chapter Five

Aidan entered his room that night with a sense of satisfaction. It was the first time he had truly felt alive in years. The injury in his leg ached less and the weight of Anni's death weighed less heavily. It seemed life in Cornwall had a way of agreeing with him.

Bevan followed him into the room and hastened across to rekindle the fire to a healthy blaze. Again, his room had become deathly cold, almost freezing. Aidan chafed his arms and settled at his desk to check his correspondence. He dare not undress or Bevan would take offense, as he considered it his job to help his master. Searching, Aidan found what he wanted. A list he had made of his tenants' needs, including grain, food, hens, perhaps a pig each and the new machinery he had read about in the *Times* with which he wanted to experiment. He scribbled a quick note to his man of business in London for the purchase and shipment, put the finishing touches to the letter, closed the envelope, and stamped it with his seal.

When satisfied with the fire, Bevan helped him disrobe, tut-tutting at the rumpled state of his breeches and shirt. He passed Aidan the long white nightgown he insisted his master dress in each eve. Dutifully, he donned the gown, then climbed into the bed, waiting patiently while Bevan folded his morning coat and placed it atop the trunk at the end of the bed. He then picked up his muddy boots and bid him goodnight. He thanked his valet, then hastily stripped off the gown as Bevan closed the door.

He rested back in bed, his hands behind his head, staring up at the ceiling. Candlelight played short and tall tricks upon the wainscoting and cast dark shadows into the corners.

He had hired most of his staff from among the locals, and new furniture would soon arrive from London. Too distracted by his thoughts, he failed to notice one certain shadow detach itself from the wall and drift closer to his bed.

He blew out the candle and stared absently up at the ceiling with tomorrow's activities already carousing through his mind. He had sent word to his cousin Freddie with a letter of credit to purchase new furniture and trimmings for the castle. If there was anything he could rely on Freddie to do well, it was to spend money.

He exhaled a satisfied breath, closed his eyes, pulled the duvet to his chin, and drifted into a deep sleep.

He was floating. Three men in armor sat on large warhorses below him. Before them, overlooking the ocean, was a squat castle of blue-gray stone. The wall had partly collapsed, hit by a trebuchet, a giant catapult powered by a heavy counterweight. A battering ram lay discarded beside the gate. Bodies littered the ground. Women weaved in and around the battlefield tending to the wounded, rifling the dead. He watched one woman cut a ring from a dead man's finger, shuddered, and looked away.

The castle portcullis rose. Two men and two women rode through the gates. The elder of the men bore a white flag.

Aidan remained, watching, waiting, those below oblivious to his presence. One of the armored men turned, his features strong, his eyes deep brown, his hair long and blond. His moustache the same color. The man beside him rounded to speak. Aidan put the man's age in his early forties. His ebony hair, sprinkled with silver, hung past his shoulders. His pointed beard of the same hue and his eyes a cruel black. His ebony breastplate bore the crest of a golden lion and a red rose. Aidan dated the armor to the mid-sixteenth century and recognized the crest as that of Thornwood.

The third man of the party spoke to the first, but his words did not register as Aidan's gaze rested on his face. Around twenty-five, dark hair, which waved and curled over his shoulders, and deep blue eyes—eyes the replica of his own.

He pivoted out of control, no longer floating, and plunged into the body of the man.

He was the man.

And his name was Cai de Morgan.

"Well," the second man said, a man he now knew by the name of Gedrych de Morgan, his father. "Shall we accept Llewellyn's terms? Will she do?"

The two men and women had stopped roughly eight feet away and sat their horses facing them. The younger of the men had a face with the stamp of a hawk, strong and ruthless. Hate burned in his amber eyes. The older man just looked weary.

"A Protestant, a heretic," de Morgan growled. "But Llewellyn's promised five thousand in gold and sworn his men to me for battle should the need arise. What do you say, boy?" He slapped Cai on the back. "Speak up." The man's words were rough and loud. "Has your

tongue frozen on seeing the wench? Has she bewitched you already?" Gedrych and the blond man gave a bark of laughter.

Cai could not take his gaze from the woman.

She stared back at him defiantly.

He urged his mount closer, but the young man from the castle rode to block his path. Cai's hand flashed to his sword and his jaw hardened.

"Let him go, Cullum," the older Llewellyn ordered, riding up alongside his son.

Cullum reined his horse around and moved back several feet, but the look he rested on Cai was deadly.

He ignored him, pulled in alongside the woman, and ran his gaze insolently down her length. She wore a dress of yellow gold, the color of hate. Hair like red fire was tucked beneath a horned headdress. Fine tendrils had escaped to fall softly against her pale cheeks. However, it was her eyes. They burned with an emerald brilliance unlike any he had ever known. They spoke of strong passion. Passion which he would like spent on him. Her full lips pulled tight with displeasure and looked in need of plundering. Something he would take his time doing.

Her breasts were high and firm, her waist thin, her hips well rounded. His gaze traveled every curve, and with every newfound asset his body tightened more. She would breed well, and he would enjoy the begetting. Oh, yes, Llewellyn's daughter would do well indeed. His lips curved in a slow, impudent smile as she turned her head away. "Let the deed be done," he said, leaning forward, snatching the reins from her hand.

Gedrych nodded to Herbert Llewellyn. "I will send men to collect the bride price come morning."

"I shall have her properly wed," the old man

growled.

"Oh, she will be wed properly, all right." Gedrych dragged his mount around. "By a good Catholic priest." He laughed over his shoulder, kicked his heels to his stallion, and rode north with the blond man at his side.

Cai brought his gelding around and followed the two men with the woman in tow. Her maid rode close behind. He had not spoken to his future bride, but he had known from the moment she had looked into his eyes that she would be more to him than a trophy of war.

Aidan sprang upright in bed. His body trembled. It had been a dream. He tossed aside the duvet, strode to the window, pushed open the shutters, and felt the cool breeze caress his cheeks.

He stared down into the courtyard. All was darkness. Nothing moved. Not a night creature called. He swung to face into the room. It was lit by only the faintest of moonlight and a low-burning fire.

It had to have been a dream.

Naked; the breeze was cold but sweat still trickled down his back. He stared down at his hands. They trembled. "It *was* a dream." If he repeated the words emphatically enough, perhaps he would believe them.

He ran a hand through his thick hair. He had been in Cai de Morgan's body. He had seen what he had seen, done what he had done, and thought what he had thought. It was as if he was a spectator in another time and all had been beyond his control. Yet, as incredible as it was, he had been there. And who was Cai de Morgan? What was the man to him? And more so, who was the woman? Why did she remind him so much of the woman in the fire? Countess Llewellyn, the woman who supposedly haunted this castle.

He pulled his pants up over his lean hips, strode to the dresser, and lit a candle. Crossing to the large freestanding mirror in the corner, he critically viewed his features. Was it his imagination, or was there the slightest hint of another image superimposed over his own? Did the face look more angular, the jaw harder? He held the candle closer to the glass, and a chill prickled the back of his neck.

The hair on the man in the mirror waved and curled past his shoulders and there, standing behind him, was a woman. A woman with a riot of deep red hair, brilliant emerald eyes, full lips, and fine brows—a woman with the face of an angel—the woman in his dream. His hand tightened on the candlestick. It felt as if it were frozen; his fingers glued and could not be uncurled.

She no longer wore the yellow gown and headdress but instead the white shift she had worn the first night he had seen her amidst the fire in the courtyard.

Their eyes met and held in the reflection.

He swallowed, trying to free up his throat, trying to force words that would not come. As he watched, she drifted closer, yet no step could he hear on the polished wooden floor.

"Who are you?" he managed at last, his words a strained whisper. He twisted around. She vanished. He swung back and stared into the mirror. She stood behind him with a look of accusation in her green eyes. It was as if he was a moth and she pinned him with her diamond bright gaze. "I'm sorry," he said. "But I had to be certain." He spoke quietly, afraid to raise his voice lest she disappear. "Will not you speak to me? Will not you tell me your name?"

She opened her mouth, and a soft sound issued forth,

almost a sigh, as if it was coming from far away. "Cai."

Cai. Had she said Cai? The man in the dream had been Cai. The man whose body he had inhabited for a short time. Inhabited. The thought disturbed him, but he could think of no other word to explain the happening. Was he going crazy? But no crazier than seeing and talking to a ghost. Again, he wondered what Cai de Morgan had to do with him. How was Cai connected to the murdered Countess?

"I have so many questions," he said, holding her reflection in the mirror.

She moved closer, pressed her warm soft body to the length of his back, and encircled his waist.

His mouth went dry. He couldn't swallow. He had always thought a ghost would be cold, but he had never felt such heat as that which now filled his body and hastened to pool in his loins at the soft caress of her silken hair and the touch of her hands on his sweat-damp skin.

She leaned her smooth cheek against his shoulder, and his body hardened with desire as she tilted her head to the side to watch him for several painful heartbeats through sooty lashes, her eyes dark, intense, wanting.

Suddenly, he swung to seize her, but his hand passed through a draught of cold air. Goose bumps raced up his arm. She was gone, and he cursed himself for a fool. He should have known better than to try to capture something as elusive as an angel.

Chapter Six

Sometime in the history of the castle, one of the lower rooms of the Keep had been converted to a morning room. Two chairs had survived the lean years of the previous owners. It was on these two chairs, one placed at each end of an extraordinarily long cherry-wood table, that Aidan and his grandmother now faced each other.

Lady Elizabeth wore a high-necked lavender morning dress and a coiffeur of delicate dark curls, which Dora had likely taken the better part of the morning to arrange.

It was not like him to disagree with his grandmother's advice, but he was about to do so now. "If you are not happy with the living arrangements, madam, perhaps it might be in your best interest to return to London or to Dunmore."

"And leave you here? I think not. There is no telling how long you might take it into your head to stay at this fool place." She raised the gold-rimmed monocle pinned to her bodice and peered around the desolate room at the dusty bare floorboards and faded maroon curtains. "I cannot see the allure of this mausoleum. Barely is it fit for the vermin I am certain it must house." She sniffed into a lace handkerchief.

Aidan thought of one good reason he would want to stay, and it included a very fine pair of emerald eyes.

However, he refrained from saying so. From what he knew, Lady Elizabeth had suffered no dealings with the lovely ghost of Thornwood, and he preferred to keep his own encounters private until he could unravel the mystery surrounding her. As far as his grandmother knew, the ghost was no more than a myth. She was disgusted the coachmen had abandoned their duties and that their London staff, who spent the night in St. Agnes, now refused to set foot on the castle grounds merely on hearsay from the coachmen about their ghostly encounter.

One lone coachman returned with their trunks and Aidan's Arabian stallion. Then after delivering the news that the rest of the servants would not be arriving, quickly departed back to London. He was thankful for the locals Jeffreys had hired the previous day, as it appeared they were of sturdier stock. That, or the ghost did not bother people from her own locality. At first, they had been a little afraid of the stories they had heard of the rumored ghost, but when the day passed with no sign of her, they grew more complacent. Still, they wished to leave for home before sundown and he agreed.

Remembering his grandmother's last statement, he answered, "As far as I know there are no mice, and if there were, I am certain the five cats I have seen parading the grounds would make short work of them." He speared a piece of fish on his plate and brought it to his lips. "It might cheer you to know that Freddie will arrive shortly. I sent a dispatch back to London with the coachman, in which I asked him to purchase furniture, material for drapes, floor coverings, and whatever trappings he thought essential in refurbishing a castle."

Lady Elizabeth continued to eat as if he had not

spoken.

Another of her ploys he recognized well to signify he was out of favor. "Perhaps we should spend a few days in St. Agnes. It might not be London, but perhaps you could discover some small trinket to take your fancy."

Lady Elizabeth dropped her fork noisily onto the table and pushed aside her breakfast. "I am not an actress to be bought, Aidan. I have coin enough to purchase my own *trifles.*"

Aidan winced. "Of course, Grandmother."

"However," she said, her voice softening, "a tour of the local village might be in order. I believe copper and tin to be mined near St. Agnes. There might be a piece or two I could purchase for this desolate abode. Furthermore, Freddie shall arrive soon. I cannot very well go traipsing off back to Dunmore and miss my other favorite grandson, now, can I?"

Aidan hid a smile. "I will have Dora and Bevan ready our trunks. How many days?"

"Three should suffice to see all of interest."

"Done. I will have Jeffreys bring the coach around before noon." He pushed aside his plate of curdled eggs and haddock and left his grandmother to finish her breakfast.

****

As the coach he shared with his grandmother jostled over the rise that would see them back to Thornwood, Aidan relaxed into his seat. One could never be careful enough while crossing the moors of Cornwall. Wild, rugged country, it was thought to harbor more than one outlaw or smuggler. Beneath his coat, an ivory-handled pistol pressed snugly against his stomach. A piece he'd purchased in the Indies after the war had proved its worth several times over.

He glanced across at his grandmother with her fur wrap and warming brick, and his lips curved. Their three-day jaunt to St. Agnes proved enlightening, to say the least. The same woman who professed to be dying a month ago and begged him to take her to Bath to bathe in its wondrous recuperative water had made a marvelous recovery since arriving at Thornwood. And their sojourn to St. Agnes had shown Aidan a side of his grandmother unknown to him previously.

Lady Elizabeth had cajoled a matching pair of hand-painted rose vases from a local porcelain maker for an indecently low sum; haggled over the price of a blue-feathered bonnet with the milliner; and browbeaten a craftsman blacksmith into selling an extraordinary cast-iron bathtub with clawed brass feet for half its worth, delivery included. However, unbeknownst to his grandmother, it had taken Aidan some time to persuade the tradesman to keep his word about the delivery because of the rumored ghost. However, it was surprising what three silver shillings could achieve.

Lady Elizabeth would have her new bathtub on the morrow.

Concluding his business with the blacksmith, he'd stepped through the door to see Landan Denero leaning nonchalantly against the milliner's doorjamb across the road, and his sense of accomplishment died. Denero acknowledged him with a dark-lidded nod, and a moment later a lovely woman in a froth of pink and maroon silk and ruffles stepped from the establishment to join him. He tipped his hat at him in acknowledgment, took the woman's arm, and they continued on their way down the deserted footpath toward the wharf.

Aidan watched until they were well out of sight but could not shake the disquiet that the sighting of Denero had conjured. The man was akin a pinprick that would not stop bleeding. What was he doing in St. Agnes? Was it by coincidence or design? And if by design, by whose orders?

The coach lurched, its wheel hitting a pothole, and Denero receded to the back of his mind. As they entered the castle grounds, Aidan noted the crushed stone drive was well on its way to being restored to a pristine state. The overgrown creepers along the drive were pruned and shaped and the overall appearance of the park much improved.

The carriage stopped, and he stepped down to speak to the head gardener as the man ambled toward him. Saul, a tall man of around forty, a half head taller than Aidan and broad as an ox across the shoulders, had a thatch of brown hair liberally sprinkled with silver. His brown eyes were akin to a doe's and his temperament matched. And his wife Eleanor doted on him.

A young boy of around twelve with sandy-colored hair ran up alongside them. Saul introduced the lad as Toby and informed him in a deep, gravelly voice that the boy was one of the cottager's sons. Jeffreys had put the boy to work with him in cleaning up Thornwood's park and the two courtyards, hoping that would suit the master. Aidan replied it suited him well indeed and complimented both on their hard work.

The big gardener mumbled a few gruff words and moved on with the boy in tow as Aidan helped his grandmother alight from the coach.

On entering the castle, they found more surprises.

Eleanor and Mary, Saul's wife and daughter, plus three other young women whom Jeffreys had hired from the village, had been very busy. The castle was sparsely furnished, but on returning to Thornwood that late afternoon, he was amazed to see that once the foyer floor was scrubbed, it was found to be a startling white marble.

The blue and red Oriental rug covering the stairway up to the first floor had been swept, and the kitchen sported a new coating of whitewash applied to the stone walls, the ancient bread oven blackened and polished until it gleamed, and the few pots, kettles, and pans that hung from the beam above the table glinted in the light of a roaring fire.

The smell of fresh herbs tantalized his nose as he moved farther into the room. Several bunches hung from overhead beams, and Eleanor, the cook, told him she brought them from home and that her husband Saul intended to plant a large herb garden along with a vegetable plot at Thornwood, with his lordship's permission. Aidan said it would be his pleasure to grant it; any improvement to Thornwood was welcome.

He sent for all the servants and, when they assembled in the foyer, promised a bonus in their wages at the end of the month. He then dismissed them, made his excuses to his grandmother, and left her sipping Indian tea from a fine, chipped china cup in the newly scrubbed parlor.

On entering his bedroom, he acknowledged the room was immaculate as ever. Not a smear of dust or article out of place. It was as if whenever he left the room it was cleaned by an unknown hand, and for the first time since arriving, the room was warm on entering. Perhaps his ghostly inhabitant had finally given her stamp of approval.

Aidan pushed open the shutters, noting for the first time the board on which he stopped creaked. Frowning, he moved aside in case the wood was rotted and swore he would have Saul repair it come morning. However, the board was forgotten as he peered down into the courtyard.

The grass trimmed short, and the garden among the stones had been tidied, the red and white roses pruned to form two beautifully sculptured archways. Large bluebells and a splash of pink daisies lined the curved beds around the edges of the tall stones, and in the center sat a carved stone bench.

He had not seen the bench before and wondered if Saul had found it somewhere else on the estate. Or had the seat always been hidden amongst the tangled growth? Again, he thought of a girl with hair like dark fire and green eyes who had cried for help from that same garden the night of his arrival and wondered if she was watching him even now. He stripped off his shirt with a smile.

Chapter Seven

Aidan stretched and came awake to the sound of birdsong. A shiver ran through his body, and he glanced at the window. One of the shutters was ajar. He could have sworn he had latched it shut the night before.

In no hurry to rise, he allowed the covers to fall down around his waist as he sat and scanned his room. His late wife, Antoinette, would have loved this castle with its sense of history. She had spoken often of her family's chateau in the heart of France, where she spent her childhood until she and her father were forced to flee during the Royalist uprising. She loved antique furniture and held a special fondness for old books, and there were plenty of those in Thornwood's library.

Two Oriental rugs added shades of red and blue to the color scheme of the room, while the whitewashed walls above the wainscoting were decorated with a delicate artwork of painted green vines and pale pink blossoms. They appeared almost lifelike in the dusty light of the solitary sunbeam streaming across the room.

He arranged his pillows and leaned back against the headboard. Who had occupied this room, with its sixteenth-century chunky dark furniture and Louis-XV writing desk, giving it an air of old-world charm? Why had Jeffreys put him in here when there had been so many other rooms from which to choose? The room being furnished was one reason, no doubt.

However, this room was almost palatial compared to his grandmother's. And that brought him to another question. Why had this room escaped Wyndham's notice? Why hadn't it been stripped, and its contents sold as the other rooms? Was it because it belonged to the woman in the mirror? Did she guard it? He glanced at the mirror he had dragged across the room last night so that he could peer into it from his bed. Alas, this morning no red-haired woman stared back. Why did the thought of her torment him so? What hold did she have over this castle, over him?

He knew he should leave, get away as his grandmother insisted, but he knew he could not. There were too many unanswered questions. There must be something he was missing. Something that would give him a clue to the ghost's true identity—a journal perhaps, a bible recording births and deaths. Some of the older families had kept them; many still did. And was she the murdered countess Wyndham indicated or someone else entirely? The woman in his dreams, perhaps. Herbert Llewellyn's daughter? She certainly looked like her.

He sighed. Too awake to stay abed, he threw back the covers and reached for his robe. He would find Jeffreys and question him again. Better still, he would search the library. As far as he knew, neither Wyndham nor any of those who came before him disturbed the library. Apparently, it was another room reputed to be haunted.

He stretched and wandered over to the hearth, then bent, poked life into the last glowing embers, and added more coal. Satisfied, he returned to his bed and lay back with his hands folded beneath his head. For the first time since arriving at the castle, he felt relaxed. He had slept well. No strange voices calling from the courtyard, no unexplained dreams, no young woman peering at him from out of his mirror. Yet still the woman invaded his thoughts, and her face danced before him.

The royal-blue curtain across the room billowed inward, almost as if someone stood behind it.

"You will never leave me." The words were so soft, he was not sure if he really heard them or if they were a trick of his mind. He shot up in bed. "Stop! Get out of my head!" Nothing moved. An eerie silence prevailed. "You may have done this to the others, but you will not do it to me. The dreams I can handle, the roses, the ploy with the mirror, and the pantomime in the garden, but stay out of my head, or I will depart here today. That I—"

A shutter crashed back on its hinges, striking the outside wall, breaking off his words. He cursed loudly, sprang from his bed, and sprinted to the window. Reaching for the shutter, he was grateful the colorful stained glass hadn't shattered.

Then his grip faltered, and his hand shook. The beautiful garden of yesterday was no more. In its place, an overgrown monstrosity from the night of his arrival, and something white moved within its tangled foliage. Swearing, he pulled back, about to turn away, and stilled. On the sill beside his hand lay a blood-red rose, wet from morning dew. With a slash of his hand, he swept it over the edge and watched, as if in slow motion, one by one the petals fall away and diminished before they hit the ground.

With another curse, he dragged the shutter closed and pulled on his riding pants and boots that Bevan had laid out the night before. The antique wall clock chimed eight as he picked up his crumpled shirt of the day before, pulled it over his head, and flung his riding coat around his shoulders. Pushing a black necktie into his pocket, he strode for the door, and snatched his hat from the stand as he passed.

Saul's daughter stood on the top stair polishing the banister, and he nodded to her as he took the steps two at a time down to the foyer. He entered the kitchen, and the fresh smell of bread greeted him, matched by the aroma of lamb's fry and bacon. Yet he had no hunger for food. Only hunger for knowledge of the woman he had seen burning in the courtyard garden.

Eleanor glanced up, and he nodded in acknowledgement as he passed her by and exited the back door.

The sun burst through the clouds as he stepped onto the flagstone path. A robin sang in a nearby blossom tree, and a puppy ran under his legs, almost tripping him. He regained his balance, breathed deeply of the chill morning air, and continued along the path, the squelching of his boots marking time on the crushed gravel.

At the stone garden, he stopped. The flora was overgrown as he'd seen from his window, but there was a murmur of voices issuing from within—a boy's and the soft lilting tone of a woman's.

He moved into the long grass and pushed beneath the overhanging roses, receiving several fine scratches. He cursed ungentlemanly and proceeded on.

The voices ceased.

He ducked a last branch of white banksia and spied a young woman seated on the stone garden bench—an angel of a woman. He put her age at around nineteen. She wore an off-white gown in the style first favored by the Empress Josephine. A little old-fashioned, but charming, nonetheless. The bonnet she sported of the same color was held in place by a blue bow tied beneath her small, pointed chin. Her hair had been tucked beneath her bonnet, but one strand of dark red fire had escaped to lay softly curling against her pale cheek. He thought her the most enchanting creature he had ever seen. And he was struck by her uncanny likeness to the ghost that haunted his room.

However, this young lady was no apparition. She was warm, vital, and very much alive. The only explanation he could give was that perhaps they were related somewhere back in their ancestry. However, he kept his counsel well hidden behind the same mask of boredom he affected when he did not want people knowing his thoughts.

The woman spoke quietly to Saul's young gardening apprentice. She glanced up as the lad swung around. Her eyes were a brilliant emerald—the exact replica of the woman in his mirror. But he quashed the thought as ridiculous as it entered his mind. That woman was spirit, not of this world, and this one was very much of the living. He stepped forward, his mouth dry, his words sticking in his throat.

Toby shuffled his feet in the grass. "Sorry, me lord. I wasn't bludgin'. Promise. The lady called to me, and I couldn't just walk by." He made to leave but turned back. "I won't forget to tell Jeffreys, ma'am. I'll do that right now." He spun to race past Aidan, but Aidan called him back.

"Milord?" Toby pivoted and removed his tweed cap.

"I would have you stay, Toby." Aidan had no eyes for the boy. He had eyes and ears for only one person in that garden. “I would have you introduce me to this young lady.” His gaze never left the woman’s face.

“Yes, milord, but Saul will have my breeches if I don’t git back.”

“I will speak to Saul. All will be well.”

“But I don’t know the lady’s name.” The boy shuffled his feet and stared at the ground. “She jist’ called me.”

“Then stay and I shall introduce myself. If that would meet with the lady’s approval?”

The young woman came to her feet and shyly held out her hand. Aidan smiled at her, and she smiled in return. Toby, seeing this, moved several feet away and settled on the thick, springy grass beneath the rose bower to wait.

A puppy ran from out of the bushes, and he was soon occupied.

****

“Lord Aidan de Morgan, Earl of Dunmore, at your service, my lady. But please call me Aidan.” He took her hand briefly and bowed low, and Alyssa gave a small curtsy, keeping her head bent so that he could not read that which was in her eyes.

“I…I could not.”

“Oh, but you can. We are in the country and miles from any polite society.” He smiled again and her heart, though she knew it should not, thudded into her ribs. It beat in so wild a fashion. She never understood how she could feel so alive and still be of the spirit world. Whatever magic some long-ago sorcerer or Druid Priest had imbued into the standing stones, she would be forever grateful, for it enabled her to appear human and alive to the one person who mattered—Cai. Yet she knew in her heart he was not Cai.

This man seemed gifted with a gentleness her husband had never possessed, except with her. Her husband had been of a sterner mettle, she supposed. A product of the warring times in which they had lived. And growing up with a father like Gedrych de Morgan, it was a wonder he had been sane at all. She laughed shortly beneath her breath. It was funny how she could think of Gedrych now without the hate that had eaten away at her for so many centuries. Perhaps it was the fact that Cai was home. Yes. Her plan had worked. He was right before her, and she supposed she should say something, but what? She searched her mind. She had not planned so far.

"Who are you?" he asked, his voice rich and smooth like a fine red wine yet holding the slightest trace of a command. "Who are you?" he beseeched again softly, tilting her chin up so that he could look deeper into her eyes. He frowned. "I feel we have met before."

"I am sorry, my lord, but that is impossible," she said, pulling her hand free from his. "However, I must beg your forgiveness. I fear I am a creature of habit. I often sit here when I visit my uncle." She crossed her fingers within the folds of her gown. "The roses are so beautiful, and if you sit still long enough, the birds will venture right up to your feet."

A small smile hovered on his lips. "No apology needed. You are welcome anytime, but you must forgive me for disturbing your quiet." He peered over her shoulder in a distracted manner, as if searching for someone or something. "I thought…" His sentence trailed off.

"Yes?"

"I thought you were someone else." He ran a hand over the back of his neck, beneath his thick black hair. "But here I am, still being impolite. I insist you resume your seat." He smiled fully this time and it near knocked the breath from her lungs.

"And if it does not seem too forward, perhaps I could join you?"

Alyssa hastily took the bench, and Aidan sat beside her, leaving several notable inches in between.

"Your uncle, does he live far from Thornwood?"

She laughed softly. "My uncle is the steward here."

"Tom Jeffreys? Impossible."

She arched a fine brow. "And why would that be?"

"Well…well you are so well spoken, and Jeffreys…" He left his sentence hanging.

She arched a fine brow. "Not so well spoken?"

"Indeed, yes." He looked away.

They sat in silence for several long heartbeats. "Perhaps if I explained a little of our family history?" She took pity on him.

"Forgive me. I did not wish to be rude."

"Not at all." She looked at her toes peeking out from beneath her hem, then realizing her breach of etiquette, hastily drew them under her gown. "My father," she began, "the second son of Henry Jeffreys, moved to Plymouth when he was fifteen to live with his uncle, Edward de Bracey, his mother's brother." Again, she crossed her fingers. The half lies she was about to spin would most probably see her in hellfire to be certain if she ever moved on. "de Bracey," she continued, "was a man of means, but unfortunately his wife bore no son. He owned a large shipbuilding business and, wishing to keep it in the family, had my father educated as a gentleman and taught the trade."

"And Jeffreys remained here? Incredible."

"It was his wish," she returned defensively. "My uncle's family has resided at Thornwood in one capacity or another since the sixteenth century. Most have been stewards." She glanced down at her folded hands, willing them not to tremble.

"So, Jeffreys gave up the chance of a proper education and his inheritance to stay here?" He frowned. "A person would wonder why."

Alyssa paused. For what could she say? That at the age of fifteen Tom Jeffreys had met and fallen in love with her and refused to leave the castle, although his father had begged him to do so? Although he knew their love was doomed? Much as her love for the new owner of Thornwood was doomed.

Alyssa had never returned Tom's affection in that manner, and he had eventually met and married Grace with whom he had sired one son. Tragically, the fever had taken the child at the age of eight. It had been a brutal blow to Tom and Grace. Tom's family had been guardians of the castle since William de Bracey had taken on the position of steward to Justin Llewellyn in 1665. She sighed. But that was another story.

Over the years, Tom's infatuation for her had turned into a deep friendship with an instinct to protect.

At last, she spoke. "My uncle is a quiet man and at times very lonely since his wife passed away this last five years."

"I fear I know so little of Jeffreys. I had not even known he'd been married." The earl paused and turned to face her. "How often do you visit?"

"Not so much as I would like. My father brought me

here often as a child. I used to play up at the keep. I thought my uncle might have mentioned I was here. Did he tell you that the castle has not been inhabited for these past thirty years?" She looked into his sapphire eyes. So like Cai's. She could have looked forever.

Instead, she said, "I am fond of my uncle. I have already had my coming out and loath the eccentricities of polite society. I visit him twice a year for several weeks at a time." Again, she looked into his beautiful, fathomless eyes and her breath caught. "I…I hope…I may continue to do so?" She shifted her gaze to her folded hands in her lap. "It means a lot to me."

"As it would him, I should think." Aidan smiled reassuringly as she lifted her chin. "I hope you find the gatehouse to your liking. If there is anything you should need…"

"That is most kind, but my uncle's family has always lived here, and it is well furnished. The gatehouse furniture was not sold off, as was the fate of the rest of the castle." A small silence fell, then she said, "My uncle told me you have ordered furniture all the way from London. How exciting."

He nodded. "My cousin Freddie will be arriving with several loads any day now. You must come up to the keep and see for yourself."

She turned away, heart sinking, knowing that would only be possible in spirit form and he would never know she had seen it. "Perhaps," she said quietly, stretching out her bare foot to contemplate her toes.

"You must not be shy." He stared at her foot as if mesmerized. "You would be most welcome, and my grandmother would be glad of some more female company. Dora, my grandmother's companion, is a most gracious lady, but she can be extraordinarily vague at times." He smiled. "Are they not cold?" he asked, indicating her small pink toes.

Realizing her *faux pas*, she dragged her foot back under her skirt. "I do not feel the cold." She flushed. "And you must forgive me, my lord. I was in such a hurry to come down to the garden this morning, I forgot my boots. I had no idea you would be here. I dare not wonder what you must think of me."

He smiled. "I think you are enchanting."

She blushed and looked away. She was beginning to hate herself for her deception, but it was the only way she could keep him here. And she so wanted him near.

The earl came to his feet and moved to lean against the post supporting the roses. "I wonder," he asked, his gaze fixated on one of the standing stones. "Have you seen anyone lurking about other than young Toby?" He threw a look at the boy playing busily with the pup, oblivious to their conversation.

"A ghost per chance?" She arched a brow and hid a smile as his mask of boredom momentarily slipped, and he looked back at her.

"Why yes."

"My uncle says I am her replica."

"Does he now?" He crossed back to the bench and turned to study her face. "What else does he say?"

"Not much at all," Alyssa countered, watching him watch her. If only she could keep him talking forever. "I would not think one as worldly as yourself would believe in such fanciful creatures."

"Have you asked him?" he replied, ignoring her statement.

"He does not like to speak of her."

He came to his feet as if ill at ease and ran a hand over the back of his head through his carefully styled hair. “Forgive me for pushing. You are not the only one lax in etiquette this morning, but the tale fascinates me.”

She rose and stood beside him. “Have you seen her?” She breathed in his scent, a mixture of wood smoke, pine, and leather. Not at all what she had expected from a man as elegant as he. It was a man’s smell. Cai’s smell. She felt her knees weaken and forced her hands not to tremble. His body was calling to her—an aged old song. She would not look away. She could not. His deep-blue eyes drew her as a butterfly to a sweet flower. She saw him swallow and nod.

“Was she as beautiful as they say?”

“More so.”

“Her hair? What color was it?”

He took the step that separated them. “Deep fire like your own.” His fingers seared her skin as they brushed a tendril back from her face.

“And her eyes?”

“Deep forest pools of emerald, and they beckon.” His hand rested upon her cheek, whisper soft, but as strong as an iron shackle. She knew it was wrong for a young woman of this era to allow a gentleman such familiarity, but for all that was holy, she was lost. His mouth lowered toward hers, and he seemed equally so.

A cough sounded behind them.

Aidan stilled and stepped back, his eyes darkening as he rounded. “Yes?”

Jeffreys peered through the vines and glared at Toby.

The boy jumped to his feet, standing mute as the puppy gave a short, sharp bark and scampered off down the path.

"You may go now, Toby. And thank you," said Aidan. "Tell Saul I will speak with him shortly."

The boy tipped his cap at Aidan, twirled, and raced along the path in the wake of the pup.

"Your grandmother's tub 'as arrived from St. Agnes," said Tom to Aidan, but he looked pointedly at her. "Lady 'lizbeth is in a quandary as where to put it. 'Er ladyship insists you come at once."

It was Tom's way of telling Alyssa it was time for her to leave. That she should never have been here.

"Thank you," said Aidan. "Tell her ladyship I will be along shortly."

The old man remained as he was.

"That will be all, Jeffreys." Aidan's tone held an edge, which the old man could not ignore. "I assure you your niece will come to no harm."

Tom's eyes widened, and again he sought Alyssa.

She nodded. "I am quite well, uncle. I will see you back at the house for morning tea, shall I?"

Tom grumbled beneath his breath and trudged from the garden. When he was lost from sight, Alyssa said, "Forgive my uncle, your lordship. He tends to be a little overprotective of me."

He captured her hand between his two. "And why should he not be when his charge is so lovely? And unfortunately, now I must go. I cannot keep my grandmother waiting or I shall be in her bad graces for the rest of the day. Which is not a good place to be I assure you." He hesitated, looking down at her, then he brought her hand to his lips, brushed a soft kiss across her knuckles, then released her and stepped back. "May I see you again?"

She smiled. “Perhaps.”

“Then I shall count the hours.” He turned about to leave but swung back. “I never learned your name…”

Alyssa had drifted out of the garden and reverted to her spirit form. To Aidan, she was invisible. Hastily, she stashed the gown and bonnet that had belonged to Meredith among a clump of bushes and, with a heavy heart, turned to watch Aidan push through the overgrown garden onto the path. There he stood, staring at the postern gate for several minutes. Then with a harsh sigh, he rounded and stepped onto the path. She watched until he reached the kitchen door and disappeared, feeling her spirit heart beginning to crumble.

Yes, she had spoken to him, touched him, and for a moment thought he would kiss her. But for some uncanny reason, now that he had returned to the keep, she felt more alone than ever. For she knew, although this man resembled her husband, he was not Cai. And although she wished it with all her heart, he could never be hers. And it would be akin to dying all over again when he learnt her true identity and she lost him forever.

****

The sun was beginning to set in shades of mauve and gold on the horizon when Alyssa met Tom in the garden.

“Now, Tom, do not scold. You agreed I could speak with him in the garden. You brought me Meredith’s old dress from the attic, remember?”

Tom shook his head and leaned back against the stone facing away from the keep. He had made his excuses to leave Aidan and Lady Elizabeth and make his way back to the garden as soon as polite to do so.

“What I saw was no’ talkin’. There were a lot more going on there than a few simple words.”

Alyssa raised her chin and set her jaw. "Now you listen here, Tom Jeffreys." Her fists clenched and unclenched in her white linen shift. "It may not be what you wanted to see, but I have waited two hundred years for that man to return to me. If I want him to touch my face, touch my hair, or touch any other part of me, you will not be stopping him. Your family has been good to me, keeping my secret all these years. But can you not understand?

"This is the closest I have felt to really living since Gedrych burned me. Although I know what I feel for Aidan de Morgan is as doomed as my love for Cai, I will have what little happiness I can grasp, until he learns my true identity and spurns me. I do not want to hurt you, Tom," she finished gently. "But I am more than capable, and you know it."

While she had spoken, Tom's lips had tightened. He jammed his hands into his pockets. "No good will come o' this. You mark my words."

"That may be so, but you will not interfere."

He moved away from the stone. "Just don't say when you get your 'eart broken that I didn't warn you." He stepped out of the garden and kept walking.

"You know I love you, Tom. You have always been my favorite."

Tom stilled. "Yes, I know. And where 'as it gotten me?" He shuffled through the grass as she moved to the edge of the garden.

"Do not forget I am your niece," she called softly to his back.

"*Hmph*," he grumbled, and kept moving.

She stepped out of the circle, and her physical body faded to nothing as she watched Tom retrace his steps and enter the kitchen. She sighed and turned away. It saddened her she had spoken to her old friend with such anger, and it surprised her. She had not felt such wrath since Gedrych's treachery, and again, it began to rise. Her nails bit into her palms, although they could not be seen.

Woe to anyone who stood in the way of her love for Aidan de Morgan, for she would have that man as surely as the darkness would claim her, if only for one night.

And in thinking of the darkness, it manifested. A shiver traveled the length of her body, and her teeth chattered. She had no knowledge of where she went when the darkness claimed her. She never wished to know. She thought it might be *the powers that be* trying to pull her through to the *Otherside*. However, she never wondered about it too deeply, or too much, or she might begin to truly believe she was dead.

A silent scream escaped her lips as an invisible hand dragged at her spirit and blackness engulfed her.

****

That afternoon, Aidan achieved two tasks that had bothered him for several days. Exercise his stallion and visit what remained of his tenants to discover what could be done to improve their livelihood. He had asked Tom to accompany and introduce him, so after riding double to St. Agnes and purchasing a small quiet mare for his steward, they continued to the cottages.

Aidan found most of the crofts little more than ruins. Two sported animal skins across their windows. On another, the door hung askew. All were sparsely furnished, and most of the tenants, quite malnourished. Five of the dwellings lay empty and in disrepair. Jeffreys explained these had belonged to the families now residing in London.

Three other cottages, he learned were once inhabited by families now working the tin mines. Eleanor and Saul, who often obtained odd jobs in St. Agnes before finding employment at Thornwood owned another.

The tenants he found at home, he spoke to, left them a few coins for repairs and food, and promised to establish a more efficient way for them to work the land. He had read in an agricultural manual; farmers were experimenting with adding sheep manure or fish offal to the soil. He had always enjoyed reading, especially anything to improve the farming land on his properties. Jeffreys could see about a few chickens, pigs, or goats for each of them. He would speak to Eleanor about baking extra loaves and have them distributed to the needy.

When Saul harvested his vegetable gardens, there would be plenty to share until his tenants could better fend for themselves. He knew many lords who would not contemplate such deeds, but it was important to him, that these people thought well of him. Whether it was in some way linked with a certain fire-haired spirit, he could not fathom.

A wife of a tin miner, a middle-aged woman with fading brown hair, tired eyes, but a ready smile, invited him and Jeffreys for tea and set a small home-baked biscuit before each. Aidan finished the tea but refused the biscuit, knowing that for him to eat it, another would go hungry. They spoke of her son, who had run off to London to seek employment, and the long hours her husband toiled in the tin mine near St. Agnes. He promised he would see her husband's burden lessened and left her a silver coin for coal, then biding her goodbye, he and Jeffreys turned their horses for home.

"You did well today," said Jeffreys, in one of his uncustomary bursts of speech, as the small croft disappeared over the hill.

Aidan pulled his triple-layered traveling cloak up around his shoulders to ward off the bite of the wind. "And what would that be? You are thanking me for?"

"Giving a penny instead o' takin' one."

"These people have it hard enough without me making it worse."

His answer earned him a quick look of respect from the old man.

Although he knew the sun was setting and shadows would soon blanket the land, he could not help but take advantage of the situation. Throughout the day he had tried on several occasions to engage his steward in conversation about his niece. But he had stoically refused to be drawn.

"Tom? Do you mind if I call you Tom? I know it is not customary, but I think we have taken each other's measure over the last few days."

"If you wish m' lord."

Aidan deliberately slowed his pace as Tom rode up alongside.

His steward, a hard man to read, baffled Aidan. He found it hard to believe this rough old man was related to the enchanting girl from the garden and that he had given up his inheritance to stay at Thornwood. He could see how Thornwood could eat into one's soul. He was proof of that. However, there was more to this story than Tom was telling, and he had an itch to find out what it was. "Your niece, Tom. She said you could have had a living in shipbuilding."

The older man scowled, and his lips tightened. “She ’ad no right discussin’ me business.”

He nudged his horse to a faster walk, but so did Aidan. He remained silent for a time, then tried another tact. “She is a handsome girl, your niece.”

Tom smiled softly—the first time Aidan had ever seen him do so. “She is at that. Always has been.”

“I did not catch her name.”

Tom stared straight ahead, his smile dropping away. Aidan thought for a moment he would refuse to answer. “Lyssa,” the old man returned gruffly.

Aidan tried the name on his tongue. “Lyssa.” It sounded good, and for some reason familiar, but he could not remember where he had heard it. “Somewhat unusual,” he said.

“Welsh. I believe ’twas ’er mother’s name.”

“You believe?” Aidan frowned. “I thought her mother was your brother’s wife?”

“Of course, she is…was,” amended Tom. “But I only met the woman once. She died at Lyssa’s birth.”

The two men remained silent for several more minutes, the only sound the clip clop of the horses’ hooves on the dirt road.

“She must have found it hard without a mother.”

“She ’ad ’er nanny and ’er brothers.”

“Brothers?”

He hesitated. “Never see the lads much. They don’t come ’ere.”

Aidan didn’t know how to answer that, so he changed the subject. “Well, you are lucky to have Lyssa to care for you.”

“That I am,” Tom replied gruffly, “and I would likely do harm to any ’oo did her ill.” He cast Aidan a pointed glance. "Now, if 'is lordship is finished with 'is questions, night be fallin', and I meself would rather be 'ome with somethin' warm fillin' me belly than wanderin' the moors at night." With that, he slapped his reins lightly to his mare's neck, and she fell into a canter.

Aidan, feeling suitably chastised, followed behind, yet he could not help thinking of the girl who uncannily resembled the woman in his mirror to the extent he found it hard to separate the two faces in his mind. Many years it had been since he had even glanced at another woman, let alone two. He had mourned his dead wife for so long he thought his heart had stopped beating where it came to the matter of love. With a ragged sigh, a face of a frail dark beauty with pale skin and masses of black hair superimposed itself over the face of any other in his mind, living or ghost, and all thought of the red-haired women vanished. Antoinette Du Bois was certainly a hard woman to forget.

Chapter Eight

Three days passed before Aidan encountered Lyssa again. Walking by the stone courtyard, the soft, gentle strands of a music box pricked his ears. He stopped and listened, recognizing the tune as Greensleeves, an old medieval song his nanny used to sing to him in his nursery. He smiled, and without conscious thought, pushed through the bower of white banksia, cursing under his breath as a branch caught his coat sleeve and he pricked his finger when stopping to fight for release. Finally detached, a rose lay crushed at his feet, withering and dying before he took his next step. It gave him pause. However, it was not the first time he had noted some unusual anomaly within the stone circle, leading him to believe it a place of mystical activity. If that were at all possible.

He moved into the garden noting also for the first time the twin carvings of the crouching lions, a rose vine twirled about their bodies at each end of the seat. The animals appeared almost in pain, but the thought soon vanished as Lyssa, perched on the edge of the stone bench, spoke.

"My lord, I did not see you there." Her voice held a breathless, husky quality, a soft melody to his ears. She lowered the lid of a golden music box and stood to greet him with a dainty curtsy.

"I heard the music. Greensleeves, a favorite of mine

as a child." He pulled a white handkerchief from his coat pocket and wound it tightly around his injured finger, which had dripped blood onto the grass.

"You're hurt." Carefully, she set the music box on the bench and hurried toward him. "May I?"

"It's nothing. A thorn scratched me as I entered the garden." He held out his finger, and she unwound the blood-soaked handkerchief. Fresh blood welled up from the wound and splashed onto her white gown. A startling stain on a pristine background. A memory of Anni and the guillotine flashed to Aidan's mind, and he pulled back. "I'm sorry. Please send the gown up to the castle and I will have it cleaned. Or better still, I will replace it."

She smiled and shook her head. "I would not hear of it. I can take care of the gown myself. Now." She took his hand. "Let me see that finger."

She singled out the digit in question, and before he could figure out her intentions, popped it into her mouth.

Surprise raced through his body. Fire and ice all in one rose up to burst upon him, engulfing him in perspiration and a powerful bout of lust. Did this small woman have any idea what torture her warm, wet orifice had set upon him? He had never had a woman do anything even as remotely erotic.

He forced his mind to a cold bath in the dead of winter and pasted a tight smile to his lips, all the while yearning to show her what her mouth was really doing to him.

Still, she sucked at his finger, not looking up, drawing her lips along the wound once, then twice more. Finally, when he thought he could hold himself in check no longer, she released him and stood back. "There." Her eyes, deep pools of innocence. "Is that better?"

Swallowing hard, he looked down. The long scratch seemed completely healed. "A miracle indeed." He frowned. "How did you do that?"

"'Tis easy." She turned and drifted back to her seat. "When you know how."

He frowned and followed her, raising his foot to the bench so he could lean upon his knee and look down at her. She had picked up the music box, clasping it in the folds of her gown.

"May I?"

She hesitated, then placed the small, bejeweled box in his hand.

Unusually cold, almost freezing, ornately decorated with emeralds and rubies, it was inscribed with a large embossed "*A*." He stilled. "Where did you get this?"

Her eyes were defiant as they met his. "My mother gave it to me."

"Your uncle told me your mother died."

"So, she did. At my birthing."

"And the 'A'. What does that stand for?"

His jaw tensed. Her hand clenched tightly in her lap. "Anne. My mother's name was Anne. It belonged to her. She left it to me." Her words seemed almost defensive. He wondered why.

He smiled thinly and passed it back. "It appears extremely old and exceedingly precious."

"That it is. I believe it belonged to my great-grandmother before that and handed down through the family. It is told it was given to her by Edward IV, who, it is said, was infatuated with her."

He leaned closer. "And this great-grandmother. Her name?"

"Alyssa."

"Alyssa." He expelled the name on a breath. Something was not right here. Alyssa, the woman from his dreams, a woman who bore a striking resemblance to the young woman who sat staring at him with guileless green eyes. Eyes he had peered into in those dreams. He dropped his foot from the seat and settled beside her, leaving a space between them. "Alyssa, you say?" He stared down at his clasped hands.

"Yes. I believe it a common name in Cornwall in the sixteen hundreds."

"Indeed?" His brow raised. "Would your family and the Llewellyn's be related by chance?" He turned toward her, his hand accidentally touching hers. He didn't move; neither did she. He saw her hesitate, but only fractionally, the air crackled with tension.

"Not that I know." Her words were slow and precise. "I am certain I have heard mention of the name somewhere, but I am not certain if we are related to them. Why?"

He shrugged and stood, breaking contact. He could see no reason she would lie. "Nothing rational. In many ways, you remind me of someone I once met."

"Do I? And what was she like? This woman you cannot forget?"

"Lovely." He caught her hand and brought the tips of her fingers to his lips, holding them there in a way he knew to be far too familiar. "But not as lovely as the woman before me." He released her hand and watched it settle into her lap, then stood.

Her green eyes sparkled up at him. "Till we meet again, my lord."

He swept her a bow. "To that, I look forward." He

turned to leave, but at the edge of the circle, he rounded. She had already disappeared, but he could have sworn he heard the soft strands of Greensleeves lingering on the breeze.

He took up the tune and continued to hum it softly beneath his breath as he moved toward the gate.

****

He floated above them, peering down. A great hall full of people. Trestle tables set with trenchers of succulent dishes. Duck, chicken, pig, jellies, and pastries. Wine and ale flowed freely. Musicians played at the end of the room.

He spied Gedrych, de Bracey, and the woman. Tonight, she wore cream, and pearls were braided through her dark-red hair. Cai de Morgan sat at her side.

No sooner had he thought the man's name than he felt an awful dragging. He toppled, spinning out of control into the other man's body. Then he was the other man, and he was speaking. "Are you not happy, my lady?"

She turned to him, her eyes wide and green and full of uncertainty. "In truth, I do not know how I feel." Her voice had a lilting musical quality. "All of twenty-one days I have been here." She lowered her head to look at her untouched plate. "And today I have wed a man I do not know."

He found her hand beneath the table. "But you do know me. I am your soul, your moon, your stars. As you are mine. Did you not feel it from the first, as I did?"

"You were horrid to me that first day," she whispered, not looking at him.

"For my father's benefit, I assure you. Have I not

spent these last three weeks constantly at your side? Courting you in the fashion a woman of your station would wish to be courted?" He leaned lower to speak into her ear. "Am I not all that you would wish in a husband?"

He broke off a small piece of succulent chicken and made to pop it into her mouth, but she turned her head away.

"I will not force you. Ever." The seriousness of his tone must have registered, as did the double meaning of his words.

She looked up, the heat in her gaze all he could have wished for. "I am grateful, my lord, but if I may be so bold, force will not be necessary." She opened her lips, and the morsel of chicken slipped delicately onto her tongue.

His breath caught at her words. He had not meant to fall in love with her. So shy, so unsure of herself when she arrived at his home. His father had been so abominable. He could do naught but take pity on her. Then it was not pity. It was love. She was the sweetest, most charitable woman he had ever known, and he knew that in all of three weeks.

She had none of the false charm and coquettish ways of the courtiers he had met—a charm of which he had soon tired. As he grew to know her, he realized she was fresh, alive, vital, and held a hidden strength of which she was yet unaware. He knew this woman like he knew his own soul, and he knew what he felt for her would not easily exist again. With her, he could be himself, not what his father wished of him.

She glanced past him to Gedrych and met the dark glint of his eyes. With a shiver, she leaned back so she could speak into Cai's ear. "He watches me. Every time I look around, he is watching me. I do not wish it, but I am afraid of him."

He turned to Gedrych on his other side, laughing at some jest of William's. He slapped Cai on the back and took a quaff of ale. "William says it is time to bed your woman, Cai. I told him perhaps you might need some help. She is a feisty one, your new bride." He peered around Cai to better view Alyssa. "I would not mind helping with that one myself."

He forced a smile. "I shall keep your offer in mind, Father, and call should the deed become too great. But do not hold your breath."

Gedrych thumped his shoulder and twisted to relate his message to William, who gave a great roar of laughter, and Cai turned back to Alyssa. Her face flushed. She would not look at him. "Take no heed to them. It is the ale talking. My father is a hard man. He has had to be, to command the respect he has and the land he owns and be able to keep it. He might appear harsh, but at heart I believe he is a good man.

"Come. I have a wish to dance with my beautiful bride." He took her hand and brought her to her feet, at the same time signaling to the musicians. As he and Alyssa stepped onto the floor, the soft lilting strands of Greensleeves filled the hall, and other couples milled around them. He bowed, she curtsied, and he took her hand. The slowness of the dance gave them plenty of time to converse.

"What do you know of William de Bracey?" she asked. "He strikes me as a man of worth."

"I would trust him with my life." His tone hardened. "But not with my wife."

She smiled and lowered her lashes. "I ask not for myself, but for Jane, my lady-in-waiting. She finds him most charming."

He laughed shortly. "That he is. William de Bracey is as a brother to me. His father, my father's best friend, was unfortunately thrown from his horse and killed not long after my birth in a freakish accident whilst hawking with my father. William has a small estate ten miles from Thornwood, but prefers to spend most of his time here, close to those who care for him."

The music stopped, and Cai brought Alyssa's hand to his lips. "Now enough talk of William," he whispered close to her ear. "It is time I took my lady to bed." He turned from the floor, took her hand, and intended to lead her through the milling crowd before his father caught sight of them and insisted on the ritual of he and his cronies seeing the newlyweds to their bedchamber. Cai, not up to any more snide remarks, wished to spare his lady's feelings. However, it was not to be. Halfway across the room, a loud pounding on the hall door interrupted the music, and the door burst open. A servant entered, followed by two men dressed in the King's livery.

Gedrych pushed from his chair. "What is the meaning of this intrusion?" His loud voice filled the room, and everyone stilled.

The first messenger removed his hat and bowed deeply.

"My lord, forgive me. But I come from Prince Rupert himself. War has broken out between the allied army of Parliamentary and Scottish troops and Prince Rupert's Royalists. The Prince requests you send men at once. He plans to intercept the Scots at Marston Moor."

"Highlanders!" Gedrych roared. "Those skirt-wearing swaggering windbags." He sank into his chair with a scoffing wave of his hand. "He can deal with them alone. I will not waste good men on such a cause."

The messenger straightened. "My lord. I have my orders. The King has men traveling the country to gather an army."

Gedrych scowled and searched the crowd. His gaze fell on Cai. "Take fifty men. Join Rupert and show him the courage of Cornwall."

Cai's heart pounded, but his tone held even. "Do you forget, father, that I am only just wed?"

Gedrych waved his words away with a flick of his wrist. "There is not a Highlander who will stop fighting his neighbors long enough to give a decent fight to the English. You will be back before the week is out to bed your bride."

A few men laughed out loud, but Cai quelled them with a look. "It will take eight days to reach Marston Moor." His tone cut an edge through the silent room.

His father's fist pounded the table, upending a flask of wine. It spilled over the rim onto the floor, pooling blood-red like a bad omen among rushes and dirty flagstones.

"I will speak no more on this," Gedrych boomed. "Take your woman, bed her, and in the morning, you ride!"

His jaw clenched, and his anger rose. "We have not spoken the last on this."

"Have we not?"

"No. Indeed we have not!" He grasped his wife's hand and dragged her toward the door. As he reached for the handle, he stopped and turned. However, it was

not he that his father's gaze rested on, but Alyssa, and he did not like the look of lust that sparked the man's eyes, nor the feeling of dread that churned his stomach.

****

Aidan sprang upright in bed. "Who's there?"

Bevan stood by the window, tying back the curtains. "It is only I, my lord."

He released a ragged breath and sagged back onto his pillows, staring unseeing at the painted lilac ceiling.

He was back in the real world. Yet even so, he could not help thinking of the man he had left behind—Cai de Morgan, forced into battle the day after his marriage by his own father. He went still. The war between the Allied Army of the Parliamentary and Scottish troops and Prince Rupert's Royalists. He tried to recall the history lessons his tutor had forced upon him.

Why did he have the dire feeling that the war had ended badly for the English and Cai? Had this something to do with Alyssa's haunting of the castle? What happened here so long ago? What secret did this castle harbor? The secret he was becoming obsessed with unlocking.

"Are you ill, sir?" Bevan stood at his side, looking down at him with a careworn look on his aged face. "You have gone quite pale."

Aidan swung his legs over the edge of the bed as Bevan moved to fetch his trousers.

His manservant handed him his pants. "I swear sleeping naked the way you do will see you taken with the ague."

"Don't fuss, man. I am quite well." Aidan pulled the trousers up over his lean hips.

"It might cheer you to know," said Bevan. "Your

cousin has arrived, and he has with him a young lady. An acquaintance of yours, I believe."

"A young lady?"

"The Honorable Mrs. Carolyn Simms, my lord. I believe I have heard you mention her name, although it be many years ago."

"Bloody hell." He groaned. "What the deuce is Freddie about, bringing *Carolyn* all the way up here? I had no idea they knew each other." He ran a hand over the back of his neck and paced. "Her husband, the admiral. Is he here?"

"I believe your cousin mentioned something to your grandmother about him being deceased, my lord."

Aidan froze. "A widow. I will be damned. Pity, I liked Conrad despite our misunderstanding."

"Misunderstanding, my lord?" Bevan raised an iron-colored brow. "From what you had implied, I was under the impression that it was more than a misunderstanding."

Aidan accepted help with a newly starched cravat as his thoughts drifted to the past and the incident that had almost ruined him.

After the French had sunk his parents' ship, he'd begged his grandfather to buy him a commission in the Royal Navy. Sixteen at the time, he'd been hell-bent on revenge. His grandfather, although not liking the idea of his eldest grandson going to sea, had reluctantly agreed.

At seventeen, he served under Nelson. At eighteen, he transferred to a place under a childhood friend of his grandfather, Admiral Conrad Simms, where he obtained the rank of First Lieutenant. He had liked the older man. He reminded him a lot of his grandfather in his ways. Stern yet always willing to give a man credit where credit was due. The admiral had taken him under his wing, inviting him home for Christmas in London.

At nineteen, he was about to make the greatest mistake of his life.

Carolyn Simms, his admiral's young wife, with her golden hair and cornflower-blue eyes, held the power to sway a young boy's heart. Smitten by her beauty, he allowed himself to be caught in her silken trap. And found in what could only be termed a compromising position. His grandfather's deep friendship with the admiral quieted the scandal that threatened to shatter both households.

His grandfather, gravely wounded by the affair, had he had any other choice of an heir, bar Freddie, would certainly have left him to rot on their plantation in India. However, groomed from the age of twelve to one day inherit Dunmore, his grandfather had done the only thing available to him. He had implored his old friend to forgive his grandson's shameful behavior.

Both old friends' pride had been wounded. Aidan had never felt so ashamed. The admiral had taken him under his wing. Treated him like a son. And he had betrayed him.

He had even laid a loaded pistol on the admiral's desk, but the man, too much a gentleman, had refused to pick it up, resulting in Aidan feeling more disgusted with himself.

He went to the admiralty, stating that he craved more excitement and volunteered for a reconnaissance mission in the heart of France, hoping a stray bullet might find him. Unfortunately, he could not even get that right.

"Your waistcoat, my lord?"

Aidan stared absently at the maroon-and-gold waistcoat Bevan held out before him. Silently, he slipped his arm into the armhole, and his thoughts returned to the past.

In Paris, he met Antoinette Du Bois, the daughter of an impoverished French count. Count Louie Du Bois, being half English, half French, had turned informant for the English Crown. He had been Aidan's contact in Paris.

Aidan and Antoinette, attracted to each other from the first, their love swift, fierce, and all-consuming. Despite the desperate times in France with Bonaparte's men guarding every front, they managed a small private marriage ceremony two weeks after their meeting. And it had been the devil's own struggle for him to leave France two months later.

Urgently summoned home to his grandfather's side. Antoinette begged him to go alone. Her people needed her, and he would be back soon, and they would be together always.

He found his grandfather dying and the following day inherited the title of Earl of Dunmore and all that it entailed.

He made an excuse to return to Paris, telling his grandmother he would be in London to resign his commission, intending to bring Antoinette back to England and surprise her. Perhaps the fact that he was married would cheer her. Instead, he returned to find his wife betrayed, captured, and soon to face death. He had watched her die on the guillotine.

Devastated, he returned to England and retired to his country estate. His grandmother had often commented on his disinclination to join in the festivities of town life, and more so his disinterest in women, yet she never pushed. Whether because she enjoyed his company at Dunmore, or she guessed at some tragedy in his past, he never knew. She hadn't known of the scandal or his mission in France, and he forwent mentioning his marriage, feeling the time inappropriate. He wondered if it would ever *be* appropriate. Antoinette seemed more like a precious dream now than reality.

"When did they arrive?" he asked, his thoughts returning to the present and Carolyn. Somehow his memories of Anni would always be tied up with Carolyn, for had he not become involved with the admiral's wife, he would never have journeyed to France.

Bevan helped him on with his navy-blue velvet frockcoat. "I believe a little after nine this morning, my lord."

Aidan glanced up at the antique wall clock and ran a hand over his stubbled jaw. "One half hour ago. Why didn't you wake me?"

"Lady Elizabeth insisted I allow you to sleep."

"Did she now? She was obviously more interested in prying the latest Town gossip from Freddie's tongue and screening Carolyn for marriage to me, if she isn't already spoken for by Freddie."

"Would that be so bad?" returned Bevan dryly. "From what I saw of the lady, she is quite handsome."

He groaned and made for the door. "If you knew Mrs. Simms the way I do and of what she is capable, you would never ask that question."

****

He opened the door to the sitting room to find the Honorable Mrs. Carolyn Simms and his distinguished cousin Freddie standing by the window.

"You really do have the most extraordinary view of the coast," he heard Carolyn say.

"Yes, it is one I very much appreciate." Aidan stepped into the room. "It can only be improved upon by the view from the conservatory, which is quite spectacular."

Carolyn swung at the sound of his voice. "Perhaps you could indulge me sometime and give me a tour." She smiled and her soot-colored eyelashes fluttered down to hide her expression. Her golden curls, artfully arranged in a topknot upon her head with only the tiniest, but tasteful, adornment of three small teal-blue peacock feathers, glinted in the sunlight. Garbed in a stunning traveling suit of lapis blue and white stripes, which brought out the cornflower of her eyes that were wide with feigned innocence. She slid toward him like a cat to a bowl of cream.

He controlled his smile. He knew personally just how innocent Carolyn Simms could be. "Later," he answered her question, "but for now I must admit," he flattered, "you are still the most ravishing creature in all England." He clasped her outstretched hands. *Too beautiful, and she was well aware of it.* "Too long, it has been," he said out loud.

She bobbed a small curtsy. "Six years, my lord, and you are most kind."

He dropped a kiss on her small, gloved hand. "Lady Simms." He met her gaze. "Or should I call you Carolyn?"

She cast a look at Lady Elizabeth, watching on from a dusky pink sofa with a look of open curiosity. "His lordship and I are old acquaintances," Carolyn hastily explained. "Before he resigned his commission and ran off to spy on France," she admonished gently. "He served under my late husband, Admiral Simms, during the Napoleonic war."

Lady Elizabeth raised a fine arched brow. "France? Spy? I do not recall you journeying to France, Aidan."

He threw Carolyn a steely look. "A small reconnaissance mission. I hardly thought it worth mentioning. Also," he chastised Carolyn lightly, "I would prefer to give it its proper name."

"Phooey. Spies, reconnaissance, what does it matter? The war is long over." She drew a lace handkerchief from her reticule and daintily dabbed at her eye. "But I was so dreadfully afraid for you."

Lady Elizabeth raised a brow.

"And your late husband, if you would forgive an old woman's curiosity? His passing is recent?"

"Gracious, no." Carolyn laughed softly. "Conrad lost his life at Waterloo alongside Nelson."

Aidan looked away in disgust as he watched her bring real tears to her eyes. From what he knew of their marriage, they had never been close. The admiral had overindulged and spoiled his young bride, and she had never appreciated him. Aidan was not her first lover and most likely not her last. Women like Carolyn needed a man in their lives.

"Tea?" inquired Lady Elizabeth into the silence that had fallen. "And do sit down, girl." She indicated the only other seat, a black-lacquered high-backed chair by the window. "Aidan? Perhaps you and Freddie could see to the unpacking of the furniture?"

Freddie straightened away from the window. "Unpacking?" He fingered a shiny gold button on the cuff of his bottle-green frockcoat. "I thought you had servants for that."

Lady Elizabeth held her quizzing glass to her eye and peered across at Freddie. "Unless you bought a bevy of your own, you will learn we have all of two housemaids, one cook, two gardeners, a stable hand, and a steward," she said softly.

Freddie glanced at Aidan.

He nodded in confirmation.

"Good God." Freddie flushed. "Don't tell me, cousin, that you've become tightfisted in your years. I have six wagons of furniture to prove otherwise."

"Not at all," chimed in Lady Elizabeth. "You should know Aidan better than that. He likes his creature comforts as well as I. No. It is that dreadful ghost. She frightens away the servants. Only the crofters stay, as they are used to the antics of the bothersome creature."

"Ghost? You mean you have actually seen her?" Freddie swallowed and peered nervously into the dark corners of the room.

"Even if she were here, dear boy, I doubt you would see her." Lady Elizabeth leaned over to pat his hand. "I have heard she is quite invisible." She glanced at Aidan. "Is that not so, Aidan?"

He remained silent as he met her steady blue gaze. Her tone had told him nothing. Only once before had his grandmother mentioned the ghost. The night of their arrival. He wondered now if she spoke of everything she knew. Or had she too seen the red-haired woman who haunted his dreams?

"My lord?" Carolyn rose and touched his arm. "Are you well? You look positively ghostly. Perhaps we should have that cup of tea before you and Freddie set about your labor."

He took her hand, squeezed it lightly, and released it. “I am quite well, I assure you. Just a little perturbed at my grandmother’s talk of the ghost. I was unaware that she still spared our little spirit a thought.”

“I can do little else when she has the servants up in arms every other day. Have you seen what she did to the courtyard garden again last night? And the room we had prepared for Freddie? She moved a trunk in front of the door inside, and it took Jeffreys, Saul, and young Toby half the morning to remove it. Toby had to scale the wall and come in through the window. And John the stableman threatened to leave after only one night. Apparently, every time he lit his candle, she blew it out.”

Aidan tried to hide a smile, but realized he’d failed when his grandmother scowled.

“If she is a pest, why not summon a priest?” Carolyn rested back in her chair, tucking her feet primly beneath her gown, her smile sugar-sweet. “I have heard tell the clergy are most successful at ridding old churches of unwanted spirits. Perhaps they could work the same wonders with your castle.”

Lady Elizabeth made to speak, but Aidan cut her off. His tone hard and laced with ice. “There will be no priests. The ghost resided here before we came, and here she will stay. We will have to learn to live with her eccentricities, not she with ours.”

Freddie opened his mouth, but a sharp look closed it again.

“Ladies.” He bowed politely to the women and moved for the door. “Freddie, I believe we have work to do.” He raised a brow. “If you know the meaning of the word.”

Freddie picked up his hat and threw Aidan a

disgruntled look. "Really, cousin, your harshness offends me."

Aidan ignored Freddie's grumblings, dragged open the door, and strode into the hall. His cousin followed, closing the door behind him.

****

Alyssa had seen them arrive. Had seen the beautiful woman alight from the coach with the aid of the young fair-haired man Aidan referred to as his cousin.

Standing in the sitting room, invisible to all, she scowled as the woman tucked her hand through Aidan's arm. And smiled when he defended her. *An exorcist indeed! It would take more than a priest to evict me from Thornwood!* Meredith's weak little husband had attempted just that, and he hadn't gotten very far.

Whether 'twas the magic contained within the standing stones and the hold they held over her spirit, she could not understand. All she knew it had not achieved Meredith's husband's desired result—her exorcism from Thornwood.

She floated down from the ceiling and stood by the window with her arms crossed, staring at the woman they called Carolyn. Golden-haired, blue-eyed, and vitally alive. All the things she was not. She peered down at the courtyard. They had given the woman a room overlooking *her* garden. Three doors up from Aidan—too close.

She could feel her rage building. She knew she should not have these feelings. She was of the spirit world, not of the world of substance. But like a living creature, her jealousy clawed at her insides. Aidan knew this woman. How well, she did not know, but already she disliked her.

She watched while Carolyn selected an intricately carved four-poster in a dark rich wood, a matching dresser, a large bevel-edged mirror, a rose-pink satin counterpane, and material for drapes. Even Lady Elizabeth insisted she have first choice of items for the chamber in which she was to sleep. Aidan, Freddie, and Saul had carted the furniture up the stairs, falling over themselves to please her.

The woman, after dismissing her maid for some small infringement, now sat before a dresser on a musk pink velvet stool in a powder-blue and white-striped satin and lace corset. With a silver-backed brush, she worked the ringlets from her golden hair, which fell to the center of her back. Alyssa knew she could move a few feet, peer into the mirror over the woman's creamy white shoulder, and probably have Miss Golden Hair running from the castle as fast as her too-perfect legs could carry her. But she would not do it. Aidan must care for the woman. He would not have invited her had he not wanted her here. And she would do naught to embarrass him.

Being a warm-blooded man, and Carolyn a warm-blooded woman, Aidan needed someone in his life. She sighed and turned to stare pensively out the window. How could she be such a fool? There would never be a time for her and Aidan. All her waiting had been in vain. What man would want a two-hundred-year-old ghost when he could have the golden goddess sitting in the room behind her?

A knock sounded, and Alyssa spun to see Carolyn hasten to the door. The blonde opened it a crack and dragged Aidan's cousin Freddie inside. "What are you doing here? You will ruin everything if you are caught."

She flounced over and flopped down onto the stool. "You were supposed to visit me tonight. Not now."

"I know." He came up behind her and trailed his fingertips down her slender throat. "But you know how hard I find it to keep my hands off you. I wanted to kill Aidan in the sitting room when he kissed your fingers." Meeting her wide-eyed blue gaze in the mirror, he trailed his hands down to capture her breasts, kneading them gently.

She arched up and laid her head back against his stomach as he caught her nipples between his forefingers and thumbs and delicately squeezed.

"You are the only one I want." She groaned as he spread soft kisses along her throat, then lower to take the place of his hands.

Alyssa, sickened, floated out through the window. Something wrong was going on here, but she would not stay and watch. There would be time enough to see what Aidan's not-so-innocent cousin and the golden-haired woman were about.

****

Aidan's head ached with dark brooding thoughts as he slouched against the stone windowsill, peering out the parlor room window at the pounding sea lashing the black rocks below. Carolyn would do nothing for naught. So why had the lovely widow Simms left London to travel to the wilds of Cornwall in the middle of the Social Season? He laughed shortly. To capture a rich husband, why else? But for whom had she set her cap?

Freddie had no fortune left to speak of, just a small annual stipend doled out by Aidan due to the proviso of his grandfather's will. He was next in line to Dunmore, yes. But unless something fatal happened to Aidan before he produced an heir, it was unlikely Freddie would ever inherit. And his health could never be better.

Still, he had not seen Carolyn in all of six years, and according to the lady herself, her husband dead for all of four. Aidan thought she would have sought him earlier, had there been an interest.

"What a delightful woman," his grandmother remarked into the silence. "Mrs. Simms tells me she and Freddie met at one of Lady Talbert's masked balls over a year ago, and you know how hard Lady Talbert is to please. She would not extend an invitation to just anybody."

He absorbed the information with barely a blink. His grandfather must have done an excellent job of hushing up the old scandal if Lady Talbert had not caught wind of it. Lady Talbert, one of the most distinguished dowagers in all of London, wielded her power with impunity. A right word from her had been known to raise a young lady in status. A wrong word to break her.

He turned and leaned with his back to the window ledge. His grandmother, seated on a new pink and white satin sofa, stitched a floral tapestry with diligent concentration. Dora perched on the edge of a matching overstuffed chair by the fire, giving her small doily the same attention. Aidan removed his dark-blue frockcoat and folded it over the arm of the sofa.

"I hope, Grandmother, this is not going to lead to another of your dreary lectures on matrimony."

"The woman is of good breeding."

"Excellent really. Her father, a lord, and I believe there is a duke to be had on her mother's side. But that is no reason I should whisk her away to the altar."

Lady Elizabeth lowered her tapestry and motioned

for Dora to leave the room. She waited for the other woman to close the parlor door, then rounded on her grandson. "Why ever not?" she demanded. "What is wrong with the girl? I declare, Aidan, I despair of any woman ever getting you to the altar." She pulled a lace handkerchief from her pale mauve reticule and dabbed at her nose. "Is it so wrong of me to want to see my great-grandchildren before I die? What more could you want in a woman?"

What indeed? Aidan looked past his grandmother at the fire as it flickered and leapt in the grate. *Except a very fine pair of emerald eyes.* He picked up his coat. "If you wish for a grandchild so, perhaps you should speak to Freddie."

"Freddie? You cannot be serious. That boy wouldn't know what to do with a woman."

Aidan threw his grandmother a look of despair. He could tell the fine lady about the succession of broken hearts and sullied reputations his cousin had left behind in London. Though to what end? It would only destroy her illusions about her only other grandson. No, it was best *he* play the villain in this piece.

"I find this conversation both repetitious and boring. I will marry whom *I* want when I am ready, and no amount of nagging will change my mind. Now, if you will excuse me, I have a craving for some fresh air." He straightened away from the window and crossed the rug. "If you wish to find Freddie, I believe he is in the stables speaking with the groom." He reached for the door handle. "Perhaps you will have more luck with *him*."

Lady Elizabeth made to rise and fell weakly back into her seat. "Please, I did not mean to offend." She brought her lace handkerchief to her lips and coughed several times, wiped her mouth, and sank back into her chair.

Aidan hastened across the room to kneel at his grandmother's side and took her hand. "Are you unwell? Should I send for a doctor?"

"So the barracuda can bleed me? Certainly not." Her voice softened, and she gently squeezed his hand. "No. I worry for you, that is all. I do not wish you to end up alone when I am gone."

"I have told you. You are not going anywhere for a very long time." He smiled softly. "I will not let you." He rose and reached for his coat. "I will speak to Freddie about his intentions regarding Carolyn. If he is not inclined to marry the woman, I will consider her." *Not if she were the last female in this hemisphere.* "But I cannot promise anything," he added quickly, turning for the door.

Teary-eyed, Lady Elizabeth nodded. "Tell Carolyn when she comes down from her nap that I am looking forward to seeing her at dinner."

Aidan closed the door with a soft click of finality, but not before he spied Lady Elizabeth picking up her tapestry and leaning back in her chair with a satisfied twitch of her lips. The old devil, he thought, with a soft smile.

He had every intention of seeking out Freddie when he left his grandmother, but as he passed the round garden on a shortcut to the stables, he spied Lyssa sitting on the stone bench. He stopped dead, caught by the picture of innocence she portrayed. The last rays of sunlight surrounded her body, enhancing it, giving her silhouette an otherworldly luminescence. She faced away, speaking to Tom.

The old man glanced at him, his expression tightening as he snatched off his cap. "M'lord?"

"Forgive me. I did not mean to intrude. Do continue. I can wait."

"I was leavin'," Tom grumbled.

Lyssa had risen and turned at the sound of his voice. She gave a small curtsy as Aidan approached, and he could not help but smile.

"Then perhaps I could impose on you, Tom, for a few words with your niece."

The old man grunted something that might have been his consent and ambled across the courtyard.

He nodded to Lyssa, indicating she should sit. He removed his hat, leaned against the standing stone closest to the seat, and crossed his arms.

She wore the same white bonnet and dress he had seen on her the first time they met and appeared just as ethereal. Like a lovely spring breeze come to settle in his courtyard. He wondered why she reminded him so much of the woman in his dreams when Lyssa was so innocent, sweet, bordering on shy, and Alyssa—*their names even sounded alike*—was strong, independent, and knew her own mind.

"My uncle was telling me your furniture has arrived. He says there are many fine pieces."

"Three more wagons should arrive come morning if all goes well. One can never eliminate the danger of the highwaymen altogether."

"Yes, but it must be exciting to furnish the castle with all that modern furniture and choose what goes where."

"My guest, Mrs. Simms, certainly thinks so," he commented dryly, then smiled. "Would you care to offer us the pleasure of your company tomorrow morning for tea? Then afterward I could give you a tour of the castle. I will have my grandmother send you her card."

She glanced away in what Aidan took as a bout of shyness.

"Perhaps," she murmured. "I will have to speak with my uncle."

"And there is our resident ghost. I hope *she* will be kind. It is said she likes to play tricks."

"Oh. As in what way?"

"The wagon drivers are housed in the old servants' quarters for the night. They will depart at dawn if she leaves them be. Perhaps you could mention the fact to your uncle, and he could persuade her to behave." He contemplated Lyssa's lovely face, flushed rosy by the setting sun. "I don't know, though I cannot help but feel Tom has more dealings with our ghostly inhabitant than he is wont to say."

Alyssa contemplated her feet, and again Aidan thought it unusual for a young woman to wander the courtyard barefooted, but he refrained from saying so. Her small perfect toes and slim ankles did things to his insides Carolyn's too-obvious charms could never do.

"I promise I shall ask, but as I have said, he does not speak to me of her. However, he did tell me just now that your guests are here for several days."

He moved to rest his foot on the seat beside her.

She glanced up at him through dark lashes, her eyes so wide, so green, he was tempted to study them closer and try to fathom the true enchantment that lay within. What color would they turn should he kiss her? If she would allow him to kiss her? Would they burn bright like Alyssa's when she had met his gaze in the mirror? When she had touched him.

"My lord?"

He straightened and settled beside her, running a hand over the back of his neck beneath his cravat. What was he thinking? Just because she resembled Alyssa and their names sounded alike, it did not give him license to take advantage. "Forgive me, you were saying?"

"You have guests?"

"Yes." He turned to face her. "My cousin, Lord Fredrick Fitzwilliam, and an old acquaintance from London, Mrs. Carolyn Simms, whom I mentioned earlier."

She studied her folded hands. "Not so old, I am led to believe."

"She is really my cousin's guest. He invited her. She is the widow of the admiral whom I served under while in the Navy."

She looked up. "You served in the Navy?"

"Yes, during the Napoleonic War."

"Oh. Of course, how silly of me. How fortunate you returned unscathed." She looked away. "My uncle tells me Mrs. Simms is very beautiful."

"Beauty is as beauty does," Aidan murmured, still thinking on her first words. He may have been unscathed in body, but he had seen a lot and done a lot during that time that would forever haunt him. Losing Anni being one of his most painful memories. He lifted Lyssa's chin to look into her eyes. Perhaps in those depths, he could lose himself and never have to remember again.

"I do not understand."

"No, you would not. It is an old saying. It means beauty is only skin deep, or more so, in the eye of the beholder. And I behold great beauty here." He breathed softly. "I have missed you."

"You have?" Her words almost as soft.

She searched his face as he smoothed a strand of dark-red hair back beneath her bonnet. For some uncanny reason, he could not look away or lower his hand, and his fingers curved of their own accord to fit the contour of her cheek. He had not bothered to collect his gloves before he had left his grandmother, and her skin seemed warm, almost hot, beneath his touch. He couldn't move and had no will to do so. "I have only met you once, but I cannot help feeling we have met before. Does that sound ridiculous?"

"No, not at all," she whispered. "I feel it too. Perhaps we met in another lifetime."

He leaned in closer. Feeling her soft breath on his face. Her rose perfume embracing him. Even her scent seemed familiar. "I would like very much to kiss you. I *am* going to kiss you, for I cannot help but do so."

She swayed into him, and his arms came around her. His lips claiming hers in a soft caress, then searing, branding. He crushed her to his chest. He had wanted to be gentle, coaxing in respect for her innocence, but from that first touch, he was lost. His tongue pushed into her mouth, and she welcomed him with a sweet sigh, her mouth a pure aphrodisiac, hot, smooth, and tasting of honey.

An image of Cai and Alyssa flashed through his mind.

Her fiery hair, wild about her shoulders, her eyes bright, and her face flushed with passion. They were in the tower room on the floor. Hot blistering desire. She melted into him as if she belonged, as if she had always belonged. Pressing, melding, bodies grinding, entwined.

Flesh upon flesh. Her hands burned feverishly as they pressed against his abdomen, dragging at the laces of his breeches.

Aidan tore his mouth from hers, and the image fled. He ended the kiss with passion riding him hard. It was all he could do to stop from tossing her to the grass like a tavern doxy and burying himself between her thighs. He shoved her from him before thought become reality, though he did not release her, and his fingers bit into her soft upper arms. He saw her wince, but she did not cry out. She was stronger than he imagined. He held her there at arm's length, his anger bubbling like an inferno in his chest.

"What was that?" he hissed, releasing her abruptly and backing away. "I thought I knew you." He shook his head, his breath coming harsh, fractured. "But I don't know you, do I? Not at all. No properly brought-up young miss kisses like that. Nor does she press herself into a man's arms in such a wanton manner. No. I don't know you at all." He twisted and strode swiftly to disappear through the rose arch at the side of the garden.

****

She watched him go in silence, restraining a wild urge to race after him, to call him back, to tell him it had always been like this between them. Her hands trembled. Confusion filled her head. Had he seen what she had seen? She had thought the vision that played in her mind while they kissed a memory. Now doubt plagued her. Had her being a ghost worked some strange power upon them both? Had they somehow been transported back to a time when he had held her so and their love had burned? Love for her and Cai had never been a gentle thing that could be mastered. It had been wild, passionate, and untamed.

They had known each other for such a short time before death had parted them, and made love only thrice, but he had kissed her many times in the days before their marriage, and each time it had been the same—bone-melting, earth-shattering, lustful, and powerful. And now she had felt it once more with Aidan de Morgan, Cai's likeness, and wondered how she could bear to be parted from him again. But there was no place in this chaste world in which Aidan lived for a love such as theirs, and now he thought her a wanton.

She sighed. Why did he have to kiss her? Everything was ruined. She had been content to see him, talk to him, and occasionally touch his hand. Now all that was spoiled.

What a simpleton she had been to think that he was a reincarnation of Cai or indeed anything like him. Aidan de Morgan had no passion in his soul. He was a stranger. A stranger she did not know. Yet still, she could not let the dream of him go.

She slipped from the circle and resumed her spirit guise, but as she did so, she glanced at the room the woman called Carolyn now occupied, and her thoughts again turned to the man who had kissed her. She did not know what Carolyn planned, but if she schemed to harm Aidan, she would have a battle on her hands. For she would defend Aidan de Morgan to the root of her immortal soul. She had lost him once. She would not lose him again. That he looked like Cai was reason enough, plus the thought of Carolyn touching him made her skin crawl.

Chapter Nine

Aidan sat in the dining room at the long cherry-wood table. Their party included Lady Elizabeth, Carolyn, and Freddie. Their chatter about the pros and cons of London society hummed around him like a bee surrounding a honey pot, but he barely acknowledged the sound. His ears were filled with his harsh words to Lyssa earlier that day.

Suddenly, he noticed the silence in the room and looked up to see the other occupants of the table staring at him.

"Aidan, the wine," his grandmother prompted with a tight-lipped smile from across the table.

The butler, standing beside him, awaited his verdict. He had not seen the man pour the sample for his tasting, so deep were his thoughts. He lifted the glass, swirled it, sniffed, and sipped. "It will do," he said, watching the new butler refill his glass with Burgundy wine.

The brew tasted sour on his tongue, not unlike his thoughts. He had acted a fool. How would he ever face her again? Dear sweet Lyssa had not deserved his display of temper. The episode was entirely his fault, not hers. He had initiated the kiss and the one who'd had the vision.

A young maid entered with entrees, including turtle soup and shrimp jelly, and again the conversation flowed. Eleanor had outdone herself with an evening meal that could have rivaled any of the fine culinary chefs of London. Pheasant, duckling, and a side of roast pork, accompanied by an assortment of steaming vegetables, spiced and cream sauces, and pastries followed. However, he barely tasted a morsel. Still brooding over Lyssa, his gut churned, and every time he thought of the words he had uttered in the garden, his food threatened to choke him. The vision of Cai and Alyssa haunted him.

Could he and Lyssa be the reincarnations of Cai and Alyssa? He had heard such tales, but had dismissed them as nonsensical. Now with what had happened, he had to consider the possibility. Lyssa certainly resembled the woman in his dreams. Even her name—Lyssa, Alyssa. He tested the words softly on his tongue. Or perhaps there was a logical explanation. Perchance the Jeffreys family *was* in some way related to the Llewellyn's. It would explain the likeness…but not the vision.

He poked at his pudding with his spoon, unable to sample it. Why had he acted so rashly with Lyssa? Why was he so affected by her fresh convent-girl innocence, then upset by what he had termed her betrayal? By nature, his ways were not rash. No schoolboy to lose grip of his emotions so easily.

Then a small voice spoke in his mind, reminding him she had deceived him. He had thought her innocent.

But no innocent kissed like that!

Her tongue matched his stroke for stroke. Her nails raked his back, and her body…her slim, pliant body, hot against his, urging him on. There had been fire, hot, burning, lustful fire that had torn at his insides and turned his emotions inside out.

And what of the vision?

He had been hard-pressed not to toss her onto the grass and take her right between the druid stones after seeing that vision. The sensation had terrified him, and he was not a man easily frightened. But then again, was she truly at fault? Perhaps it had not been Lyssa at all. Perhaps the ghost planted the vision in his head.

It would not be the first time she played tricks upon he and his. He'd read of people being possessed by spirits. Perhaps neither he nor Lyssa were at fault. He relaxed back in his chair, only for his mind to take another track.

Or maybe his conscience was rebelling with guilt? Had he conjured the images himself? He thought of Antoinette, with her cloud of dark hair and deep violet eyes, and guilt washed over him. He had betrayed the memory of his dead wife. Promising he would never love again, here he was with not one, but two women playing with his mind. Or did it go deeper? Was he afraid of being hurt? Of giving his heart? Could that be why the ghost woman held such an attraction? She could never leave him, never be taken from him, because she was already dead.

He stopped poking at his food and leaned back in his chair, staring across at his grandmother but not really seeing her. No. What kind of sick masochist had he become if this was the case? So locked in his own personal world of blame and despair that he had taken his frustration out on a young woman who had shown him naught but kindness?

"Aidan, are you well? You look positively ghastly, and you have been unusually quiet all evening, as if you are not really here. First, the wine, now staring straight through me as if you don't know me." His grandmother frowned. "You do worry me at times."

He pushed his plate to the side, took up his napkin, and wiped his lips. "Do not concern yourself, grandmother. I am quite fine. I am contemplating if I should start breeding my stallion now or when I return to Dunmore."

"Really, Aidan, that is no talk for the dinner table."

"You did ask." He smiled.

"Yes, well. I must despair of you ever becoming a proper gentleman. I don't know what happened when you served in His Majesty's Service, but it certainly did not refine your manners."

"No, fortunately, I was too busy making certain you and Freddie were safe in your beds."

Freddie opened his mouth to speak, but Carolyn cut him off with a pointed look. "Aidan, you must allow me to guide you on your arrangement of the furniture tomorrow. I did so enjoy myself today." Carolyn's forget-me-not eyes smoldered at him across the table.

Wearing a white gown trimmed with thin gold tassels along the hem and short sleeves, the neckline fashionably low, barely covering her breasts, she looked amazing, and she knew it.

He could not help comparing Lyssa's high-necked, outdated dress to Carolyn's gown of the latest fashion. Sometimes a woman's charms were better left to a man's imagination. A steely edge crept into his tone. "Of course, I am certain my grandmother would be most approving."

Carolyn paled and raised her fingers to her throat. "I must beg your forgiveness, Lady Elizabeth. I hope you did not think me overindulgent."

His grandmother patted Carolyn's hand. "Of course

not, my dear. Aidan and I would be delighted to have your assistance. You have such a wonderful eye for color. Has she not, Aidan?" His grandmother glared at him across the table.

He met her steady gaze with a somewhat wan smile, but deep inside his stomach churned. He'd been considering a way of dodging Carolyn's company when his thoughts turned to his dilemma with Lyssa. "I look forward to tomorrow with anticipation." He cringed and changed the subject. "Jeffreys' niece may drop by in the morning." He took a sip of his wine, contemplating its rosy hue and its bitter fruity flavor on his tongue rather than looking at the two women. "I have promised her a tour of the castle."

"Oh?" Carolyn queried.

"Yes. She is visiting from Plymouth. Did I not tell you, Grandmother?" He gave Lady Elizabeth a charming smile, which his grandmother met with a frown.

"No. You did not."

"Jeffreys? The steward, you mean?" Carolyn's smile slipped.

"Yes. Her father, Jeffreys' brother, owns a shipping company in Plymouth."

"How quaint." Carolyn peered down her nose at her barely touched Manchester pudding. "Though I suppose, if one is not born into the gentry, one must make a living."

Eleanor helped the maid clear the plates with a noisy clatter and disappeared through the door at the back of the room.

"I never knew Jeffreys had a niece." Lady Elizabeth dabbed at her lips with her linen napkin. "Let alone that she was staying with him. Wherever does he hide her?"

She raised her quizzing glass at Aidan. "You have actually met this girl?"

"Lower your monocle, grandmother, you make me feel like a bug beneath a spyglass. Yes, I have met the young lady twice in the garden between the standing stones."

"Alone?" Carolyn asked with a rise of a shapely brow. The look she threw Lady Elizabeth spoke volumes.

The older woman arched a brow in Aidan's direction.

"No. Of course not alone. If that is what my words implied, I must apologize on her behalf. Jeffreys introduced us and stayed while we spoke." Aidan shaded the truth. He didn't know why he felt so protective of Lyssa, only that he didn't want his grandmother or Carolyn thinking ill of her. He knew firsthand how cruel society could be to any who did not conform to its strict code of etiquette.

If anyone deserved their contempt, it was not Lyssa, but himself. It had been he who had flaunted convention at their first meeting. Insisting Tom leave when he had discovered them, speaking with only Toby in attendance. He then sent Tom and the boy on their way. On the second occasion, he had asked Tom for time alone with Lyssa, knowing it would be unlikely he'd refuse.

It had been he who initiated the kiss, though he never expected the outcome to be so dramatic. A flush of heat suffused his body at the mere thought of Lyssa's soft, pliant form clinging to him. He scowled into his empty wineglass. Why should such images haunt him? There had to be a reason his thoughts would give him no peace.

Out of all patience with himself and his company, he pushed back his chair and made his excuses before another word could be said. He could no longer stay and pretend to be something he was not, like agreeing to his grandmother's plan to see him and Carolyn wed. He just wanted to seek his room, where he could mull through his thoughts, no matter how twisted and confused. Where he could stare down at the garden between the stones and imagine a lovely red-haired girl looking back at him, hoping she would forgive him.

****

She watched him enter his room and close the door softly behind him. He leaned back and breathed what seemed a sigh of relief, then tossed his frock coat to the bed and continued on to the window. She had watched him since he left her earlier in anger and saw him defend her to his grandmother and his guests, and her love for him had grown tenfold.

Light droplets of rain touched Aidan's face as he leaned out the window to gaze down into the dark courtyard. With a disgruntled groan, he drew back and slammed the shutters. Turning abruptly, he strode straight through her, and she fought to control the sick feeling that lurched in her stomach. She heard the loose board creak and saw Aidan drop to his knees to peel back the rug, and her nausea dissipated to be replaced by the pounding of her heart. She knew she shouldn't feel it, but it beat in her breast like a war drum. He had found her journal. Her hopes, her dreams, her cry for help!

Aidan tried to push his fingers into the crack between the boards and pry the loose board from the floor, but with the gap being so narrow, he could gain no purchase. He pushed down on one end to lever the other end up, but again met with failure. The board had loosened, but it refused to cooperate. He scanned the room for a lever, saw a shoehorn upon the dresser, rose, snatched it up, and dropped to his knees again before the board. Pushing the wide end of the shoehorn between the boards, he forced up the edge.

Alyssa knelt across from him. His face alight with the same anticipation she knew hers must show, had it been visible. His hands trembled as did hers as he lifted the board from the place it had rested for almost two hundred years.

Then suddenly, she felt it. The deep abiding cold, the same familiar chill, an ache in her soul. The hand of darkness rushed closer, surrounding her, merging, drawing her along, tearing her from Aidan's side. She screamed silently into the void. Not now, not when he was about to discover her secret…

****

Aidan stared down into the cavity beneath the board, his breath stilling, almost afraid to move, lest the book within the dust and cobwebs should vanish. His assumption about the loose board had been correct. Beneath the board lay a secret. How big a secret, he was yet to discover. Dust layered the small book's black-and-gold-engraved cover, and his hands shook. Reverently, he lifted what looked like a journal from its ancient resting place only to make another precious discovery. Beneath it, glinting through a thick layer of cobweb, sat a small golden key. He plucked the key from its hiding place and fit the board back into place. "Dear lord," he breathed, "let it be hers." He replaced the rug and carried his treasure to the bed, stripped off his clothes, and hurriedly climbed beneath the covers.

He sat leaning against the headboard, staring down at the closed diary, seeming utterly out of place, yet…belonging perfectly. Finally, he slid the key into the lock as though made of spun glass and carefully turned. The mechanism gave immediately with only the slightest catch.

One simple action and the private thoughts of a woman ages dead lay revealed before him.

His hands shook at the prospect of unraveling the mystery of Alyssa, if that was indeed to whom the book belonged. With a deep breath, he carefully opened the journal partway through. Pages yellowed and brittle with the passing of centuries stared up at him. He focused on the first line of the left-hand side and read the delicate intertwined script, which could only belong to a woman.

Today Jane and I came to Thornwood. My father has given me to Gedrych's son in marriage, bringing an end to the siege. He is a strange man, Cai de Morgan, this man to whom I am pledged. Cold, remote on the outside, I think he pretends to be something he is not. I see a warmness within him, which presented itself this eve when he gifted me with a perfect red rose. It sits beside me now even as I make this entry.

The entry was dated May 19, 1644. The same day he arrived at the castle except it had been May 19, 1824. One hundred and eighty years later.

A soft knock sounded on the door, and Bevan poked his head around the edge. Quickly, he covered the diary with the duvet.

"I thought I would see if you needed anything, my lord?"

Aidan frowned at the other man, uncomprehending as Bevan looked pointedly at his bare chest. Then, remembering where he was, shook his head. "No. Goodnight, Bevan." Although he knew Bevan to be loyal, he could not trust his manservant with such a precious discovery. He heard the door close, and his lips twisted wryly. He knew he had disappointed his grandfather's former manservant yet again and wondered if he would ever become the gentleman the older man hoped for.

However, Aidan had no time to ponder thoughts of proper bedtime etiquette. Already he reached for the diary. The last entry had told of the siege of Herbert Llewellyn's castle—about Cai and Alyssa's first meeting. He had been there. He had lived it, and he now knew beyond a doubt that what happened was no dream, but a digression into a past life. And he could not help himself. Although the hour grew late, he felt driven. He moved the candle closer and read more of the beautiful spidery script that spilled out the life of a young woman who had become almost an obsession to him since arriving at Thornwood.

May 25th

The wedding is in five days. I must confess Cai has stolen my heart. Something I thought impossible in such a short time. To fall in love with the son of my father's enemy, and a Catholic.

But it is Gedrych I fear. He watches me. Even when I cannot see him, I feel his demon eyes upon me. I swear the man is the devil reincarnate. Jane told me today, she heard from a servant that he strangled his wife after she gave birth to Cai, for it was thought she had taken a lover. And it could not be proved the boy is his. He is a cruel, brutal man who is a law unto himself. I could believe well that Cai is no kin of his!

May 26th

I rode the moors with Cai this day. We picnicked between the strange stones in the valley below the castle, and he stole a kiss for the first time. 'Twas all I thought it would be—fire, ice, hell, and heaven. Fire for the way he makes my blood burn. Ice for the deep cold blue of his eyes. Hell, because the kiss did not stretch into eternity. Heaven for the way he makes me feel protected when his arms surround me.

Mid-Morning May 30th

I have taken this moment to write in my journal. The wedding was all I could hope for. My Lord husband is the most handsome of all men and I am truly blessed. 'Tis beyond doubt a marvel how fate can twist something as ugly as war and hate into a thing of love and beauty. If not for the feud between our families, I would not now be the wife of Cai de Morgan. I only wish my father and brothers could have attended, but Gedrych would not sanction it. Though he has in a rare act of kindness hired an artist to capture the wedding on canvas—his wedding gift to us. Still, the man frightens me. His eyes are like living creatures. Whenever I turn, they claw at me.

Evening May 30th

A terrible tragedy has occurred. A royal messenger interrupted our wedding feast. War has broken out between the allied army of Parliamentary and Scottish troops and Prince Rupert's Royalists. Rupert is demanding men be sent to join him. Gedrych has ordered Cai to go. I cannot help feeling that it is a ploy of Gedrych's to separate us. Cai is determined to speak with his father in the morning, but I feel it will be in vain.

Aidan laid the book aside and glanced unseeing at the dying embers of the fire.

He had experienced the banquet with Alyssa. Had held her while they danced and heard her tell of her fears of Gedrych. He remembered Cai's anger at being told he must lead Gedrych's men to battle the next morning and the look of lust he had caught in the older man's eyes as he stared at Alyssa on the way from the hall.

The ink was blotched in several places, and Aidan's hands clenched on the bedclothes. He could see far too clearly—the new bride, sitting alone with her diary, tears spilling from her eyes. What had started as such a joyful day had ended in sorrow. How he wished he could have held her close to comfort her.

May 31st

My fears are realized. Cai rode from the castle this morning with fifty men. Gedrych would not relent. He says Cai will return before the week is through, but I despair of ever seeing my beloved again.

Last night my husband held me in his arms, and we pledged our love and our souls for eternity. I pray to God for Cai to come back to me. I do not know if I can survive in this dreadful hellhole without him.

June 3rd

My intuition served me right. I knew I did not imagine it. No sooner had Cai ridden from my side than Gedrych's attitude changed. He is too friendly, overly so. He brushed past me today in the hallway, then caught me in his arms as I would have fallen. His touch way too familiar and he held me far too long. I can still feel the imprint of his wretched body against mine, and the imprint of his talon-like fingers on my arms, and I shiver. The man revolts me even as he terrifies me.

He is prone to fits of unreasonable anger, as I witnessed this evening. He had a servant thrashed in the great hall to within a breath of his life for spilling a goblet of wine. He is a cruel and despicable master, and all my father's words ring true. He is no godly man.

Aidan flipped through several pages, skimming the words. All telling of Alyssa's fears of Gedrych.

July 5th

Today I had word from Cai. My heart soars. He is well. He promises to be home in ten days.

I have made a new friend. Jane's William de Bracey is a great comfort to me. He fills my days with tales of Cai's childhood. He and Cai grew up together. At least when I am with him, Gedrych cannot happen upon me alone.

July 8th

William asked for Jane's hand in marriage and Gedrych refused. Jane is devastated. She threatens to kill herself. Gedrych says Jane is not to leave the castle. She is a trophy of war, and he will hear no more talk of a man of William's station asking for the hand of a commoner. I have tried to explain to Gedrych, that Jane is the daughter of a noblewoman. A lady-in-waiting and of no low station, but he will have none of it. He forbids William to see Jane alone, but they have already plotted to meet in secret.

Aidan closed the book gently and, with a clenched jaw, climbed from his bed to replace the diary beneath the loose board. He had no desire for Alyssa's personal thoughts, feelings, or words to be read by any other.

Even though he felt like an intruder, he doubted she would mind too much, if the way she had touched him and looked at him that first night in his mirror gave any indication of her feelings toward him. But his fist bunched as his thoughts turned to Gedrych, and he knew something of Cai's frustration. If he had been sent from her side, he knew he would have fought with every fiber of his mortal soul to stay. Yet from what Alyssa had written and from what he had viewed in his dreams, Gedrych de Morgan was a formable man and not easily denied.

Chapter Ten

Aidan had no time to read more entries from the diary, as the second shipment of furniture arrived. Lyssa sent word that she could not accept his invitation to tour the castle due to a family emergency. And any discussion he attempted with Tom had been virtually ignored. He could have called the old man to account but thought it best to let it lie.

Distributing the furniture among the various rooms of the castle helped fill his next few days. Then afterward, Carolyn insisted they take a jaunt to St. Agnes to hire a seamstress to fashion new drapes. He realized Carolyn's enthusiasm stemmed from her hopes that he might ask for her hand, but he had no intentions in that quarter. Although, as Lady Elizabeth pointed out, Carolyn was of good birth and she had given him no obvious reason to distrust her, the woman instilled an uneasiness in him.

Overall, the outing to St. Agnes rang with success. Rugs procured, drapes ordered for the twenty bedrooms and the living areas, and his grandmother had purchased a fine porcelain teapot, saying she could no longer abide tea from the old, chipped relic at the castle.

They returned to Thornwood early afternoon with Carolyn pleading tiredness and Freddie making the excuse he had to check on his new gelding.

Aidan left Lady Elizabeth in the sitting room sipping

tea with Dora and wandered out to the courtyard in hope of finding Lyssa. He needed to apologize for his behavior at their last meeting. However, the garden was empty. The weather was cooling, and a north wind whistled through the courtyard. The scent of roses was thick in the air and heavenly sweet to his senses, reminding him of Lyssa. The garden lacked life, despite the fragrant flower beds. Or was that just guilt gnawing at his senses.

Determined, he set out for the gatehouse to see her. The desire more desperate as his footsteps ate up the white gravel beneath his boots. Lyssa must know he was sorry. He'd no right to blame her when it was he who was at fault. He had taken advantage of her. However, even as the thought crossed his mind, he knew, should the situation arise again, the outcome would be the same. He was drawn to the girl unlike any before, even Anni. Whether it was her uncanny resemblance to the ghost or her blend of sweet innocence and sensuality, he had yet to decipher. He knew he had to see her, and the feeling was becoming as imperative as air to his lungs.

A small blue bird flew, startled, from a berry bush as he marched past. Late spring and the park abounded with color. Dainty pink and white flowers laced the branches of the ancient trees lining the drive. A multitude of blossoms swirled toward him, caught by a light breeze, and sprinkled down upon the newly manicured lawn. Toby and Saul had worked the grounds diligently, trimming hedges and sowing flowerbeds of yellow daisies, pink and white hollyhock, and bluebells.

The ancient fountain in the small court out front of the gatehouse gleamed, and a splash of crystalline water sprayed into the air from a cherub's mouth to tinkle into the surrounding bowl. Aidan barely noticed any of this

his resolve to see Lyssa, so strong.

He reached the bottom of the five steps leading up to the gatehouse and as if on cue, Tom emerged from a heavy oak door to greet him. "She ain't 'ere."

He admired the old man's courage. "I'll wait."

"Won't do you no good. She's gone t' St. Agnes."

"I just returned from St. Agnes. I did not encounter her."

Tom shrugged. "You wouldn't 'ave been lookin'."

"She told you what happened?"

"No." Tom peered over Aidan's shoulder with a scowl. "Now, I must be gettin' about me business." He made to turn, then pulled himself up. "She said if you came 'ere to tell you she needs time t' think. She said not to look for 'er."

Aidan held himself rigid, realizing he'd just been chastised. "I see. Well, tell her I'm sorry for any misunderstanding."

Tom grunted and made to turn into the house.

"And tell her—"

"Yes." The old man rounded, folded arms across his chest, his lips thin in his weathered face.

Aidan looked away. "Don't worry, I'll tell her myself."

"I said no good would come o' this." Tom reached for the door handle.

"Wait."

He stilled and turned.

"Tom, I meant no disrespect to your niece. I think she is…a most charming and lovely girl."

Tom's jaw hardened. "But?"

Aidan folded his hands behind his back and studied the old man's face. What could he tell him? That although he thought Lyssa lovely, he could not dismiss the thought that her resemblance to Alyssa and his curiosity about the castle's beautiful ghostly inhabitant might be her only attraction.

"There is no but," he said, taking a step backward down the steps. Though as he did so, he caught a movement of the curtain at the top window of the gatehouse. Perhaps the wind, or Lyssa watched. He could place no blame on her for not wishing to speak to him. He'd not exactly acted the gentleman at any of their meetings.

Confusion filled him about who he really wanted. When with Lyssa, he wanted only her. When he thought or read or dreamed of Alyssa, every moment was consumed with her image. One thing he did know. If he didn't leave this castle soon, it would see an end to him. And yet he was compelled to stay, for the thought of leaving filled him with despair.

****

Alyssa watched Carolyn choose a bottle-green evening gown with golden thread, low bodice, and wide skirt when a light tap sounded at the door.

Carolyn's maid traipsed across the room to open it and stood aside for Freddie to enter.

Carolyn's dark gaze rested on her maid. "Not a word, hear? Or I will see you dismissed."

The young maid blanched. "Yes, milady."

"Good." She smiled briefly. "Now go."

As the maid pushed past Freddie into the hall and shut the door, Carolyn swept into Freddie's arms, and his mouth claimed hers in a hard kiss. He released her and eased back, holding her loosely in his grip.

She lifted her hands to the sides of his face. "What

are you doing here?"

He broke free and fell theatrically back upon the rose-pink counterpane. "I cannot stand that stuffed shirt near you. I cannot abide the way he touches you."

"Now, darling." She knelt between his legs on the Oriental rug and ran her slender hands up over his muscled thighs. "You must be reasonable. It is all part of our plan."

"To hell with the plan," he ground, staring sulkily up at the ceiling, pushing her hands away. "Your way is too slow, and I am not a patient man."

But Carolyn would not be deterred. She cupped the bulge in his riding breeches and squeezed gently. "You promised we would do this my way," she murmured as a hiss of breath escaped his lips.

He took her hand and brought her to her feet, turning her quickly toward him. With both hands, he tore her dress from neck to waist. A soft sigh escaped her lips as the satin-covered buttons flew around her and her gown slithered to the floor.

"You've ruined my gown," she admonished, stepping from the pool of satin and lace.

"When I am earl, I will buy you a thousand new gowns. Now come, my beauty. I have missed you."

With a satisfied smile, she turned into his arms, and he fell backward onto the bed again, taking her with him with her short, sharp squeal of delight.

"Hush," he admonished, covering her mouth with his hand. "Do you want my cousin in here with us?"

She smiled wickedly into his eyes. "The thought of having you both at once intrigues me."

"It would give me an excuse to shoot him. We could say he went mad with lust." His teeth glinted in the sunlight filtering into the room. "That I found him forcing himself upon you. We struggled, and I shot him in self-defense."

She laughed softly and leaned forward, running her small pink tongue down the thick curve of his throat. "Not yet, darling. Keep your plans for the honeymoon."

Standing in the corner, Alyssa went still. So they meant to do Aidan harm. Now it all came clear—Carolyn's play for Aidan and Freddie standing by all innocent, saying naught. They planned for Aidan to marry Carolyn, then kill him on their honeymoon. As the grieving widow, an inconsolable Carolyn would naturally turn to Freddie as an old friend, and the soon-to-be Earl of Dunmore. After a decent interval, he would marry her.

She wondered how they meant to do it. A feigned robbery? A carriage accident? Bile rose in her throat, then her fists bunched in her gown. She had to stop them. She would not let Aidan be stolen from her, as Cai had. She had lost her love once to Mistress Death. She would not allow it again.

"I don't know if I can bear seeing you married to that stuffed shirt, even for an instant," Freddie murmured, trailing soft wet kisses down Carolyn's slender throat, finally coming to rest over her breast. "Allowing him to touch you like this." He kneaded her breasts with his hands, watching her nipples pucker and shrink. "And like this." One hand disappeared between her thighs, and her eyelids lowered.

"Help me off with my stays," she purred.

Alyssa swung away toward the window. She had heard all she needed to hear. She had to warn Aidan, but first she must speak to Tom. She willed herself to materialize in a different part of the castle, but as she began to fade, she cast a last look at the two on the bed, and in that instant, an idea formed.

Carolyn slid from the bed, her gaze going to the mirror across the room as she waited for Freddie to deal with her undergarments. Alyssa saw her chance. Moving up behind her on the far side of the bed, she peered into the mirror and locked eyes with Carolyn.

The woman's bright blue eyes widened, and she spun. "Who are…?" The color drained from her face as she realized there was no one behind her but Freddie.

Or no one she could see.

She turned again quickly.

Alyssa met her gaze with a mocking smile.

Carolyn's face burned red as she held her breath, then white as she released it in a long, piercing scream. Two more screams followed in quick succession, her eyes remaining fixed on Alyssa in the mirror.

Freddie scrambled from the bed and slapped a hand across her mouth as she fought for control.

"What is it?" He dragged her into his arms and shook her until her fair hair tumbled down around her shoulders, and a loud bang sounded at the door.

"Carolyn?" Aidan shouted. "Are you well? I heard a scream."

She sucked in her breath, blinked, and pulled from Freddie's arms. Straightening her dress she turned to search the mirror.

Alyssa stood by the window watching, smiling inwardly. She could no longer be seen.

Freddie cast a desperate look around the room. "What was that about?"

"Hush," whispered Carolyn. "He will hear you. That

ghost was here. She merely startled me, but the wretched creature will not have me at a disadvantage again."

"Ghost?" Freddie paled. "In this room?" He peered into the shadowy corner where Alyssa stood, but could determine nothing. "What will we do?"

"About the ghost, naught. She's gone. But you best hide." She threw back the lid of a carved wooden trunk at the foot of her bed. "Quickly. In here."

Freddie frowned down at the box half his size. "Don't be ridiculous."

"Carolyn. Are you in there? Open this door at once." Aidan pounded three more times in quick succession.

"Under the bed."

Freddie dropped to his knees and slid beneath the four-poster as Carolyn grabbed up a blue silk robe from the open trunk and tossed it around her shoulders. She pulled the sash tight, emphasizing the smallness of her waist, the lushness of her breasts, and marched to the door, dragging it open as Aidan raised his fist to pound again.

Pasting a sensual smile on her face, she ran her hands back through her bountiful blonde hair, arching her throat and pushing out her chest. "You wished for something, darling? I was sleeping, but now you are here..." A red-tipped nail trailed down his lapel. "It would not be the first time we shared a bed."

Ignoring her innuendo, he took a step back. "I heard a scream."

"I assure you. I heard nothing, but you are welcome to search my room." She flicked a lock of golden hair over her shoulder, allowing him a better view of her scantily covered breasts, and smiled coyly. "But there is no one here but me, and as I said, I am perfectly well."

Aidan straightened, and Alyssa, who had moved into the hallway on hearing Aidan's voice, smiled as she noticed the worried look drop from his face to be replaced by one of guarded indifference.

Carolyn glanced both ways, making certain no one approached, and stepped boldly into the hallway. "I lie. Your little ghost paid me a visit," she said, curling her hand about his arm. "I'm afraid I allowed her to catch me unawares." Her voice softened. "Perhaps you could come in and see if the creature has gone? I have missed you these long, dreary years. And town life can be tedious at this time of year."

Aidan's expression remained guarded. Stepping into her room would be akin to stepping into a matrimonial noose. She would have to do better if she wished to capture him in *that* trap. "I promised I'd ride out and check on my tenants. Word is, there is a fox pestering their chickens."

He smiled thinly, about to turn away, but Carolyn's hand clamped onto his arm, and her bow-like lips formed a pout. "A smelly old fox. You would prefer a fox over me?" Her hand dropped to her side. "Really, Aidan, I swear I do not know you anymore. You have become such a bore."

Aidan peered down at her, trying to read her face. Was she right? Had he become boorish? Had two years of abstinence done that to him? Shutting himself off to every female he met, afraid of being hurt again. Afraid of losing the one he loved. Perhaps Carolyn was right, for were they not the same sentiments he had voiced about himself only days before? He relented and moved closer. "And is that so bad?" he asked, trailing a knuckle down her smooth, perfect cheek. "I am only acting the gentleman my grandmother wishes me to be. Although I find it decidedly difficult with such a vision of loveliness within my walls."

****

Aidan gave Carolyn a charming smile, and Alyssa could only watch disheartened as he captured Carolyn's hand and brought it to his lips.

"Yes, but there are gentlemen," she heard Carolyn murmur, "and *then* there are gentlemen."

Hearing enough of their banter Alyssa faded out of the hallway, with a hope that Aidan would not succumb fully to Carolyn's charms before she could seek Tom's advice on what she overheard. She coalesced in the shadowy corner of the rose garden, about to don her dress when another thought occurred. Why should she make things easy for Carolyn? After all, she intended to hurt Aidan. And no one hurt Aidan while she was around to stop them.

****

Aidan touched Carolyn's hand to his lips, pretending to succumb to her charm. Her words struck a nerve, yes, but he wished also to discover Carolyn's intentions. At the moment, she held her cards close to her chest, and he was not naive enough to think the woman loved him.

She sought marriage, though what kind of marriage he had yet to decipher? A marriage in name only? He doubted that, as she was too hot-blooded. An open marriage, perhaps, where they could both seek pleasure outside the marriage bed? He shuddered inwardly. The thought sickened him after the love he had shared with Anni. He could not live such an existence. Yet Carolyn would never be faithful. Faithfulness did not feature in her vocabulary. He knew that much about her.

She peered up at him through dark lashes. "What manner of gentleman do I prefer? You should know the answer to that. You were once *my* gentleman." She pressed against him boldly, and her hands snaked up around his neck; however, their interlude broke when a loud thump sounded from the bedroom. She paled and backed up so she could peer through the crack in the door. The four-poster under which Freddie hid began to rise into the air.

She pulled her hand from Aidan's and stepped into the room, leaving the door ajar so that she could peek out at him.

"I heard a noise?" He frowned. "Have you someone in your room?"

"Of course not. My gown slid off the bed onto the floor. My silly maid forgot to hang it in the dresser. I will have to reprimand her. However, I do feel a sniffle coming on." A lace handkerchief appeared, and she touched it delicately to her nose. "Perhaps we should postpone this…ah, conversation, until later?" She gave him the benefit of another wide-eyed smile. "I will see you at dinner." She made to close the door but changed her mind. "Oh, I am wearing green."

He gave a perfunctory bow. "I will remember and dress accordingly. Until tonight then, my lady. I wish you a speedy recovery."

****

He gave her a quick, penetrating look and took off down the hall, and Carolyn slumped with her back against the door, her hand pressed to her heart.

"You can lower the bed now, you little hussy," she hissed, hastening farther into the room. "Do not think your parlor tricks frighten me."

Freddie crawled out from under the four-poster and climbed to his feet, brushing down his buff-colored breeches and maroon-and-gold waistcoat. "Who the deuce are you talking to?" The bed crashed to the floor, and he leaped back, knocking into Carolyn.

Carolyn regained her balance. "*She* is still in this room, or returned, if you failed to notice the bed floating above your head."

"Who?"

"The ghost, of course."

Freddie peered around, swallowing hard. "A ghost. Where?"

Carolyn breathed deeply. "She is invisible, you dullard.

Freddie's palm cracked against her cheek. "Don't call me names, ever, hear?" His fingers dug into the fleshy part of her shoulders like small blacksmith vises. "My father called me names. I didn't like it then. I don't like it now. I will not have it from my future wife."

Carolyn tried to wrench free, but he held tight. "You're hurting me."

"Understand?" Freddie's voice grew softer, deadlier, his dark gaze more intense. His hand tightened.

"I hear." Tears welled in Carolyn's eyes.

"Good." He smoothed his hands across her shoulders and down her arms in a soothing gesture. "It will not happen again, will it?"

"No." She looked away. "It will not happen again."

The tension seeped from his body, and arms came around her to force her face back so that he could claim her mouth in a quick, hard kiss. He set her aside and picked up his top hat and coat. "Excellent. Now I best go. I will see you at dinner, shall I?"

Carolyn nodded and waited until the door closed softly behind him, then dropped onto the padded dresser stool. Picking up her monogrammed brush, she sat staring at her hands as her knuckles whitened on the silver handle. If Freddie were not so imperative to her plans, she would see him dead for this infringement. No one manhandled her in such a manner and lived. Her husband had only done so once…

"I know you are still here," she said into the silence. "I can feel your presence. I don't know if you speak, but I am certain you can hear. So hear this, little ghost. Aidan de Morgan is mine. I will not be chased off by you or anyone else. I will be Mistress of Thornwood and Mistress of Dunmore, and no one will stand in my way, living *or* dead. So be wary, very wary. You would not wish to see me your enemy."

Alyssa listened to Carolyn rant, but the woman had no command to frighten her. Only one man had ever held that power, and Gedrych de Morgan had lain in his crypt for over two centuries. Funny how his name could still instill fear in her.

She blended with the darkness.

Chapter Eleven

The journal had vanished. After a night of Carolyn's cloying company and insincere ramblings, he had needed to immerse himself in the purity of Alyssa's simple words. Returning to his room, he intended to study the diary, but after peeling back the rug and pulling up the board, he discovered the book was missing. His first thought was Alyssa had taken it, but if she had that power, why had she not removed it before now? Surely any of the past owners could have found it. And he was certain Alyssa wanted him to have it. So who else did that leave? Bevan? Tom? His grandmother? He gave a mental shake to the latter. His grandmother never entered his room.

He hurried to find his aged manservant.

He burst into his room unannounced as Bevan pulled on his nightcap. "Have you seen Alyssa's diary?"

The old man raised himself to his full height and looked down his nose at him with an air of disapproval. "I assure you, sir, I know of no young lady called Alyssa, and I know naught of any diary. And had I, I would not think this the appropriate time for discussing such matters."

He had been suitably chastised. "Of course, and please accept my apology for the intrusion." He backed out of the room. How utterly stupid of him. Of course, Bevan knew nothing of the diary's existence. Neither was it his want to search his master’s room. He was far too dignified to even contemplate such proceedings.

Therefore, who did that leave? There was only one person he could think of, and that was Tom.

Tom Jeffreys, who had grown up at Thornwood.

Tom, who, if he was not mistaken, knew Alyssa well.

Had Alyssa told Tom to take the diary? And for what justification? What did she not wish him to read?

****

The next morning dawned dark and brooding. Storm clouds gathered on the matt gray horizon. Not a day Aidan would choose to go riding. He had yet to question Tom on the matter of the diary. However, he had received word late the day before about the tenant’s wife, who had been hospitable to him on his first day at Thornwood. She was ailing, and he thought he would check on her. Tom would still be at Thornwood when he returned.

Eleanor had made a pot of chicken soup, which she packed for him to deliver to the ailing woman. At the same time, he would determine whether he should send for a doctor. Freddie decided to accompany him to St. Agnes later on, stating he wished to seek a cobbler to fashion him a new pair of riding boots. “That is, of course,” he added disdainfully. “If a decent cobbler can be found in such a quaint seaside village.”

He had treated those words with the brusque rebuke it deserved.

He arrived at the cottage near midday to find the woman gravely ill. She seemed to be suffering all the symptoms of the lung sickness, which had claimed his grandfather’s life.

He left the soup with Toby, who he discovered to be the woman's son, and rode on to St. Agnes with his cousin. On arrival, he found and paid the doctor handsomely to attend the woman. Though he doubted much could be done other than make her last days comfortable.

It was late afternoon when Freddie, at last, decided on a pair of pre-made black, knee-high riding boots, and the weather had become even more overcast. He was undecided about starting back. However, Freddie insisted he would rather risk a soaking than sacrifice his body to the bedbugs in either of the town's two inns.

Aidan lent a small thought to Lyssa, glancing toward one of the inns which Freddie had spoken of so disparagingly. He wondered where she would be sleeping this night or if she had returned to the castle. However, he pushed his thoughts aside as his attention fell to a tall man in dark trousers and long black coat lounging in the shadowy doorway of the inn. The man's top hat was pulled low, almost covering his dark eyes, but there was no mistaking Landan Denero. He had a certain noble carriage about him that was unmistakable.

Aidan stilled.

What business brought Denero to St. Agnes? And why did he have a feeling the man watched him from beneath the brim of his hat?

Freddie tapped him on the shoulder, and he glanced around. When he looked back, the man had disappeared as if vanishing between the cracks in the pavement like the worm he was.

With narrowed eyes, he searched the street, but Denero was nowhere in sight. Only three people occupied the quiet street. A woman with a small squealing child in her arms, a young boy running with his spotted dog, and a small rotund man he recognized as the blacksmith. He turned toward the stables with Freddie.

Failing to talk any sense into his cousin about riding home, they set out.

A half hour later, the storm hit.

Fork lightning streaked the blackening sky, thunder cracked in a deafening crescendo, and fat raindrops fell.

Aidan dragged his stallion to a halt. "I told you this was a fool's idea. We should have stayed in St. Agnes. We better make for one of the tenants' cottages."

"Never took you as fainthearted, cousin. Thornwood is no more than two miles cross-country. If we pick up the pace, we could make home before nightfall."

"Cross-country? Are you mad? You will risk your life and that of your horse, should you step into a hole or be lost on the marshes."

Freddie's teeth gleamed macabre in the dimming light. "I'm game if you are."

Aidan shook his head and tugged the brim of his beaver hat low, attempting to stop the rain lashing at his face. He had a bad feeling about this. Dark clouds hung overhead. He'd experienced one such premonition on the night of his crossing back to France and had arrived to find the Royalists had arrested Antoinette. He dragged his triple-layered traveling cloak more securely about his shoulders to ward off the chill seeping into his flesh. "I don't think—"

"That's the trouble with you, old chap. You think too much." Freddie grinned again. "I'll race you!" He brought his crop down cruelly on his gelding's neck, and Aidan heard the horse scream as it bounded forward into the driving rain.

Bloody fool. His jaw tightened. He hated Freddie's callous way with animals. In all other matters, except perhaps his excess when it came to gambling, he had found his cousin a man of high character, but when it came to animals, it was as if he thought they harbored no feelings at all.

He once witnessed him flog a horse till it dropped from beneath him. He had come close to killing his cousin that day and had ordered him from Dunmore out of his sight. The willful cruelty had sickened him. Freddie would probably break his neck or his poor horse's before this night was through. As if the man did not realize what a lethal situation he placed himself and Aidan in with his stupidity. Even on a clear night, which did not occur often in this part of England, the moors held treachery at every turn.

With a sigh of resignation, he touched his knees to his horse's flanks and urged him to a slow canter.

Icy needles of rain struck at his face, and a flash of lightning lit up the ever-darkening sky, followed by thunderous cracks of thunder. Not a soul stirred, and no sound registered except for the steady slap of rain against his cloak and hat, and the thud of his horse's hooves on the muddy road.

He should never have listened to Freddie. His cousin had forever led him into trouble.

As children, he would produce some hare-brained idea, and he, Aidan, would end up weathering the brunt. At twelve he had visited his Uncle Cyrus's estate in Hampton with his parents. Freddie had made two pairs of wings from broom handles and white linen tablecloths and dared Aidan to jump with him from the barn window. Of course, he had ended with several scrapes and bruises. Freddie had broken his arm in two places, and somehow it ended up being Aidan's fault. He'd been confined to his bedchamber for three days.

Aidan's horse stumbled, and it jogged him from his reverie. He could see no more than three feet in front of him. Freddie had long since disappeared into the looming night, taking the more perilous path across the fields. He hoped his cousin gained Thornwood safely. Tired and cold, he did not relish sending out a search party on such a night.

No sooner had the thought left his mind than he was propelled through the air. He hit the ground with a sickening *thud*, the wind expelling from his lungs. The rain cut at his body, and a short distance to his left, he heard the soft whinny of a horse in pain. Thick mud oozed between his fingers as he pushed to his knees, but pain slashed at his heart harder than any rain or bruises he might have received from his fall. His stallion, Rajah, lay several feet away, making a valiant attempt to rise. For one agonizing moment he managed to gain his legs, and then staggered, fell heavily to his knees, and toppled to his side.

He crawled the several paces that separated them and ran a hand gently down the black's front legs. The left leg was broken in two places.

Rajah whinnied softly beneath his touch. The bone beneath the knee shattered and protruded in stark white contrast through his black hide. He could just make out Rajah's face as he stroked the white blaze on his forehead, and his heart broke as his horse focused on him with trusting dark eyes.

He had bought Rajah on his return from France after

Antoinette's death. He had in a small way reminded Aidan of his dead wife, with his high spirit, delicate lines, and exotic ebony coloring. Now death would take him too.

He swallowed the lump in his throat, and his fist bunched as he cursed Freddie's name to the starless heavens.

Oblivious to the rain and descending darkness, he cradled his horse's head in his lap, coming to terms with the hurt and knowledge of what he must do. Rajah made another gallant bid to stand and failed, as Aidan knew he would. Feeling for the pistol he carried tucked beneath his coat, he placed the muzzle to the head of the best horse he had ever owned and pulled the trigger. A loud bang shattered the night, and the horse expelled his last agonizing breath and lay silent.

For several minutes Aidan remained where he sat, filled with numbing guilt, then he laid his faithful friend's head to the ground and pushed to his feet.

What a stupid, wasteful thing to have happened. What a brainless situation to get himself into—trapped on the Cornish moors at night in a rainstorm with a dead horse and not a soul to lend him aid.

He stared up at the sky and considered his options. He could wait until daylight, then walk home, or head off now. If he didn't succumb to the treachery of the night, he might make the castle before Freddie sent out a search party, for he had faith that his cousin would do just that when time passed, and he did not arrive home.

The rain eased to a misty veil, and a small slice of a moon peeked periodically through thick black clouds, allowing him an occasional glimpse of the road. He thanked Jove the rain had kept the fog at bay. However, as he sloshed through the mud and water on the uneven ground, the heavens conspired against him to send down another deluge of stinging rain, and with the pain as it slapped at his face came the image of a dark man slinking around the corner in St. Agnes.

What had Landan Denero been doing in the village? What business had brought him to this part of the country? Was he on assignment? Or acting of his own accord? And why did he have the feeling he was connected to this? He rubbed at his old leg wound even as he dismissed the thought as foolish. He doubted Denero would be out on the moors at night. A body would have to be daft. Or very single minded.

Deep in thought, he stumbled and tried to right himself, but the ground crumbled beneath his feet, and he slid, crashing, and sliding stomach-first among mud and rubble down a steep incline. The air expelled from his lungs as he landed face-first in a gushing stream. Dragging his face from the water, he gulped for air, trying desperately to determine his surroundings. All was darkness, but by instinct, he knew he lay in a gully. Shivering from the cold seeping into his bones, he pushed to his feet, knowing he had to get back to the road, and fast. Gullies could turn into raging torrents in minutes with heavy rain.

Then he heard it. A low rumbling in the darkness, growing to a thunderous roar that only water could produce. And a lot of it.

He fumbled to pull his fingers free of his leather gloves, which had turned to icy weights on his hands. Then, grasping the tufted grass, tree roots, rocks, or anything he could use as handholds, he began his slow, hazardous climb up the steep embankment, all the while the sound of raging water growing louder in his ears.

Then it hit, tugging at his feet, almost ripping him from his precarious position. One boot tore loose, and he swore, gritting his teeth, holding on for dear life. The bladed grass bit into his palms as he struggled for another foothold. He found a rock jutting from the bank, pushed up, found another, and did the same, all the while conscious of the water rising below him.

The moon left him, and the rain struck his face and back like grapeshot, and he prayed like he had never prayed before. But it was not God that gave him the strength to push one hand and foot after another. It was the image of a red-haired woman looking up at him so trustingly beside him in a mirror. And as he thought of Alyssa and what she must have endured in her lifetime and in death, his strength grew. He must discover her secret and what bound her to Thornwood, and to him.

After what seemed like a lifetime, he touched the road's gritty surface, pulled himself up over the edge, and collapsed to lie in the rain, breathing heavily. Then realization hit. He had only escaped one danger to face another. It was a long way home and still he found himself lost on the moors in the dead of night.

He came to his feet, took two steps, and tripped over his dead horse, to land heavily on his hands and knees. Rajah's body was cold, but the rain had kept it supple.

What a strange thought to run through his mind when there was so much more he should think about. A small bubble of laughter burst from his lips, and he clamped a hand over his mouth to stifle it, determined not to lose his wits.

He had survived the climb, and he'd lived through worse during the Napoleonic War. He rolled from

Rajah's body and pushed to his feet. He would not be beaten by an enemy he could not see.

One careful foot after another, he limped along the road. If he stuck to the path, eventually it would take him home, or Freddie's search party would stumble upon him.

By the placement of the moon, as it drifted from the shadows, he reckoned it to be several hours since Rajah had gone down. Freddie would be well home. He was confident he would soon be found and have a generous plate of pickled meat and crusty bread to see him to his bed. His stomach grumbled at the thought. It had been a long time since his last meal.

However, as the night wore on and the cold prickled his skin and each step grew more laborious, he realized there would be no search party, or it had certainly not stumbled his way. Hour upon exhausting hour he trudged the road, one foot blistering in his remaining waterlogged boot, his bare foot cut to ribbons by the small sharp rocks in the uneven road. He had never felt more alone or more thankful for his life when the first rays of bright sunlight hit the moors, turning the heather to a bouquet of purple, and he spied Thornwood, eternal, stalwart, and welcoming upon the hill.

Each stride now had a purpose.

Freddie. Why hadn't he instigated a search? Why had he been left on the moors? Surely, he knew the dangers.

Not a soul stirred as he passed through the iron gates of Thornwood. Wet white stone crunched beneath his feet, gaining him more pain, feeding his anger.

He took the side entrance, as he'd given orders for the front door to be bolted after ten every night, and entered the kitchen.

Eleanor glanced up from baking the bread, an expression of horror crossing her face at his muddy clothes and missing boot. “My lord, what—?”

He raised a hand. “Do not ask,” he growled, stopping to tear his remaining boot from his foot, tossing it into the fire, then continuing through the kitchen. He entered the foyer and climbed the stairs that led to Freddie’s chambers, two at a time, to face a locked door.

He did not falter.

Instead, he put his shoulder to the oak door and, on the third attempt, sent it crashing back on its hinges, thanking his ancestors for a weak lock. He stopped beside Freddie’s bed as his cousin pushed upright, rubbing the sleep from his blurry eyes. He opened his mouth to speak, but Aidan was in no mood for babble. Grabbing Freddie by his nightshirt, he half dragged him from his bed. His cousin came to his knees, his mouth working in a silent plea, his pale blue eyes wide, his face white as Aidan’s fist struck his chin.

Freddie grunted as a cut opened in his lip and fell backward onto the bed. Aidan dived after him, but Freddie, with an uncharacteristic show of agility, scrambled across the counterpane and onto the floor.

He lunged after him, but his cousin snatched up the bedside chair and held it feet-first before him. “No more! What is wrong with you? Have you taken leave of your senses?”

“What’s wrong with *me*? Why you…you ask that after what you did?”

He grasped the legs of the chair with both hands and ripped it from Freddie’s grip, tossing it to the far side of the room.

"Are you mad?" His cousin glanced around and, seeing no escape, backed up against the wall, holding his hands up before him. "What is this about? What am I supposed to have done?" His eyes widened as if noticing Aidan's appearance for the first time. "How did you arrive at such a state?"

His anger drained. Exhausted. His hand fell to his side as he studied his cousin. Even after sleep, the man's hair appeared immaculate, his blue-striped nightgown uncreased, but his face wore the shade of tallow. Perhaps he had misjudged his cousin. Perhaps there was a logical explanation for him being left on the moors. He pushed a hand through his hair and dropped onto the side of the bed. "Why didn't you send out a search party?"

"Search party?" Freddie frowned. "Whatever for?" Then his face whitened, and he settled heavily onto the bed beside Aidan. "You mean…by Jove. You've been out there all night." He shook his head and searched Aidan's face. "But your horse—you should have been home not long after me."

"Rajah's dead," he answered flatly. His jaw set hard. "He tripped—broke his leg. I had to shoot him."

Freddie's hand touched Aidan's shoulder. "I am so sorry cousin, really, I am. I know how much Rajah meant to you. You could have died out there yourself. I cannot help feeling at fault. If I hadn't left you…" A stricken look entered his eyes. He grasped Aidan's shoulders and pulled him into a brotherly hug, but Aidan, still not convinced, pushed back. "You must have known I was missing when I did not attend dinner."

"I arrived home soaked to the bone. Grandmother and Carolyn had already eaten and retired to their rooms. Done in and in need of a bath, I ordered water brought to my room and a cold plate. I thought you were not long behind me. Little did I dream…" He stopped and fingered his jaw, giving Aidan a reproachful look.

"No." Aidan came to his feet. "I suppose you did not." He studied Freddie's eyes for some sign of malice, but could find none. Either a competent liar or he was telling the truth, Aidan could not guess, but he knew he would not rest easy until he got to the bottom of what happened last night. "Sorry about your jaw," he said, not really feeling it.

Freddie grinned. "Guess you owed me, since it was my idea to ride back in the rain. But your horse…" Freddie's sentence drifted off lamely, and his smile dropped. "What happened out there?"

Aidan held up his hand and backed toward the door. "Later. I am tired, in need of food, and I have to find Bevan. He'll be fretting." He dragged open the door and stumbled into the hallway.

The door closed with a soft click, and Freddie's fist hit the counterpane.

"Damn you to hell, Aidan de Morgan. Could you not die on the moors like a normal man?"

Chapter Twelve

Aidan and Tom rode from the castle the next morning. The weather still bleak, the wind a bite to the soul, but the rain stayed at bay.

Little was said between the two.

Aidan, still uncomfortable about the episode with Lyssa in the garden and uncertain how much the older man knew of the affair, remained silent. He'd had no intentions of trifling with Lyssa's affections when they first met. He had been attracted to her, yes, but his initial thought was to befriend her, as she seemed a sweet but lonely soul.

A young woman of her age should have been enjoying tea parties, soirées, balls, and society in general, not playing companion to an old man, no matter how fond she was of him. As for the matter of the diary, he had not initiated the topic, for he was too preoccupied with reaching the place of last night's fiasco. Hopefully, he could unearth clues as to who or what had caused his fall, other than a slippery road on a storm-filled night.

Tom brought him from his reverie as he pointed up ahead. His horse lay prone across the road where he'd fallen last night.

The two men slipped from their horses.

The stench of death lay heavy in the air. Already the carrion were busy. Two crows flared up in a flurry of screeching and wings as Aidan waved his arms. *Rigor mortis* had set in, making the horse hard to maneuver, but with Tom's help, he dragged his old friend to the side of the road. The horse's front leg was broken, as suspected, but a dreadful rope burn also ran along his lower chest.

A few paces away, he found a thick snake of rope with one end attached to a stump. The other end had torn free from the old stone wall running parallel to the road. "Hell and damnation!" His horse had not stood a chance. This was no accident. Rajah had been deliberately tripped to either kill him or strand him on the moors in hope of death.

He told Tom before they left home what happened the night before. The old man maintained his stoic silence, but the look he bestowed on Aidan said he had his own ideas on the subject.

He wondered at his steward's silence. However, his thoughts soon turned to the dark-haired man he had seen in St. Agnes. What secrets did Landan Denero harbor? Had he tried to kill him? And if so, for whom was he working? Denero had been at Whites the night he won the castle. If it truly was Denero in the village, it would have taken no time at all for him to ride out here and set the trap while Freddie haggled with the bootmaker over the price of his boots. Perhaps Freddie had been his target? But as far as he knew, his cousin had not an enemy in the world, as Aidan always cleared his gambling debts.

No. Aidan was Denero's quarry, to be certain, and it was all tied in with Ireland. As far as he knew, Freddie did not even know Denero.

Tom pulled a small hunting knife from the pouch at his waist.

"Well, what do you think?" questioned Aidan, stretching out his hand for the weapon.

"Bad business. 'oo would do such a thing?"

Aidan knelt and cut the end of the rope still attached to the stump, passed back the knife, and began making a coil. "I don't know, but I intend to find out. I'll ride to St. Agnes and speak with the constable. See if there were any highwaymen sighted out this way. Perhaps it was meant as a robbery, but when the weather grew inclement, the robber abandoned his plan." Aidan kept his association with Denero silent. Tom need not know about that part of his life. He glanced down the road in the direction of the castle. "But first I have a few questions for my cousin."

****

Aidan did not remove his muddy boots, nor change from his riding clothes. He entered the morning room with the rope still looped about his arm.

Lady Elizabeth, Carolyn, and Freddie were seated at the breakfast table.

"Something wrong?" Lady Elizabeth spoke first, frowning at his muddy attire.

"As a matter of fact, yes. Last night, somebody tried to kill me."

Carolyn coughed, almost choking on a piece of herring, the other half perched on her fork. She stared at him, open-mouthed.

Freddie paled. "Murder," he repeated, pushing back in his chair. "You mentioned nothing of murder last night. You must summon the magistrate at once."

"What do you mean, last night?" Lady Elizabeth recovered her composure. "In this house?"

"No. On the road from St. Agnes." Aidan strode to

the hearth and turned to warm his back at the fire. "I spent the past night on the moors, finding my way home."

Carolyn dropped her fork. "The moors. Sweet Lord. You could have perished with exposure. Or fallen into a bog." She shot Freddie a hard look.

"All of the above," Aidan countered stiffly.

"Freddie, did you know about this?" Lady Elizabeth laid down her knife and turned her eagle eyes upon her second grandson. "I thought you rode to St. Agnes with Aidan. Why were you not with him?"

"Aidan and I spoke this morning and resolved everything. I saw no reason to worry you. Though"—he shot a look of accusation at Aidan— "at the time, there was no mention of an attempt on his life."

Aidan held up the rope. "I did not have this then. I rode out this morning to where my horse fell. I found this rope lying across the road."

"A child's prank," Freddie offered.

"I doubt, cousin, that a child would be playing in the middle of nowhere in the midst of a storm in the dead of the night." Aidan raised a brow. "And *you* never met with the rope."

Freddie leaped to his feet. "By Jove, what are you suggesting? That I had something to do with this? I took a shortcut across the fields. You know it wasn't fully dark when we parted. I was home well before nightfall."

Carolyn grasped Freddie's arm. "Calm yourself, my dear. I am certain Aidan is not suggesting anything of the sort. In fact, it seems to me only one person, or should I say thing, would be capable of such a depraved act."

Aidan stilled. "That being?"

"Our resident ghost, of course."

For some uncanny reason, he knew Carolyn was going to say just that, but from all he knew of the supernatural, ghosts did not leave their place of death. Also, it took him all night to walk home. It would be quite a distance for a spirit to travel. Moreover, ghosts were ethereal and could not interact with material objects and thus would not be able to use a rope. But he kept what knowledge he had on the subject to himself, more interested in why Carolyn would suggest such a thing. "And to what end would she want me dead?" he asked at last.

"Why, to have the castle to herself again of course. She has already given me one dreadful fright." She faced Lady Elizabeth. "You said she harassed the London staff. Why should her next step not be to be rid of Aidan? For in doing so, would she not also clear the castle of us all?" Her blue-eyed look was even more innocent than usual. Or was it just his imagination? He saw guile in every smile lately.

Freddie leaned forward and patted Carolyn's hand. "Your beauty is matched only by your wit, my dear. Of course, you are right. Who else would have motive to harm Aidan?" He glanced around. "Certainly, none of us."

Who else, indeed? mused Aidan. First and foremost, Denero sprang to mind. But could he have another enemy? Someone closer to home? His gaze rested on his cousin, smiling handsomely at Carolyn as he topped up her rose-patterned cup from a fresh pot of tea. Could he have planned their late leaving from St. Agnes, raced purposefully ahead, and tied the trip rope across the road? Could he have instigated such a diabolical plan?

He had spent much time with Freddie as a boy and

more so as an adult. He had always been a prankster, but was Freddie capable of conceiving a plan to kill him? His head had always been so high in the clouds. And why would he do such a thing? It was not as if he ever went without.

Carolyn laughed out loud at one of Freddie's ridiculous jokes, turning Aidan's attention to the two. Freddie indeed. No. His near-death experience had made him paranoid. He dismissed his thoughts as foolish. His cousin did not harbor a malicious bone in his body except, unfortunately, when it came to animals. And that was an inherited cruelty from his father. A story he had no time to ponder this morning.

He murmured something about seeing Jeffreys and turned for the door, but was trapped by the look of concern in his grandmother's violet eyes.

"You will tell me if there is anything I can do? Are you sure you are well?"

She looked worried and old, and he gave her a reassuring smile. "Apart from an attempt on my life, I am well, I assure you, madam. I will not be so careless again." The last thing he meant was to upset his grandmother. Her health had been good of late, but she had always been delicate. He gave her a small perfunctory bow and made for the door, closing it softly behind him.

He would seek out Tom and hear his thoughts on Carolyn's suspicions. Could Alyssa have meant him harm, as the other woman suggested? Or had it been as Freddie had first put forth, children playing with a rope they had forgotten to remove? However, something did not ring true with that explanation either.

He would speak to Tom about sending Lyssa home.

It would be wiser with this new development. If there was a murderer at bay, the castle would not be safe for anyone.

Chapter Thirteen

It was late afternoon when Aidan finally located Tom. His steward had ridden to one of the cottages to supervise an extension and had not returned until well after lunch. Aidan knew he would have to postpone his excursion to St. Agnes until the following day, and most likely miss Denero altogether.

His mood was not amenable when he stepped into the library, but he endeavored to keep his feelings hidden. With Tom surly enough, it would not do to agitate the man further, especially when he wished to extract more information pertaining to a certain female ghost.

He stopped inside the door, his eyes adjusting to the dim light. The atmosphere in the library was bitterly cold. The only burning candles stood on the desk of his steward. The rest of the room was cast in shadow, except for the flickering firelight. Tom rose and acknowledged him, and Aidan motioned for him to sit and stepped farther into the room.

"I thought it might be best, Tom, after what happened on the moors, if Lyssa was to return to Plymouth. It is not that she's not welcome..." He shrugged, leaving the rest of the sentence hanging.

"She'd intended to stay till summer." The old man laid down his quill. "She won't be 'appy."

Aidan moved to the sideboard, sloshed a measure of

whisky into a cut glass goblet, and turned. "You could explain that it's for her own safety. If there was any other way…"

The old man peered down at his work ledger. "I'll see what I can do."

Aidan nodded, though even as he did so, he wondered why the thought of Lyssa leaving disturbed him. She had wormed her way into his heart with so little effort. Thornwood would be a barren place indeed with her gone. He enjoyed their talks in the garden—perhaps a little too much. "On second thoughts, do not worry," he said. "I will investigate a little more and see the magistrate before making a final decision. For the moment, she can stay. But please caution her to be wary of strangers."

He downed his whisky and scanned the room. He had visited the library only twice. Once when he conducted a search for any writings that might pertain to his resident ghost. That time Tom had interrupted him by informing him of the arrival of another load of furniture. The second time, he had stopped by to speak to Tom about the farm accounts.

The library was in the oldest part of the keep. Row upon row of ancient books on shelves that rose to the ceiling covered two walls. A large red-and-blue oriental carpet had been added to the floor, and the same musty tapestry hung in the shadows on the far wall, depicting a scene of horses, hounds, blood, and roses. He strode over and carefully lifted the ancient tapestry away from the wall, searching underneath for a trigger or false panel. He knew old castles sometimes harbored secret passages or priest holes.

"You are looking for something, milord?" He

glanced around to find Tom watching him with keen interest.

He lowered the tapestry back into place and wiped his hands on a handkerchief he pulled from his pocket. “Do you have note of any priest holes or tunnels?”

The old man leaned back in the leather chair behind the rosewood desk. “The castle is old, milord. It ’arbors many secrets, some known, some not.” He looked away, his gaze going over Aidan’s shoulder to the hearth.

He spun. Above the low-burning fire, there was a painting of a red-haired woman. At first, he thought it was Alyssa, but on stepping closer, he realized this woman’s eyes had a different slant, her cheekbones were higher, and her lips were full and bow-like. He bent to place another log on the fire, and the flames burned brighter as they caught at the wood and danced in the grate. He straightened and studied the man standing next to the woman in the painting. Painfully thin, fortyish, with a receding hairline and a drooping moustache. Not at all a match for the beauty beside him.

He breathed into the heavy silence. “Who are they?”

Tom lifted his gaze from his ledger and peered at Aidan over the rim of his glasses. “The late countess and her husband. God have mercy on their souls.”

He brushed aside Tom’s small prayer. “That painting did not hang on the wall last time I ventured into the library.”

“No. I kept the portrait ’idden to stop it from being sold.” The old man closed the ledger with a snap. “’Tis part of the castle ’istory and wasn’t for the likes of those gold diggers. I’m sure the past in ’abitants would ’ave wished it so.”

Aidan poured a glass of port from a cut-glass

decanter at the side of the room and slowly sipped. Old, the brew held a mellow warmth and strength of character, not unlike the man across the room. "Did you know the Countess Llewellyn well?"

"I was ten when she died. She was kind to a small boy."

He considered Tom's words as he finished his port. "Are there any other paintings about which I should know?"

The old man hesitated. "A few. I will have them brought up from the lower levels."

"Lower levels?"

"That's where I 'id 'em. Most of them 'igh-nobs didn't venture down that far or didn't know of the places below, and me nor me father weren't for tellin' 'em. Too damp and dirty for the likes of them, anyway."

"Would not the paintings have been ruined by the damp?"

"The chamber where I hid 'em is dry enough, but they never would 'ave found it without a guide. And me forefathers nor I was prepared to lead 'em. They 'ad no right to those paintings. No right at all. They belong to…"

"Yes?"

"Nothin'. I wasn't goin' to say nothin'."

"And *her*…are there any paintings of her?"

Tom stilled. Aidan knew he knew exactly of whom he spoke. For a moment, he thought the old man wouldn't answer.

"There was only one painting of her ladyship. A wedding portrait. Gedrych ordered it destroyed the day 'e had 'er burned."

He felt his stomach churn. He had the feeling that

portrait could have told him much more than the old man in front of him was willing to. He moved to the desk. "You know of Gedrych de Morgan?"

"Of course," the old man replied. "Every de Bracey knows of Gedrych de Morgan and his treachery."

Aidan's heart slowed a beat. He leaned his hands down on the desk. "de Bracey. *William* de Bracey." He ran a distracted hand through his hair. "I should have known. Of course, this all makes sense now." He searched Tom's face, his faded blue eyes. "You are William de Bracey's descendant?"

Tom raised his chin and met Aidan's eyes. "That I am, and proud of it."

Aidan sank into a nearby chair. "No wonder you are so protective of Alyssa." He folded his hands between his knees and leaned forward. "Carolyn and Freddie say it was Alyssa who tried to kill me. In doing so, she could rid us all from this castle. Except perhaps you."

"And why would she be wantin' t' do such a thing?" Tom came to his feet, and his glasses dropped with a clatter to the desk. "I've never 'eard such rubbish. What would that pair know, anyway? Alyssa would rather die a thousand deaths than see any 'arm come to you again." The old man's face flushed, and he sank back into his chair, looking down at his book.

He picked up Tom's glasses and handed them back. The old man took them without a word and popped them on his nose. He certainly believed in Alyssa's innocence, but why wouldn't she want him dead? Something was not quite right here, and that something had to do with Alyssa and him.

It was so frustrating. If only Tom would open up…but it was as if he had been sworn to secrecy and no amount of prying would loosen his tongue. He was certain the old man held the key to this mystery, but he would only be pushed so far. If Tom up and left, he would never know the answer to the riddle of Alyssa.

“Seeing as you are a respected member of my household, I will allow the disparaging remark about my cousin Freddie and Mrs. Simms to go unpunished, but in the future, watch your tongue.” He crossed to the sideboard, poured another port, and held the glass up to the firelight, noting how the red reflected in the cut glass, turning the wine the color of blood. His fist tightened on the goblet. He downed his wine and turned. “If not Alyssa, then who tried to kill me? And why doesn’t she want me to leave here?”

“Don’t know. Just know it wasn’t ’er ladyship.” Tom fidgeted with his quill.

“How do you know that?”

“She would never see you hurt.”

“Why?” His fist crashed onto the desk, causing ink to splatter across Tom’s ledger. He discarded all thought of not badgering Tom. He had to know!

“That’s ’er tale to tell, not mine, and no amount of bullying will ’ave it from my tongue.”

“You stubborn old bastard.” Aidan’s glass hit the back of the fireplace and shattered into a thousand glistening pieces.

Tom did not look up.

“Then tell me this.” He grasped Tom by the shoulders, forcing him to look up. “What happened here? I know Alyssa married Cai, Gedrych’s son. That Cai was sent to the war between the Highlanders and the Parliamentarians. That Gedrych lusted after Alyssa, but what then? What befell her? Why was she burned? What could she have done to deserve such a fate?"

Tom's gray eyes burned like bright lanterns in his face, and his voice grated from his throat as Aidan released him and stepped back. "She refused Gedrych de Morgan 'er bed, that's what she did. Not once, but over and over. And nobody refused that fiend anything. This castle was a long way from the civilized court. If you could 'ave named the English court of the sixteen 'undreds civilized, with all its intrigue, lies, deceit, and blood.

"Gedrych, a powerful man, and a law unto 'imself, ruled these moors with the might of 'is army and the fear of God. No one defied him."

"Alyssa did?"

"Aye, and look where it got 'er. She wouldn't 'ave 'im so 'e 'ad 'er tried 'ere at the castle in a closed court. 'E accused 'er of being a witch because she used 'er skill with 'erbs to cure a servant of the fever. That same woman stood up in front of the ten members of the court and a priest and testified against 'er. Gedrych also 'ad her accused of being an adulteress and trying to seduce 'im. When anyone close to them knew it was 'e who pursued 'er for months on end and caused 'er the final blow, which resulted in the loss of 'er babe. You know the rest." He sounded tired.

Aidan sank into his chair. "Not really."

"Well, I beg your lordship's pardon, but I ain't up to speakin' of it no more." The old man came to his feet, turned to the over-cluttered bookcase behind him, and dropped to his knees. Aidan rushed to help the older man, when he attempted to pull a large, leather-bound tome from the very corner of the bottom shelf.

Taking the large book from Tom's hand, Aidan

carried it back to the desk and stood looking down at it, knowing before Tom spoke it was the book for which he had once searched. The tome that would hold the key to the mystery of Alyssa de Morgan.

"That there is the Llewellyn family 'istory. Perhaps you will discover within its pages the answers you seek. There be a section written by Alyssa's brother that deals with Gedrych and 'is betrayal of the Llewellyns. 'Is treatment of Alyssa and 'is final reckoning. That might be of interest."

"Thank you, Tom. I know you do not give your trust lightly."

The steward nodded as if in dismissal and reached for his quill marking down a final figure in his ledger. "The book is rightfully yours, anyway. You would 'ave found it, eventually." He snapped the ledger closed and glanced up. "She'd want you to 'ave it."

"But why?"

"As I said, 'tis 'er story to tell, not mine."

"I could order you."

"You could, but I would rather be sent packin' than betray 'er ladyship's trust."

He nodded and brushed his hand almost reverently over the embossed leather cover. "How did I know you would say that?" He smiled.

The old man maintained his silence until Aidan took the tome from the desk and settled in an armchair in front of the fire, then he ambled to the door. As he reached for the handle, he turned. "It couldn't have been 'er you know, that tried 't kill you. She is bound to the castle grounds and keep. She cannot even visit the gatehouse." With that, he stepped through the door, leaving it open.

A moment later, it closed quietly of its own accord,

and Aidan could have sworn the room warmed by several degrees. He stared at the door, waiting for the prickles on his nape to subside, then he glanced down at the book on his knee and froze. On the black leather cover, blood red in the firelight, lay a perfect rosebud. He closed his eyes and counted slowly to ten, clearly hearing each number in his head, each word louder and louder in his brain. Then he opened his eyes and looked down again. The rose was gone.

He sat for several more minutes, not moving, then, shaking off his disquiet, stood to stack several more pieces of coal on the fire before fetching the candelabra from Tom's desk, placing it on the mantel and sinking into a green corduroy armchair. He soon found himself engrossed in the long and illustrious history of the Llewellyn family.

Apparently, at one time, King Henry VIII had favored the family. While on a short stay at their castle, the King had first made the acquaintance of their distant cousin. The fair Anne Boleyn. Unfortunately, the family had fallen out of favor after Anne's premature death, then later, more so with Mary's succession to the throne and her deep hatred of Protestants. However, they survived her reign and fared somewhat better under Elizabeth's rule, but the family never regained the power it once held.

Aidan skimmed several entries, each made by a different hand, each with the name of the one who had made it in bold lettering. He wished he had asked the name of Alyssa's brother, but when he saw it, he realized he already knew. *Cullum Llewellyn,* the young blond-haired man he had seen in his first dream of the past.

Cullum's masculine script flowed in such a way that

it made his words come alive.

Sept. 26th, 1644

Oh, such treachery. We have learned today that my beloved sister is dead! Burned at the stake by Gedrych de Morgan! Oh, what deceit. Could I take a dagger to his heart, I surely would.

A rider came this morning. He said to journey swiftly. Death and foul deeds abounded at Castle Thornwood.

I write only this night so that there be a record of the injustice and wrong this man has caused.

Cai is dead. He has been dead for almost a year now, and this knowledge was held from us. He died on Marston Moor. The Royalists lost 3,000 men, plus their artillery train. York was forced to surrender to the Parliament and the North of England was effectively lost to the King. Prince Rupert lost his reputation of invincibility in battle, but Marston Moor made the reputation of another man, Oliver Cromwell. However, that does not relate to this story and my pen runs away on me. What does relate is, before Cai was even cold in his crypt, Gedrych attempted to force himself upon my sister. It is said, she defended herself with a candelabrum by cracking him over the head. I smile now, even in my sadness at my young sister's audacity.

That same night, it is reported she attempted to escape and be reunited with us. She was betrayed, caught, and held under guard in her room.

Again, Gedrych endeavored to force his attentions upon her. She confessed she was with Cai's child and from all accounts, he struck her, and she lost the babe. As if this was not punishment enough, he accused her of being a heretic and using black magic to coerce him into falling in love with her. He claimed she cursed his son and caused him to die in battle, for Cai was a warrior of great skill.

He bribed the captain of the guard to swear to the chapel priest that she was a witch. Even though Gedrych needed no other law, with the church on his side, he had no one to stand in his way. She was condemned and spent the night in the dungeon.

It is told he sent her an ultimatum: marry him or die. She tried to send word to us of Gedrych's treachery, but her message was intercepted.

Losing all hope and all that she loved, she chose death over being bound to a man she despised. The next morning, she burned even as she cursed de Morgan's name.

I know only this account from William de Bracey. Who it seems befriended my sister, and it also appears, married Lady Jane Beaumont, my sister's Lady in Waiting.

William was ordered by Gedrych to be rid of Jane but could not find it in his heart to do so, for he secretly loved her.

September 26th, 1645

For one whole year, William and Jane were married, and in all that time he hid her beneath the castle in a large chamber he made their home. It was too dangerous for Jane to attempt to leave, for Gedrych's soldiers were forever on guard against strangers going to and through from the castle should they learn of Alyssa's death and report to our father.

But it was learned yesterday a maid in their confidence let slip to her lover, their secret. He, in turn, wishing to find favor with Gedrych, betrayed them.

Gedrych sent soldiers below into the tunnels to find Jane. William, hearing of Jane's peril, and dodging Gedrych's men reached her side. Alas, too late. She lay dead and Gedrych's soldiers stood waiting.

William de Bracey, a master swordsman and trained alongside Cai for battle, dispatched his enemies. Hearing a whimper from a large chest, he found his son of nine months in the arms of his nursemaid. He bid her wait and he would return. His only thought to exact revenge on the man who ordered the death of his beloved.

William had long lived in the castle. He knew the tunnels well. He stepped from a passage and slew Gedrych's guard before he could awaken, then put his boot to Gedrych's bedroom door.

Gedrych, in the midst of tossing a kitchen maid, had no time to concern himself with the woman before William pushed her aside. Gedrych looked up and his eyes widened as William drove his blade through de Morgan's worm-infested heart. He then returned for his babe and rode to castle Llewellyn to acquaint us with the situation.

Two months have passed since Sept. 26, 1645. We have petitioned the King and lay before him the black deeds of Gedrych de Morgan. He has granted my father Thornwood Castle and all holdings surrounding it in compensation. But even in doing so, the blood can never be wiped from the hands of the de Morgans. The Llewellyns will forever curse their name!

Aidan's skin crawled as he skimmed several more entries made by Cullum Llewellyn. Then suddenly he stopped.

Nov. 30, 1645

Today at Thornwood I found a rose. Blood red. It was left for me on my desk.

Red roses were Alyssa's favorite flower.

In a rush, Aidan scanned several more entries, attempting to learn more of what Cullum meant. A rose. Could it be the same sort of rose Alyssa left for him? Did she also leave roses for her brother? Had Cullum seen Alyssa's ghost?

He searched several more pages, but it was as if that entry had never been, for there was no more reference to Alyssa, her ghost, or roses. Cullum's words told only of William de Bracey's appointment to the Steward of Thornwood Castle, then petered out completely, the rest of the pages lying empty.

He closed the book with a snap and gazed blankly into the fire. So, here lay the answer. How the de Morgans lost Thornwood Castle, but more importantly, what he would have found in the diary beneath the floorboards had it not been taken, Alyssa's thoughts, her fears of her last days. He knew now he would never open the diary again, even should he find it. Some things were best left unknown.

He heard a soft click and glanced up to find Carolyn closing the library door behind her. Her eyes glittered strangely in the dim light as she leaned back on the door as if guarding her prize. "Here you are," she purred silkily. "I have searched everywhere. You must tell me when you are going to hide. We could hide together." She gave him a sensual smile, which would have made a weaker man's heart flip over.

Lazily, he climbed to his feet, all the time his mind ticking over what she might want. "I was reading and lost sway of the time. You wanted to see me?"

"Of course I *want* you, darling." She stopped in front of him and traced a long, pink-tipped nail down the lapel of his blue-velvet riding jacket.

He stepped around her and crossed the rug to replace the tome in the bookcase. When he turned, she stood directly behind him, watching.

"The book looks old." She arched a brow. "Anything fascinating?"

He straightened, took her arm, and guided her toward the door. "Family history. Boring stuff, nothing that would hold the interest of a lovely lady like yourself."

She stopped. "Try me."

He looked into her face and, for the first time, saw more than flirtation in her eyes. They were filled with an unfathomable shrewdness and warranted him a moment of disquiet. Then she smiled, and the look disappeared to be replaced by one of wide-eyed innocence.

"Very well." He tucked her hand through his arm and drew her along. "Did you know that this castle once belonged to my ancestors?"

"Really?" she peered up at him from beneath her lashes and laughed softly. "You must tell me more."

"Not much to tell, really. Delightful chap. Enjoyed burning beautiful women at the stake."

He felt a shiver go through her body.

"How horrid. Perhaps I do not want to know after all."

He laughed softly and stopped as he reached the door. "Rightly so." He looked down into her too-perfect features and tucked a soft tendril of golden hair behind her ear. "Not at all a story for your pretty ears."

She moved closer, and her hands swept up to rest on

the velvet lapels of his jacket. “I thought you had forgotten how to be a gentleman and flatter a lady.” Her thick sooty eyelashes swept down to fan her rosy cheeks.

“Indeed, then I must rectify that, and smartly. Is this gown new?” His voice deepened as he trailed a knuckle across her cleavage. “It brings out the blue of your eyes.”

“It was delivered from the village today.” She stepped away and gave a dainty pirouette. “Who would suspect such a quaint town could turn out something so lovely?”

“Did you wear it for my benefit?” He steadied her and took her hand.

“You know I did.” Her voice softened.

He smiled. “My cousin is quite taken with you.”

She rose onto her toes, her arms snaking around his neck. “Freddie is sweet, but he is not you. I have never forgotten our time together.” Her lips sought his, and her small tongue slid into his mouth.

Aidan braced himself, allowing her to have her way, urging himself not to pull from her cloying scent and the too-sweet taste of her mouth. How he could have once desired this woman fell way beyond his understanding. He blamed his youth and his naivety with women. Her brazenness now sickened him.

However, her curiosity over the book had been worrisome, and if he had to succumb to a few kisses to keep her mind from wandering back to it and move her from the room, so he would. For some uncanny reason, he was loath to let her read about Alyssa. Her story was too personal, too close. He pulled away, still holding her, and reached for the door. “I smell like horses and am in need of a bath.”

She put a hand up to straighten her already perfect

coiffure. "Of course, darling, but I must say the smell does not offend me in the least. In fact." She leaned into him. "I find the scent of stallion most alluring."

He smiled thinly and ushered her into the hallway before stepping from the room, but as he looked back, he stilled. A red rose lay on the green corduroy armchair that he had just occupied. He smiled, closed the door, tucked Carolyn's arm into his, and began to walk. "You wished to see me for a specific reason?"

"Freddie and I were speaking…" She hesitated, something unusual for her. "We thought it might be grand to have a ball at Thornwood." She stopped and looked up at him, giving him the full brunt of her forget-me-not eyes. "Please say you will sanction it."

He released a heavy breath. *Bloody hell.* That was all he needed. A ball at Thornwood to bring the ghosts bouncing from the stonework and give his nemesis another opportunity to kill him. Then again, perhaps that might be what the castle needed. To be filled with gaiety once more. Surely Alyssa would approve, and he would invite Lyssa.

"If it will make you happy," he answered at last, studying the change in her face. It was positively glowing.

Carolyn stood on tiptoe and pecked his cheek. "Oh, Aidan, I do feel you are the most wonderful of men. You do not know how much I have missed the balls, tea parties, the theater, and town life. I must hurry and tell Freddie." She clasped her hands together. "Fancy, a ball here at Thornwood. It will be the talk of all of London. Just brilliant!" With another quick peck, she scuttled off down the corridor with unladylike haste, and Aidan could not help but smile. If all he had to do was agree to a ball to be rid of the woman, he wished he had begged her to speak her mind earlier.

Chapter Fourteen

Aidan strolled from the stables after his early morning ride as Tom hastened toward him with a milk bucket.

"Have we not someone else that can do that, Tom?"

"Betsy would miss me," the old man countered.

It would probably be the opposite way around, he mused, but let the matter rest. "I just"—he cleared his throat—"wanted you to know how grateful I am that you allowed me to read the book."

Tom glanced away. "I thought you 'ad a right, seein' as you…" His words trailed off.

"Seeing as I what, Tom?" He searched his steward's craggy face. But Tom refused to elaborate.

"A more stubborn man I am yet to meet." He frowned, crossing his arms over his chest. "You know, if I was any other employer, I could have you dismissed for insubordination."

The old man's head snapped up, but he maintained his silence.

"Why is it that you always seem on the brink of telling me something, then close up?"

Tom shrugged and contemplated his feet. "Ain't important," he grumbled. "Now, I best be gettin' to me milkin'." He cast a glance at the stable doors as if willing them to draw closer. "Lady Elizabeth will be up an' about and wantin' 'er milk." He made to step around

Aidan, but he was ready for him, and grasped his steward's elbow.

"Damn the bloody milking, man, it can wait! I wish to speak to you on another matter."

Tom's scowl darkened.

Aidan lowered his hand and stepped back. "We are having a ball next month. You might wish to inform the staff."

Tom looked to his left and right, then leaned forward in a guarded manner. "Do you think that wise, with…" He peered around, and his voice softened to a whisper. "Her ladyship?"

"I want you to tell her to behave. Not to frighten my guests."

"Are you mad?" He flushed and glanced down. "Forgive an old man, milord, but what makes you think I can speak to 'er? Or, if I could, that she would listen?"

"You have lived here all your life, right?"

Tom grunted an affirmative.

"And you are a descendant of William de Bracey?"

The old man nodded, still not meeting Aidan's gaze.

"I know you talk to her, and I think you talk to her often."

Tom rose to his full height of just below Aidan's shoulder. "Do you now?"

"Yes." Aidan's voice hardened. "I do."

"It does not mean she listens," he grumbled, relaxing back into his normal slouch. "She's a stubborn lass. Yet so would you if you 'ad been around so long, or through so much."

"Rightly so. But tell her anyway—I mean," Aidan corrected, "ask her if she will do it for me. I don't know why, but she seems to want to please me."

Tom raised a brow. "Aye, she does at that."

His lips thinned. "I suppose you would not say why?"

The old steward opened his mouth to speak, but Aidan cut him off. "Do not bother. Let me guess. It is her story to tell, not yours."

Tom's lips curved in what could have passed for a smile, then he coughed to cover it. "About that milkin'."

Aidan relinquished his stance and moved aside to allow the old man to pass. But as Tom neared the stable doors, he called to him again. "I would like your niece to attend the ball. As you are her guardian…"

Tom stopped but did not turn. He was a long time in answering. "I don't think that would be wise."

Aidan's voice hardened. "It was not a request."

The old man's shoulders slumped. "I will do what I can," he murmured, stepping into the barn, his voice floating back through the door. "But she 'as a mind of 'er own."

****

The next three weeks were full of plans and excitement. Tom spoke to Alyssa, and she promised not to upset the staff. The castle was in an uproar with the preparations for a country ball. The wooden floor of the grand ballroom glowed with polish. Lady Elizabeth ordered more gilded mirrors for the walls, new wine-colored velvet drapes dressed the high narrow windows, and four massive crystal candelabras hung from the ceiling housing hundreds of candles.

A menu was decided upon, cast aside, and compiled again. A mountain of food ordered, from ice sculptures, suckling pigs, and peacocks with real feathers to the most delicate of wine and pastry truffles. Invitations were dispatched to London, and everyone who was anyone was invited.

At midnight, Tom slumped exhausted onto the stone bench in the courtyard. "'Twill be just like the old days when I was a boy," he mused. "When the Countess Llewellyn lived. I 'ave never seen so many people at the castle, but I remember my father once telling me—"

"I'm going to the ball," announced Alyssa, appearing in front of Tom, almost stopping his heart.

He ceased speaking and clutched his hand to his breast, regaining his breath. "But my lady…I thought we discussed this, and you decided."

"No, Tom, *you* discussed it, then *you* decided. I did not say a word. Now *I* have decided, and *I* am going to the ball. After all, he did invite me." She began to pace up and down in front of the stone bench. "You must bring me a dress." She stopped, clasping her hands together. "Yes, the green one with the sash, ruffle around the hem, and the Italian lace on the bodice." Her tone became wistful. "I loved that dress on Meredith. I am certain she would have wanted me to wear it."

"Yes. Yes, I'm certain she would 'ave." He folded his arms across his narrow chest, shaking his head. "But 'is lordship invited Lyssa, who 'e thinks is my niece. Who 'e thinks is flesh and blood. A real live human being."

Alyssa stopped pacing. "I am a real woman. I think, I feel…" She looked away. "I…hurt."

Tom swallowed the lump in his throat. "I know you do, lass, but you 'ave t' be practical. 'Ow can you go to the ball when you cannot leave these stones except as a spirit? And then only for a short time."

"I shall wait here," she said quietly, flopping onto

the bench. "I will sit in the garden and listen to the music, and if Aidan should venture out…"

"Which 'e won't," Tom warned, "with Lady Carolyn 'angin' on 'is arm every minute."

"But if he should, well, perhaps we could talk a little." She leaped to her feet and gave a small pirouette. "He might tell me how pretty I look…and I could pretend for a short time he was…" Her words ebbed, and she settled beside him on the seat to fiddle with the hem of her shift. "I am being silly am I not? To think…"

Tom took her hand, and his gnarled old fingers tightened around hers in a gentle squeeze. "I'll look for a dress, but that is as far as it goes. And…" His eyes met her dark emerald gaze beneath the stars. "I want you to know I don't approve of these shenanigans one bit. But…what 'arm can one night do? An' you might not even see 'im."

She smiled through teary lashes. "I do love you." She touched her lips to his wrinkled brow. "I cannot fathom what I would do without you."

He shook his head. "Neither do I. Now you best let an old man get to his bed."

"Would you like some help, I could…"

"No." He pushed to his feet, holding up his hands. "I think I will sleep well tonight, although I cannot fathom why." His lips twisted into a wry smile as he watched her rise and glide effortlessly from the circle to blend with the night. He shrugged and turned away. She was certainly a trial to him, but a trial he would not have missed for all the education and coin on God's green earth.

Chapter Fifteen

The day had dawned bright and sunny, surprising for that time of the year, as summer was almost spent. Carriages had crunched up the drive into the courtyard since early morning and continued to do so throughout the day. There were a goodly sum of rooms at Thornwood, but even so, some would have to be shared as most were still not furnished or take rooms at the two taverns in St. Agnes.

Among the guests were earls and dames, dukes and duchesses, ladies and lords, and anyone who was anyone in London society.

Aidan had hired more cooks, and the great feast to be had that evening had been cooking since dawn. Bowls of freshly picked flowers filled the house, merging their perfume with the savory fragrances of baked ham, fish, succulent goose, and freshly baked pastries.

Earlier that eve at the other end of the park, Aidan had held a feast for his tenants and put in a brief appearance, but none of this registered now as he stood in his room waiting for Bevan to add the finishing touches to his new white silk cravat.

He was as nervous as a newly purchased pup. All he could think of was seeing Lyssa again. He had not seen her since their misunderstanding in the garden the day he had kissed her. He had visited the garden between the stones several times and been disappointed when she had not appeared. On one occasion, he had waited for two hours on the off chance that she might show, but she hadn't. He had tracked down Tom and inquired of her whereabouts and been told she had gone for a walk on the moors.

He released a breath and surveyed himself in the mirror, finding that he was pleased with what he saw. Bevan had chosen ebony trousers, dark-blue velvet frock coat, maroon waistcoat with gold buttons, fob watch, and crisp white shirt and cravat. He glanced down and let out a breath of satisfaction as he caught the shine of his black Hessians peeping out from beneath his trouser leg. Yes, he was very pleased indeed. Now all he need do was slip from Carolyn's cloying attention and procure a dance with Lyssa and he would be very grateful indeed to the powers that be.

However, as he ascended the winding staircase, he realized his objective of seeking out Lyssa was not going to be as easy as anticipated. Lady Elizabeth, Freddie, and Carolyn were all waiting in what he immediately likened to a pack of wolves, all vying for a piece of him, at the foot of the stairs.

He pasted a smile to his face and took the last step from the staircase as he caught up Carolyn's outstretched hand and brought her gloved fingertips to his lips. "Mrs. Simms." He looked into her over-bright eyes. "As beautiful as ever. Your loveliness is matched only by this gracious lady's." He released her hand and took up Lady Elizabeth's, tucking it into the crook of his arm. "May I have the pleasure of the first dance, madam?"

Lady Elizabeth gave an uncustomary girlish giggle. "Of course, my dear, I would be delighted."

Aidan smiled down at his grandmother and led her

with an air of satisfaction across the foyer into the ballroom, leaving Freddie to follow with a not-too-happy Carolyn. He had caught the twisted look of displeasure on her brittle, beautiful face before turning away.

****

At the familiar ring of Carolyn's high-pitched laughter, Aidan pulled away from the balcony rail and slipped into the shadows. It had been almost midnight before he finally extracted himself from her clutches. He had no need of her cloying company again so soon. He had danced a lively eightsome and the Allemande, had fetched her several glasses of champagne and lemonade, and at last managed to hand her over to Freddie.

He had been pressed upon, eyelid-fluttered, and his toes stepped upon by every debutant and divorcee from here to London in the last three hours, and he was well in need of a break.

As the evening air wafted over him cooling his face, he released a heartfelt breath. He had found no joy in the night's festivities, as he had only agreed to the ball for the sole purpose of holding Lyssa in his arms, and she had not appeared.

Carolyn's laughter cut through the night again, and he glanced over to see her standing several feet away with a tall male companion. This was not unusual, as when she had not been clinging to *his* arm, she had had no shortage of admirers lining up to fill her dance card. Cautious not to draw attention, he edged along the balcony the few paces that separated him from the small side staircase leading down to the inner courtyard. On impulse, he descended the stairs and was instantly struck by an urge to seek out the seat between the stones.

Pale gravel crunched beneath his boots, marking his

path in the moonlight. Wishing not to be discovered from the ruckus he was making, he stepped onto the grass. At last, the giant standing stones rose before him. As always, he felt overwhelmed by the presence of the tall monoliths. Oh, what secrets they must guard and tales they could weave if only they could speak. Possibly they even knew Alyssa's story and what transpired to hold her prisoner within these castle walls.

He stepped into the garden, and immediately sensed a presence. A shadow rose from the bench and drifted across the grass toward him. The darkness manifested as a woman, and he searched her features. Pale and beautiful beneath the stars, Lyssa's resemblance to the woman he had seen in his mirror struck him again. But that woman had been of the Otherworld.

This woman was of flesh and blood, and he drew in her rose-scented fragrance wafting toward him, smelling like he could only imagine heaven would smell should he ever be granted the pleasure of entering that most holy place. Lyssa could also give him what no ghost could give. Her heart. She was dressed in an off-the-shoulder gown that could have been green or blue beneath the evening sky. Lace fell in delicate folds around the sleeves and neckline, and she robbed him of his breath.

"What are you doing here?"

"Listening to your musicians," she said softly, turning to drift across to the stone bench. "They play well." She smiled wistfully. "And the night is so wonderful and full of stars. If you look hard, it is said you can see all of the Greek Gods." She pointed. "Look, there is Aphrodite. It is told she—"

He grasped her hand. "I know, the Goddess of Love." Lyssa's hand was cold. Freezing. He took her other one and tried to chafe them between his own, but she pulled away and hid them in the folds of her gown.

"I do not feel the cold. Remember?" She gave him the oddest kind of look, and he smiled as again he noted she had no shoes.

"Why did you not come up to the keep? I told Tom—"

She leaped to her feet.

"Please do not seek to blame my uncle. It was I…" Her lashes fanned her cheeks. "I did not have a gown, and…" She clutched her skirt in her fists and spread it out for him to see. "All I could find was this old evening gown of my aunt's, and I had no proper shoes. Then, I thought with all the finery that would be present…well…that they would laugh at me, look down on me." She glanced up at him with tear-bright eyes and clutched his arm with her small hand. "I really did wish to dance with you. Believe me."

He studied her defiant, woebegone face and felt the numbness surrounding his heart melt a little more. She had arranged her hair atop her head, and her likeness to Alyssa was even more pronounced. Shadow and pale planes, coldness and warmth, a chameleon of emotions, innocence, and brazenness rolled into one sweet package. However, Alyssa was a ghost, and this woman was very much alive. He wanted Lyssa in his arms so badly it was all he could do to stop himself from claiming her mouth.

"Then why shall we not dance?" he said after a long pause.

"Here, now?"

"Why not here and now?" He swept her a regal bow. "My lady, would you do me the honor?" Straightening, he drew her into the curve of his arm, took up her hand, and whisked her into a few brisk steps, but she broke free, and a girlish laugh escaped her throat.

"The *Valtz*, my lord, indeed." Her lashes fluttered down as she followed his charade. "Is the Waltz not thought improper?"

"Magnificently so, but a country ball is such a marvelous place to flout convention. Is it not?"

****

Alyssa had no time to answer, for again they were swept up by the sweet notes of violins filtering through the courtyard, creatures singing in time on the breeze as around and around she and Aidan twirled.

His arms were warm and tight about her as they waltzed through the small garden between the standing stones surrounded by the scent of roses. The night balmy, the stars bright in the heavens, and it *was* heaven in Aidan's arms. She floated on the breeze, young, alive, and in love again. It was like yesterday when she and Cai had danced at their wedding. Well, not exactly. The Waltz had not been invented then, but oh, it was wonderful! She willed the music to go on forever as they whirled to the rhythmic strands of Strauss.

Unfortunately, all too soon, it was over. Yet Aidan did not release her. The music had stopped, and she stood encircled by his arms, listening to the sounds of the night, her head pressed to his hard chest, his heart beating wildly against her cheek, matching the rhythm of her own. His heady masculine cologne filling her senses, calling to her. She loved this man, as a wildflower loved the rain, as a robin gloried in the first days of spring. She had never stopped loving him, even in death. How could she let him go? When it was in his arms, she longed to stay forever.

He tilted her chin to look into her eyes. "I want to kiss you," he breathed, his mouth so close. It was not a question, but a statement, and her lashes fanned down over her eyes at the first touch of his lips, so gentle.

She felt the tenderness of his arms and body pressed around her, against her—she felt the wildness of his tongue in her mouth and savored his taste with a heady rush of euphoria. Then suddenly all changed…

She was in his arms, but they were no longer at the castle, but on the moors below Thornwood. The heather brushed her ankles. The stones were their haven, their shelter from the light summer rain that fell about them. Wind ruffled her hair, rain wet on her fingertips as she ran her hands through his silken locks. The smell of the earth filled her lungs, and his mouth sought the pulse in her throat and trailed lower to her breasts. Her breath labored, and she clutched at his tunic. Her knees weakened, and they could no longer hold her weight. He knew just the right time to lower her to the grass—

"Aidan! Aidan, are you there?"

Alyssa's vision shattered as Carolyn's strident voice filled the small, enclosed garden. Her eyes flickered open. They were back in the courtyard, and Aidan was looking down at her as if he had never seen her before.

****

Aidan ran his fingers through his hair, and they came away wet. It was akin to last time. Hot, heavy, passionate. Lyssa appeared flushed even in the moonlight, and her eyes filled with stars. Light raindrops still glistened upon her hair like fine diamonds. Had they really been below the castle on the moors, about to make love? And the stones…how had the stones moved?

With a touch of her lips, he had been transported. Was Alyssa using Lyssa as a channel? He had read of such happenings taking place in a small town in Ireland, but surely Lyssa would have sensed something too. The look she bestowed on him gave nothing away, and he had no time for questions, for Carolyn spoke again. This time from the edge of the circle, her words cutting into his thoughts. He cursed below his breath and answered her. "I am over here, Carolyn. I took a stroll. I needed some air." He also needed answers from Lyssa.

He pushed her to arm's length. He hadn't realized he was still holding her, and she remained quiet. Uncannily so under the circumstances. He shot her another glance. Her face appeared even paler than usual. The transportation must have come as a shock to her as well if she had experienced it with him. But again, he had no time to ponder the matter as Carolyn stepped into the garden clinging to a man's arm.

Aidan's fist bunched and his jaw clenched, but he gathered his wits. *What the bloody hell is Denero doing here?* He hadn't been aware the man had received an invitation. But Carolyn's, "Well, darling, here you are. I was beginning to worry," soon diverted his attention. "I thought I saw you scuttling along the path, but you were nowhere to be found when we came after you." He could have cut glass on her smile. "Have you met the count? He says he is an old acquaintance of yours." Her words were for Aidan, but he could see she was straining to see the figure standing beside him in the shadows.

"I first made his acquaintance in Italy a few years ago. When I happened upon him in St. Agnes three days ago, I thought you would not mind too terribly if I invited him to our little gathering." She tapped Denero playfully on the arm with her fan. “He just arrived by carriage from St. Agnes and looked to pay his respects.”

Aidan nodded coolly. Respect my ass! Likely the man was trying to worm his way further into his circle in order to get another chance to do him in.

Denero’s dark patrician features were highlighted in the moonlight. He wore a snowy shirt and cravat, somber dark trousers and tails, and his smile was cynical as he returned Aidan’s nod. “Forgive me for arriving late, Your Grace. I was unavoidably detained in St. Agnes.”

“Old friends are always welcome,” Aidan countered with graciousness he didn’t feel.

Carolyn left Denero at the edge of the garden and swept across the damp grass toward him and Lyssa. “We searched the garden and were about to return to the ballroom when I heard a noise…” Her gaze flittered to Lyssa’s face, and she blanched, taking a step backward, her mouth working but no sound coming out, her hand pressed to her throat. “Who *is* she? I mean…” She recovered quickly, as only one of her station could. “Might we have an introduction, Aidan?”

****

Alyssa smiled inwardly. She could have sworn the blood momentarily drained from Lady Carolyn’s face. She must have been reliving their first meeting in her bedroom. She wondered what thoughts flittered through the woman’s mind as she faced her.

The blonde took a hesitant step closer. “Have we met? You look slightly familiar—at a ball in London, perhaps?” A small, nervous laugh escaped her lips.

“I have not ventured to London in a very long time,” Alyssa returned evenly. “Not since I was a girl.” Which was the truth, and she had not enjoyed it one tad. Her father had forced her to endure a long stand in the rain to capture a glimpse of Queen Mary as she rode at the head of a Royal assemblage. "Perhaps you have traveled recently to Plymouth?" she asked, knowing already what Carolyn's views would be on a city whose core industry was shipbuilding. She was not disappointed.

The woman's gaze turned leaden as she raked Alyssa's length. "Not recently, indeed, never."

"Pity," said Aidan, taking Carolyn's arm, nipping the conversation in the bud. "I have heard Plymouth is quite stunning this time of year." He threw Alyssa a look of apology, which she readily accepted.

****

"Yes, well, that is to be seen," returned Carolyn dryly. Then she smiled. "I must insist you introduce your new…friend."

Aidan schooled his features. It would not do for him to show Carolyn how angry he was at her lack of manners. He would make the introductions, and hopefully, she and Denero would disappear into the night, anything to save Lyssa a further lashing from Carolyn's tongue.

Though he prayed there would be no more cutting words to come, he had seen Carolyn in action. The ugly scene still played in his mind. The year he met her, a pretty daughter of one of Nelson's officers at a New Year's ball, a cutting remark from Carolyn had sent the young girl fleeing the room in tears. He forced a smile. "Mrs. Carolyn Simms." He shot a look at Denero. "Count Landan Denero, I would like you to meet my good friend, Miss Lyssa Jeffreys."

Lyssa curtsied to Carolyn, and the blonde had no choice but to follow suit with a quick bob as Aidan looked on.

"Your friend is quite enchanting, darling," said Carolyn, curling her gloved hand possessively around his arm. "But shouldn't you be getting back to your guests? You *are* the host after all, and the count wishes to speak to you on a matter of importance." Her hand tightened on his arm, and she tried to lead him away. "I believe he breeds Arabians. Yes, I know it is no subject for a lady." She turned on the full force of her charm. "However, I thought you might be interested, seeing as your own mount met with such a dreadful accident."

Aidan shot Denero a daggered look and forced himself not to challenge the man then and there to pistols at sunrise. If he had one shred of proof… Instead, he smiled down at Lyssa and took her hand, bringing it briefly to his lips. "It seems I must return to my guests. Are you sure you will not join our dreary lot up at the keep?"

"Thank you, my lord, but I told my uncle I would not stay past the witching hour, and I fear it is already so late."

A thin smile curved Carolyn's lips. "Hardly dreary, darling," she said, tapping Aidan's other arm lightly with her fan. "But of course, do join us, Miss Jeffreys. You *must* meet Freddie. He would adore another young Miss to parade on his arm. Would he not, Aidan?"

He ignored Carolyn's jibe. "At least allow me to escort you back to your uncle's house."

"No need. Landan will escort her, will you not, dear?" Carolyn looked pointedly at Landan, and he had no choice but to step out from the shadows and come forward.

"The pleasure would be all mine. She will be quite

safe with me." He offered his arm. "Shall I have my carriage brought around?"

"That will not be necessary." Alyssa took a pace backward. "Really, I have no wish to make a fuss. My uncle is steward here, and I have been playing on these grounds since a child." She crossed her fingers in the folds of her gown. "I could walk this place blindfolded, but there is no need. My uncle will be by at any moment. He will be checking on Her Ladyship and her pups."

"Her Ladyship?" prompted Carolyn.

"A certain hound for which Mr. Jeffreys has a fondness," answered Aidan, not taking his gaze from Lyssa. He knew by the breathless timber of her voice and the way she refused to meet his gaze she was lying, but no notion why.

"What a pity you will not be persuaded to attend the ball." Carolyn switched her look to Aidan. "Now you will just have to keep all your dances for little old me. Won't you, darling?"

Aidan patted her hand. "You are anything but old, Carolyn, and you know it."

"How gallant you are, but now we have chatted long enough. We must get back. Lady Elizabeth will be worried. It has been some time since she sent me to fetch you."

"You never mentioned my grandmother."

"You never asked, darling." She raised a finely arched brow.

He gave Lyssa a despairing look, almost begging her to save him from an evening filled with Carolyn's suffocating company and the anything-but-jubilant companionship of his archenemy, the man who tried to kill him in Ireland and perhaps again on the moors.

Although he wished to question Denero on his whereabouts the evening of his accident, he did not wish to do so now. He had more pleasurable pursuits in mind. If only he could be rid of Carolyn. “Are you certain you will not join us?” he pressed Lyssa.

****

“Quite.” But although she said the words, misery was a rope twist in her chest, and she longed to beg him to stay. He had danced with her, kissed her, and now he was leaving her. She could not stop him, and she could not go with him. Never go with him! Never leave this stone prison that encircled her! Oh, how Gedrych would laugh now. Could he only see the pain she suffered. She would have surrendered to a thousand searing pyres for one night of freedom as a woman. And at that moment, as she watched Carolyn clinging to Aidan, attempting to draw him away, she realized the hopelessness of her love for him. Her shoulders slumped even as her nails scored furrows in her palms. Who was she fooling? A man like Aidan de Morgan would never love her once he knew her true identity.

“Good,” said Carolyn. “It is settled, but you must visit us up at the keep in a day or two. I will insist Lady Elizabeth send her card. I am dying to know the name of your dressmaker. That little gown is just…” She smiled cruelly. “Otherworldly. Indeed, out of this century.” She stifled a giggle behind her fan.

“That’s enough, Carolyn.” Aidan grasped her arm and gently but forcefully turned her away.

Alyssa watched them disappear from the circle with a sinking heart and listened as the crunching gravel marked their path back to the keep.

The Count stood a little ahead of her, watching them

go. He hadn't followed. He rounded, his mouth opening, about to speak. However, she would never know what he was about to say. She had already drifted from the circle, and as he did not see her, he did not speak. She watched him search the small garden in the moonlight before finally giving up and, with a shrug, followed the other two along the path.

She wondered who Denero really was, and what part he played in this charade. She sensed a mystery about him, and she had the distinct feeling that Aidan didn't trust him. Yet she could ascertain no evil in the man. Not like Aidan's cousin. Evil pervaded Lord Frederick Fitzwilliam's very aura. He was of the same ilk as Gedrych de Morgan. A betrayer of family—a Judas, and he deserved no better fate than that man himself. *To be cast into the deepest level of hell.*

Chapter Sixteen

Aidan escaped from the ballroom as early as politeness allowed. He pleaded a headache and retired to his room. Even so, the wooden antique clock read almost two in the morning. He could still hear strands of music drifting up the stairs and along the corridor.

He strode to the window and stood momentarily, looking down into the stone courtyard, thinking of Lyssa and his strange vision on the moors. Had it really happened? Could he really have been transported? He smiled and turned away to stoke the fire. It was frightening to think it was real, yet he knew he would not have missed it for all the tea in India. He had kissed Lyssa. He wondered if she was asleep. Had she thought of him before she closed her eyes? He doubted he would sleep, with all the why, what, and who's filling his mind.

He crossed to the bed and stripped off his formal attire, thankful for his dismissal of Bevan earlier that eve. He was in no mood for his fussing. He slipped beneath the covers and hauled the duvet to his chin, rolled over, and fell promptly to sleep.

He was in her room. His room. Alyssa stood by the window, her fiery-red tresses loose about her shoulders. Aidan floated weightlessly, an invisible observer, looking down at the young woman in a long white nightgown. She appeared delicate, ethereal. Tears shone in her eyes as she observed her young husband across the room examining his sword.

Cai, noting her concern, stood and dropped his sword onto the table. "He cannot make me go. I will not allow it." He dragged off his shirt and tossed it on the bed. He looked dangerous. His grim expression lethal.

"You know him. You heard him. In the morning, you will ride from here." Alyssa wrung her hands. "I might never see you again." Her gaze met his, her tone beseeching. "I am afraid, Cai. I cannot stay here. He looks at me with eyes that strip me bare."

Cai opened his mouth, but Aidan never heard his reply. He was falling, spinning helplessly out of control. His head pounded as if about to burst. Pain ripped through his vitals. He dropped and merged with Cai de Morgan...

Then he was Cai in every feeling, every nuance, every fiber of his being.

He could see the hurt in Alyssa's eyes and hear the strain in her voice. He was no longer an observer. He strode toward her, his arms going around her to cradle her face to his chest. "I will not let anything happen to you. I promise. He is my father. He would dare not touch what is mine." The tone of his voice, possessive, deadly. "I would kill him."

"You cannot protect me if you are not here. Can you not see that is what he wants?" She pulled back to look into his eyes. "That is why he seeks to send you from me."

"No." He shook his head. "He is a hard man, a ruthless man, but I cannot believe he would purposely seek to harm his only son. Or steal his wife."

Alyssa rested back against his chest. "Then we are both lost." Her words were a murmur, yet he still heard them.

He turned her and lifted her chin to smile reassuringly into her eyes. "I will not allow these dreary thoughts to spoil this night. This is our night. And if it is to be the only night we will share for some days to come, then it will be shared in love, not woe. For I do love you, Alyssa de Morgan."

She nodded. "And I, you." His mouth came down on hers, and there was no more talking as he pressed her back against the windowsill.

Alyssa tore her mouth away, inhaling deeply as he trailed ravaging kisses along her jaw, down her neck, and across her shoulder. Cai watched the firelight play over her pale golden skin. She was warm, vital, and smelled like roses, and he had never wanted a woman more than he wanted this woman, his wife, right now.

She gasped as he took hold of the neckline of her nightgown and, with one swift yank, ripped it down the middle. He saw a shiver travel along her body, but her lips and tongue were hot as he sought her mouth.

Her fingers slid from his hair down over the rounded muscles of his bare shoulders. She grabbed at his biceps, pulling him in, arching her hips toward him. He stepped between her legs, pressing hard where she most needed to feel him, and she cried out against his throat when he reached to pull one leg up over his hip. She dug her heel into his buttocks as he moved against her.

Then his mouth was on her again, forcing her leg to drop as he fell slowly to his knees, leaving a damp trail on her breasts and nipples and down the center of her belly. He ran his tongue down her ribcage, tasting the salt of her skin, then dipped it into her navel. Her soft gasp was an aphrodisiac to his senses.

In answer, he cupped her buttocks and pulled her to his open mouth. His tongue went straight to her core, and her knees buckled, her hands grasping at the sill for support.

He drove his tongue inside her over and over, her fingers tangling in his hair, her breathing a ragged sigh in the still room. He pushed her higher, harder, further than she had ever been, but still, in her pleasure, she took it.

He wanted to take her to the stars. He wanted to show her the world. If they had only this one night, he wanted her to experience everything their love could be, all she could be. She tensed as his fingers curved around her thighs and eased between her legs. She jerked against him the minute he entered her.

No longer able to stand, she sank to the floor, and Cai's fingers slipped from her as he pulled her under him.

She grappled at the laces of his breeches, but he ripped them from her hands and pulled them down and off. As he moved over her, she ran her hands across his buttocks and down the hard curve of the backs of his thighs. He pressed into her, resting his weight on his elbows, and her fingertips sank into the slick skin of his back as she slid her legs up to lock around his waist.

In the dim light of the room, he cradled her face in his hands and lowered his head.

"Alyssa, look at me."

In that instant, two things happened. A woman spoke.

"Alyssa? Alyssa who?"

The voice was not Alyssa's. And a candle flared, momentarily blinding Aidan by its light.

He held a hand to his eyes and blinked. When he regained his sight, he stared with a sinking heart and sick disappointment into the flushed face of Carolyn Simms.

"What the bloody hell!" He shook his head, trying to clear his mind. He had been dreaming. He had been with Alyssa. It was Cai's last night, and Alyssa had been upset. He had started out comforting her, but it had turned into something more. Something wonderful. Something magical.

Then he had awoken or been dragged from Jove knows where back to his own bed and Carolyn Simms. Annoyance killed any desire that might have lingered. He pushed away from the woman beside him and ran a hand through his sweat-dampened hair. "What the hell are you doing here?"

She smiled and trailed a red-tipped nail up his thigh. "Darling, do you really need to ask?"

He rolled from the bed, looked down at her pale, lush body plastered to his white sheets, and winced. Squeezing his eyes closed, he tried to block out the sight of her golden curls, plump breasts, and the triumphant look on her face. Perhaps when he opened them again, she would be gone. He would be back with the fresh lovely woman he had just left, and away from this nightmare.

He opened his eyes and Carolyn still sat on his bed, looking up at him with feigned innocence in her wide, forget-me-not gaze. "Come back to bed, darling. I'm getting cold." She held out her multi-ringed hand, but instead of doing as she asked, he picked up her pale blue nightgown, pushed it at her, and curled her fingers around the silk. "Out."

"But, Aidan," she pouted. "We were enjoying

ourselves. Whatever happened? Why are you acting so strange?"

He breathed deeply, forcing his temper under control. "No, Carolyn, you are wrong. I am finally being myself." He'd never felt so like throttling a woman in his life. Only the thought that she might come back to haunt him stopped him. "I don't know what you think you would gain by this, and I am in no mood to discuss it."

"But, darling." She tossed a tangle of golden curls over her creamy shoulder, exposing a rose-tipped nipple. "You were perfectly amenable earlier." She ran her gaze slowly down his body. "I am certain we can find it again."

"I was not myself earlier." Truer words he had never spoken. He grasped her hand, dragged her abruptly from the bed, and in one swift movement, tossed her over his shoulder.

She gave a gurgle of laughter. "Oh Aidan, you are naughty. This is not exactly what I had in mind but—" Her sentence was cut short as he strode to the door and wrenched it open.

"What are—?"

Unceremoniously, he dumped her onto the hallway floor to land with a thud and a loud gasp.

"I would suggest, madam, that you scamper back to your room before you catch a chill."

"Why you…" Her surprise turned to cold fury. "I will ruin you for this. I will tell everyone we are lovers. You will *have* to marry me."

"I am not the one sitting in the hallway naked. And this is my room, not yours. I would watch very carefully what you say, madam, for there will be no marriage." He closed the door as she opened her mouth.

Listening on the other side, he heard her mumble a few unladylike expletives, then a creak of a board as she moved away. Still, he waited, leaning against the door, his heart pounding against his ribcage. What happened? One minute he was making love to Alyssa, then he'd awoken to find Carolyn naked in his bed. He shuddered.

It had been a dream, yet not a dream. Where had the dream ended and reality set in? How much had been Carolyn, how much Alyssa? Sick and physically ill with the knowledge he had no way of telling which woman had been which.

He stared down at his hands. They were shaking, and it was not from the cold, although only a few coals burned in the hearth. Fury fired his blood. He knew Carolyn was spoiled and headstrong, but he had not thought she would go so far. What would have happened had he continued to make love to her? Would she have trapped him into marriage? Had Alyssa lit the candle? Had she saved him from Carolyn? Instinctively, he knew she had.

Aidan had no intentions of being trapped into marriage by the lovely widow Simms or anyone else, as much as his grandmother wished for it. He would do his own choosing, and at the moment there was no thought for any other woman but the one he could never have.

"Alyssa."

He whispered her name, a sigh on his lips. Though even as he spoke, his thoughts strayed to another red-haired girl who lived at the entrance of his property. However, he pushed the thought of Lyssa aside. Although their names were similar and they bore a striking resemblance to each other, that was where the similarities ended. They were as different as wine and water, and this matter did not concern Lyssa. He had made his choice. If there were any way known to man that he could move heaven and earth to be with the woman he loved, he would do it.

He stood perfectly still. "Alyssa, are you there?" He strode to the mirror and peered into the dark corners of the room, but they remained empty. "Come to me." His voice was ragged. "I need you as I have never needed another woman in my life." He took the few steps to the bed and sank onto the edge, cradling his face between his hands. "Alyssa." The dream had been of Alyssa and Cai's wedding night. He had been making love to her in this very room. Yet he knew now it had not been Cai's actions. It had been his.

He crushed the duvet hard in his fists. Cai would leave in the morning to fight with the Marques of Newcastle's troops, and he would never see Alyssa again.

Would *he*? He wondered? How could he separate himself from the other man when it was becoming hard to tell who he was himself? He felt divided. His anguish a living thing, tearing at his entrails.

He had to get back to her.

He had to know what happened after they made love.

He smashed his fist into his hand. He wanted that woman as he had never wanted another. "Alyssa!" Her name was torn from his throat—so soft, a torture to his mind. He had tasted her. She'd been like sweet ambrosia, the texture of her skin like silk. His mouth went dry as his body quickened, and he found it difficult to swallow. Could a man die from the want of a woman? He lay back and stared at the flickering candlelight dancing on the ceiling. She had been vital, so alive. "Alyssa." He drifted into a restless, dreamless sleep with her name still on his lips.

****

"Aidan, my love. Come to me. Come now!"

He sprang upright in bed. It was her. Alyssa! He would know her voice anywhere. Across the winds of time, he would answer her call, soft, urgent, like that of a siren.

The candle beside his bed still burned. He could not have been asleep long. Pushing back the covers, he reached for his pants in one fluid movement, pulling them up as he ran through the door, then dragging his shirt over his head. He moved quickly down the hallway in the dark.

He had been at the castle long enough, made this trip enough times, to know his way without the aid of a light. He passed down the steps, feeling his way along the banister, and with the help of the feebly burning torch in the foyer, made his way to the hallway that would lead to the kitchen. He knew exactly where he was heading.

The fire still burning in the hearth gave off a dim light. He fumbled for the door latch with trembling hands and broke into the cool night air without a shiver. Perspiration dampened his forehead and soaked his back. He strode along the path without feeling the icy gravel beneath his bare feet. His heart pounded so hard he thought it would burst from his chest.

She stood in the stone garden. He knew she would.

She wore a snow-white shift, and her hair like dark red fire tumbled down her back and wreathed her face in the pale moonlight. He broke into a run and caught her as she launched herself into his arms.

He pushed back and cradled her face, placing small urgent kisses on her eyelids, cheeks, and lips.

"I knew you would come."

"I knew you were real."

They both spoke at once, then laughed softly.

"How—?" he asked, then frowned, studying her face more closely. "Lyssa?"

Alyssa pressed her finger to his lips, then removed it and kissed him to silence, but only for a moment. He pulled away.

He stood silent, watching her, waiting, still trying to decide who she was. She had called, and he had come. Or could it only have been another dream or the wild beating of his heart? Yet here she was, looking beautiful, ethereal in the moonlight. But just who was she? Was she Lyssa, sweet innocent seductress, or Alyssa, wild, wanton, tragically sad, and beautiful, and did he really care?

This was his dream, and he would make it what he would.

"Lyssa?"

****

So, he thought she was Lyssa. He had called for her, and she had come, but he could not accept her as reality. To make her real, to make her substantial, he had to make her Tom's niece. He had to make her Lyssa. It saddened her that he could not trust his heart. Then again, why should he? He had only ever seen her in his dreams, in his looking glass, and once in the courtyard on that first night. Why should he love her or want her as Alyssa?

What was he thinking, now he stood silent before her, watching her. She had beckoned, and he had come. She had brought him here, but would he stay?

She had been in his dream tonight. The darkness had claimed her while she had watched him sleep. However, she had been swept back to a time long ago—to a time when she and Cai had lived. But she had known it was not Cai who made love to her tonight. For she remembered that night well, and although it had been wonderful in her memory, he had never... She swallowed as quickening sensations rampaged through her body—desire, wanting, urgent hunger.

"Lyssa," he murmured again urgently, and stepped forward to gather her into his arms.

She drew an unsteady breath and closed her eyes, letting her head fall back as he stroked the line of her throat as though she were a frightened wild creature who might flee. His fingertips trailed slowly down across her collarbone, and though the fine linen of her shift separated her skin from his, it did not matter. She could feel the heat of his touch, the vibrant passion of it through the soft cloth, as if she were naked.

His fingers lightly circled one breast, then the other. She did not have to look to know her nipples were pressing tautly against her shift. The barest touch of his lips came to her throat. She arched involuntarily and sought the cool, thick silk of his hair, her breath breaking as his hand cupped her breast possessively and his arm came around her back to pull her fully against him. The heat of his flesh branding her through the barrier of their clothing, quickening the pounding of her blood.

Of their own accord, her hands slid around his neck, along the delineated muscles of his arms, his shoulders, telling him without words his beauty struck her to the heart, that she loved him, that she had always loved him, that she wanted him.

He whispered words of endearment against her throat as his hands worked on the laces of her shift, bearing more skin to his eyes, to his mouth. Lips and teeth captured the tip of one breast, scalding hot through her gown, loosening a burst of fire deep in her belly. Her hands clenched on his shoulders, for the strength was flowing from her legs and she felt perilously close to falling. His arms tightened around her, lifting her, drawing her flush against his lower body. "I want you, badly."

She nodded. She was hot and damp, and her heart pounded in fear and desire.

He caught her face in gentle, urgent hands. Then captured her mouth with his own, invading, searching, promising things she knew could never be hers, as he rocked himself against her once, slowly, devastatingly.

The only sound their ragged breathing in the cool silence between the stones.

Slowly, he released her and stepped back to arm's length, features taut with hunger, eyes blazing like dark sapphires in the moonlight. He shrugged out of his shirt, letting it drop to the grass, his gaze never leaving her, only growing hotter at the knowledge that she was watching and glorying in the sight of his muscled torso.

But when his hand went to his trousers, her courage deserted her. She looked to his face instead. There was a smile there, the tiny curving of his lips as he shed the rest of his clothing and stepped toward her. She trembled as he gathered the fabric of her shift and drew it over her head.

"Are you cold?" he asked.

She shook her head, not wishing to speak, not wishing to break the spell, fearing that if she spoke, things would become too real, and he might guess the truth. That she was not the woman he thought she was, that he might leave her and that she could not bear it.

"You are so beautiful."

She flushed hotly at his intent perusal, watching the lowering of his thick sooty lashes, the tightening of his features in stark hunger. He caught her up against him and lowered her to the clothing that he had spread carefully on the grass. Then he came down over her, hot muscle and hard skin fitting perfectly against her, shutting out the world, his touch almost desperate in his intent to love her.

Now, more than ever, she yearned to tell him of her feelings for him. To whisper words of undying love, of endless devotion, but she knew she would not. It might remind him they were worlds apart. That their love could never be and had been doomed from the beginning, just as her and Cai's had.

His sapphire eyes remained fixed on her face, searching. Searching for what, she wondered. He drank in every nuance of her reaction as he parted her legs with his own and shifted his body against hers. He kept his eyes fixed on hers as he pressed slowly, inexorably inside her. They both groaned at the possession.

When he was solidly inside her, he lowered his mouth. His kiss wasn't gentle, but it was slow and incredibly thorough. His tongue took swift possession of hers and coaxed it into his mouth. When she boldly pressed past his teeth, he groaned and pulled her tongue deeper. Alyssa's answering moan came from deep in her throat, and she instinctively lifted her hips in response. Her nails dragged down his back as his measured movements swiftly increased until they were both driving at each other in a frenzy to be closer. Yet he was still not close enough, never close enough.

She spread her hands and slid them wantonly down his back, lower still, urging him on without words to fill her, to make her his.

Her climax overtook her in a blinding rush, and she cried out as she clamped her legs tightly around his waist. He lifted her off the grass with one arm to hold her close as he drove into her one last time—one devastating time. She clung to him, soaring with him as one into the storm-tossed heavens, which knew neither kin nor creed, living nor spirit.

When they fell back to earth, he did not pull away but gathered her close to his chest. His still-hard length twitched and throbbed inside her, and she tightened convulsively around him. For several long minutes, they lay in each other's arms, panting heavily. Then he raised up and looked down at her, cupping her face gently in his hands. "Lyssa. My beautiful Lyssa, what a wonder you are." He smiled down at her, kissed her gently on the brow, and slipped from her body to hold her in his arms.

Alyssa fought to center her mind, to bring rational thought back to her brain, but finally, she gave in to the comfort of his hard, smooth chest under her cheek and his strong arms encircling her. She was aware enough to know that she might never know such a total sense of protection and fulfillment again. She held him tightly, willing each instant of time into a picture-perfect memory—another moment to remember when he was gone—and lay quiet, listening to him breathe, knowing instantly the moment he drifted into sleep. She stayed for a few minutes more, savoring the feel of him, so alive, so vital, and then quietly she moved from him and drifted out of the circle, out of the world of the living, to a place where he could never follow.

****

A shiver washed over him, and he sprang awake. His breath pluming into the frosty morning air. Lyssa was gone. He lay in the courtyard, still naked. Someone had thrown a cloak over his body while he slept. Had it been her? He remembered a lot of things from last night. The smell of her hair, the taste of her skin, the white shift she had worn…a white shift so much like the one Alyssa had worn the first night he had looked down on her from the courtyard.

He touched the ground, frowning when he found it ice cold. He had made love to Lyssa, a young woman he had respected for her innocence. Yet earlier he had decided it was Alyssa he loved. What happened last night? What madness had overtaken him? Could it have been another dream? Yet he would swear she had been there, looking beautiful, ethereal in the moonlight. He sat up and pushed a hand through his hair. But just who was she? Was she Lyssa, sweet innocent seductress, or Alyssa, wild, wanton, tragically sad, and beautiful, and did he really care?

What sort of scoundrel was he? He was torn in infinite directions. He could not think, and he had to think. But first, he needed to get back to his room.

He reached for his crumpled evening trousers and pulled them up over his hips, but as he did so, he noticed Lyssa's shift and plucked it from the grass. He had been lying on it. It was still warm. Tentatively, he brought it to his cheek. The soft material caught at the rough stubble on his jaw, reminding him again of last night—he so hard, she so soft. He groaned and breathed in her scent. *Roses.* Not unlike the scent Alyssa wore. He crushed the gown in his fist.

There were so many similarities between the two women. Sometimes it was hard to distinguish who was who. Sometimes he felt as if he teetered on the edge of madness. He dropped the gown, hastily pulled on his shirt, then scanned the garden. No other soul stirred. *Good.* The last thing he needed was to be found naked in the garden and for a scandal to erupt. Hopefully, he could keep the escapade secret, and no one would be the wiser except for the kind soul who had draped the cloak over his body. He wondered why his savior hadn't shaken him awake, then decided his mysterious benefactor must have thought he'd overindulged the previous evening.

He stifled a laugh at the picture of old Lady Hornblower stumbling upon him. Her complexion was almost purple now, and it would not have stood for one more blush. But no, his guess was Tom on his way to do the milking. He always went by way of the kitchen to see if Eleanor had arrived for work, or so Bevan informed him.

He smiled, snatched up Lyssa's nightgown, and touched it softly to his lips. He would seek Lyssa and return her shift. It would give him an excuse to see her. He would have to make a wide berth around Tom, of course. If the old man should catch wind that the reason for him being naked in the courtyard had anything to do with Lyssa, he would be far from pleased, and Aidan wouldn't blame him.

However, all that would soon be rectified. He had every intention of asking Lyssa for her hand in marriage. After all, she had been an innocent, and he had taken advantage of the situation. He looked down at the virginal white shift and smiled. She hadn't seemed so innocent last night. Yet he was certain it was all wrapped up in the dream he experienced earlier with Alyssa and the images evoked when they kissed. It certainly seemed that way in the moonlight with the stars shining overhead and in her eyes, the silk of her hair in his hands, and the satin of her body against his. Oh, yes, he needed to see Lyssa very badly. He needed to kiss her again and claim her as his own.

He smiled and stepped from the circle, but as he did so, his smile faltered. For the gown in his hand turned to fine powdery ash, and he watched with a sick feeling in the deep pit of his stomach as the ash sifted through his fingers to be taken by the wind. His jubilant mood dissolved. Anger rose up like a fiery furnace. His fist thudded painfully into the nearest standing stone.

"Alyssa." It had been her doing all along. How could he have ever thought he'd been in love with a ghost? She had tricked him, deceived him into thinking he had made love to Lyssa and had not corrected him when he had spoken her name. He ran both hands over the back of his head and turned toward the stables. He had no idea what was going on here, but he would lay a wager Tom did.

He'd had enough of Alyssa's charades, enough of being twisted and torn in two. He had to know Alyssa's real motive and of what she was capable.

Had Lyssa been an innocent, unwitting participant used in some sick game? Had she been possessed? Had she even been here last night? Or—he could barely contemplate the thought as he strode toward the barn doors and burst into the dim interior—could Alyssa and Lyssa be the same woman? Had she been playing him for a fool all along?

****

Alyssa trailed after him and saw him open the postern gate and hasten through. She had seen him wake, watched the surprise register on his face as he'd discovered the cloak she had Tom throw over him. Saw him pull his trousers up over his lean hard hips and admired his muscled beauty in the sunrise as much as she had loved looking at him in the moonlight. He had found her shift. She had caught her breath as he had held it to his cheek and almost wept when it had turned to ash when he stepped from the garden and his smile had turned to fury.

He knew.

She was sure he knew, and if he did not, he was on the way now to find Tom, and there was no way she could warn her old friend. The barn was not part of her domain.

With a fearful foreboding, she knew Aidan would question Tom and that this time he would confess to everything.

Aidan would hate her.

She had deceived him, confused him, until he had not known who she was. He must have been certain he had been making love to a living woman, not a spirit who had been dead for two centuries, or he would not have stayed.

This time, she feared she had truly lost him.

****

"Very well, old man, it is time I was told the truth. All of it." Tom was not where Aidan had expected him to be in the stables. It had taken him all morning, but he had finally tracked his old steward to the library. He slammed the door behind him. "There never was any ship-building brother, was there?"

Tom slumped back into his chair and snapped the ledger shut. "That was the truth."

"Then nothing else was. Who *is* Alyssa, or should I say, Lyssa? For if I am right, they are one and the same. Are they not?" He had thought about it all day, and it was the only logical conclusion he could draw without marking himself a complete fool.

"'Ow did you guess?" Tom sounded weary.

"Every time I kissed Lyssa, I had visions of Alyssa. And if that was not enough, the small matter of her shift turning to ash as I stepped from between the stones."

"Ah, her shift," Tom murmured, resting his head back and closing his eyes. "So, it has gone so far? I told 'er this would come to no good, but she's such a stubborn lass. I told 'er, but she wouldn't listen. She 'ad to meet you, and she 'ad to attend that fool ball." He sighed. "So, what now? Do I pack my bags and be gone from here?"

"Don't be daft, man, this place would fall apart without you, and there is no telling what she would do if I sent you packing." Aidan stalked across the carpet to a small rosewood table and poured himself a brandy, quaffed it, poured another, downed it, then rounded. "No. I want some answers, nothing more. The first being, how does she do it? And what is her interest in me? From the moment I stepped into this castle, I felt it. A feeling as if I had walked these halls before. As if I had been in her room…" He shook his head. "I have these visions that I cannot explain." He studied Tom's face. It seemed more wrinkled and weathered than usual. "But perhaps you can."

The old man rose, crossed the rug to stand in front of a ceiling-to-floor bookcase, counted six shelves up and fifteen books in from the edge, and reached up to pull forward a large, red volume.

A door-sized portion of the bookcase swung inward. "Come," he said, looking over his shoulder at Aidan. "There is something you should see."

Aidan followed him into a dim tunnel smelling of mold, damp, stale air. He watched the old man take a rusty oil lantern from beside the door, scrounge in his pocket for a flint, and set the wick to light. For a moment he didn't think the flame would take, but after an initial splutter, it flared, and Tom replaced the glass. He then pushed on a brick on the tunnel wall, and the door slid silently closed.

"This way." Tom set off at a brisk pace down the corridor.

He followed him through a series of tunnels. Tom opened ancient doors, closed them again, and continued on only to open up another, until finally, Aidan felt as if he had delved into the very bowels of the earth. Water ran in small rivulets down parts of the ancient lichen-covered walls, and moss had formed on sections of the stone path, making it hazardous. Once, Tom stumbled, but Aidan caught him and held him until he could right himself and go on. The old man thanked him gruffly, the only words he had spoken until then, no matter how often he had tried to press him into conversation.

Finally, they stopped, and it seemed Tom was loath to open the next panel. He looked deep into Aidan's eyes and must have seen what he was looking for, because he nodded, and his hand went to a jutting rock in the tunnel wall.

A panel, a little under Aidan's height, slid open, but this was no tunnel, this was a room, and from what Aidan could see, quite a large one.

Tom trudged across a red and gold faded oriental rug, which decomposed beneath each footfall. Dust and ancient fibers plumed into the air, forcing both of them to cover their noses.

Waiting for the dust to settle, Tom used the edge of his woolen shirt to lift the glass from the lantern and light the three thick, white candles that stood on a table at the side of the room.

"This 'ere is where William de Bracey 'id his wife for over a year and a 'alf after he married her," informed the old man, breaking the silence.

He stepped gingerly into the room. "They were betrayed, and Jane slain. I read it in the Llewellyn family history that you gave me." A large dust-covered bed, a baby's crib, lovingly carved with hearts and roses, a large, black, wooden dresser—how they had managed to get that in here, he could only imagine—a wooden, studded chest, and a tall swivel mirror stood in the room.

The whole place cried of tragedy and told the story of a doomed love. He could only feel sorrow for Jane through Gedrych's appalling cruelty of having her killed, having forced her to spend her last days in these close quarters. However, this was not why he had come. "What has this to do with Alyssa?" He turned abruptly to Tom, who had cleaned off a chair and was now seated at the table.

He looked up as Aidan spoke, then stared down at his hands. "Jane loved her mistress, you see?" He smiled softly as if thinking back. "I was sixteen when Alyssa first told me of this place." He cleared his throat. "But that is neither 'ere nor now." He sighed. "They were more sisters than lady and lady-in-waiting. After

Alyssa's death, Jane had William take the wedding portrait that hung in her lady's room and bring it down here. Gedrych never noticed. 'Ad too many other concerns, I dare say." Tom gave a toothy grin. "Alyssa had already begun to haunt him, and nothing anyone could say would make him set foot in Cai and Alyssa's old room. In a small way, I suppose it was a comfort to Jane to have her mistress's portrait with her."

"Did she never see daylight again?"

"Jane?"

Aidan nodded.

"I believe William 'ad several sympathizers whom he trusted. When those guards were on duty, 'e would sneak Jane up to the battlements late at night. Or that is what Alyssa told me." Tom ambled over to the corner of the room to where a portrait sat on the ground, leaning inward against the wall. It was large, around three feet wide by five feet high, so it took him a few minutes, but he finally twisted it to face Aidan.

Aidan's breath caught in his throat, and he thought he would stop breathing. For several painful heartbeats, he stood perfectly still. So, this was what it was all about. This was the answer to the secret that plagued Thornwood. That plagued him. He should have guessed at, but he was too blind to see. He had been used. Despicably so! He had not only taken the place of Cai in his dreams. He had been his likeness, and Alyssa had taken advantage of the fact. Of him.

She looked so lifelike. Like a beautiful red-haired goddess of deception, standing before him, beckoning. She wore a gown of cream with roses of the same color woven through her veil of fiery tresses. She could have been real, as real as last night. He felt a pain shoot through his vitals at her betrayal. For beside her, on what must have been their wedding day, stood Cai de Morgan, the man she really loved. A man made in his own image.

Tom nodded. "Now do you, see?"

"Oh, I see all right." His jaw hardened as he tried to rein in his anger. "That Lyssa, your Lyssa, the one who professes to be your niece, is naught but a lying she-devil in spirit form."

Tom came to his feet, but he held up his hand.

"That the woman who appears in the stones is the wife of Cai de Morgan, born 1624 and burned as a witch in the year 1644 by Gedrych de Morgan. Yes, I see that and that the man bears an uncanny resemblance to me. But that still does not explain how she can appear alive, when she is in truth dead. How she can appear solid living flesh, speak to me, breathe, press her heart, beating, to mine…" He stopped and swung away, pushing a hand through his hair. "I just don't understand. What am I missing? Was Alyssa really a witch? She certainly bewitched me, and there is no other logical explanation."

"My lord, she wished *only* to be with you." Tom shook his head and stared at the floor. "She has this foolish notion that you are Cai reincarnated, that you have come back to her, that some miracle will occur that will allow you to be together."

Aidan ignored Tom's words, and his jaw hardened. "You still have not answered my question."

Tom lifted his chin. "Which question might that be? There have been so many."

"How she does it. How does she appear so real?"

"May an old man sit first?"

Aidan nodded to one of the high-backed chairs, and

Tom sank onto it, folding his hands before him on the dusty table. For a long moment, the old steward stared down at his hands, then slowly he began to speak. "She cursed him, you see."

Aidan took the chair opposite. "Gedrych?"

"Aye. He 'ad tried her as a witch, accused her of sedition, thievery, and umpteen dozen other trumped-up charges. All because she would not fall into 'is arms and become 'is whore. Cai had only been in his grave a month. But it 'ad begun even before that."

Aidan nodded. "I know."

Tom frowned, "You know?"

Aidan didn't elaborate. "Go on."

Tom eyed him suspiciously, no doubt wondering where he had gained the information because it was not in the book. He had read it in Alyssa's diary. However, the old man went on without further question.

"de Morgan was a blackguard, yes, of the worst kind, but he was also a strict Catholic and as superstitious as they come. The worst thing she could have done was curse him, for he already carried the burden of guilt for his son's death on his conscience, and her curse only proved to bring home to him what he had done. If William had not killed him, he no doubt would have killed himself or eventually gone insane. He was already headin' that way."

"The curse and the stones," Aidan reminded, drumming his fingers on the table. He knew he was being hard on the old man, but he would have his answers.

"Sorry." Tom scratched at his balding pate. "This mind of mine tends to wander. The curse. Ah, yes. *'I curse you, Gedrych de Morgan!'* she cried, as the flames rose up around her. *'Curse you for the murder of your son, the murder of my child, and the murder of me! May your line be cast from Thornwood until Cai walks its halls again!'"* Tom straightened and met Aidan's gaze, and the old man's eyes were clear gray. "So, you see, you are he, for the curse be broken. You have walked the halls of Thornwood. You have come home! And Thornwood is restored to the de Morgans."

A shiver raced down Aidan's spine, and his gaze slid from the old man's face to the portrait.

"May your line be cast from Thornwood until Cai walks its halls again!"

Well, the de Morgan line had certainly been cast out, and now here *he* stood in the bowels of Thornwood. Could Tom be right? Could Alyssa? Could he be Cai de Morgan, reborn, living, breathing, and walking the halls of a castle after two centuries of the de Morgan's banishment? A shiver prickled his nape and washed down his spine. His hands shook, and he jammed them into his pockets.

He scanned the room, noting for the first time the dark stains upon the rug and duvet, which could only be blood. This place stunk of death. Of tragedy for a love doomed, as Cai and Alyssa's love had been doomed. He came to his feet. He had to get out. This room held too much sorrow. But first, he would know more. Questions were like opium eating at his brain, the knowledge that there could still be matters of which he did not know.

This old man before him held the key, and he was darned if he was not going to turn that key, no matter the consequences. He searched Tom's face and saw a glimmer of fear in the old man's eyes. But who did he fear, him or Alyssa? Or was Tom still afraid that he would exile him from Thornwood? He relaxed his features and strolled over to observe the craftsmanship of the baby's cradle, so lovingly carved.

"It is a wonder William didn't take this up to the keep when he returned. So much time must have gone into its carving."

"Perhaps there was too much un'appiness associated with the crib and this room. Alyssa says William never returned down 'ere. He couldn't bear to look at the place where Jane had died."

Aidan nodded. He could understand that. He'd felt the same about Paris after Anni's death. How long ago and how far away that now seemed, as if it had happened in another world and to someone else entirely. He thought he would never love like that again, but he had been wrong. So wrong. He knew now what he had felt for Antoinette was nothing compared to what he felt for Alyssa. It had been strong, fast, and heady, like young wine. What he felt for Alyssa was a love that seeped into his bones and grew with every breath he took. Yet, he was still to discover if it was a sweet elixir or a drug that would lead to his doom. "The standing stones," he said, speaking at last on another subject. "They once stood on the moors below the castle, did they not?"

Tom nodded. "Gedrych 'ad William and 'is men drag 'em up to the castle. He believed they 'arnessed an ancient and forgotten power." He chuckled. "I think old Gedrych got more 'an 'e bargained for with that lot."

"How so?"

Tom sobered. "'Tis the stones that brought Alyssa to life. Don't ask 'ow. No one knows. My father, being something of a scholar devoted 'is life to studying Druid lore, but 'e died not knowing the secret that would unlock the key to the stones and send her ladyship on her way."

"So, she is bound to the stone circle?" He realized now that whenever Alyssa had been posing as Lyssa, she had always been within the circle. He stopped to stare down at the wedding portrait, refusing to look at Cai. "But I have seen her in my room. One night not long after I arrived. I was looking into the mirror and…she was behind me."

"Yes, she used to appear to Jane in a similar way, in that there mirror." He pointed to the large, freestanding looking glass beside Aidan. "She can only be seen within the glass."

It was Aidan's turn to nod. "And it was not even as if I was really looking at my own image. It was as if I was looking…" He paused. "…at Cai. My hair was longer, and she…touched me, and when I spun around, she was gone. And there have been dreams, but not dreams…it is as if when I sleep, I travel back…"

"To a past life?"

"It is so unbelievable, but yes."

"It could be what me father called regression. He was a learned man, you know. Taught me to read and write and keep the ledgers."

He gave an absent nod. "So, what does she want from me?" His hands began to clench and unclench at his side as his anger resurfaced. "She deceived me. She tricked me. She made me fall in love with her. A woman I can never have. Unless…it was she who tried to kill me. Who else would want me dead? In some warped way, she might think it would bring us together…" He made for the door. "Come, I've got to get out of here. This place reeks of death."

Tom pushed to his feet and grabbed up the lantern.

"What about the portrait?"

He headed for the door. "Leave it, and you are not to tell her I know." He stopped to wait in the hall. "I will handle this my own way."

"She wouldn't 'urt you. She can't leave the courtyard. She can't even come up to the gatehouse. She can only enter the castle proper, and that's in spirit form. She cannot touch anything."

"She touched me."

"She loves you."

Aidan grunted and started down the passageway in the direction they had come. "Love. How can a ghost love? If she does love anyone, it is not me. It is the man who she thinks I used to be. A man who died two-hundred years ago. A man who no longer exists."

"And are you not the same person? Did your dreams not prove that?"

Tom's words echoed after him as he headed off down the tunnel.

****

By the time Aidan reached the library, most of his anger had dissipated, but not all. He told Tom he wanted to see Alyssa in the garden the next morning. "Be sure she is there," he emphasized before pulling open the door and stalking from the room.

Drained and deflated, he now stared out of his bedroom window into the courtyard. The light was fading, but the stones were still visible. Solitary, defiant, undying…like Alyssa herself.

How could he have been so deceived, when all along the evidence had been right before him? The first time he had met her, she had worn no shoes. Not the thing for a properly brought-up young miss. The clothes in which she dressed were at least thirty years behind the times and must have been the Countess Llewellyn's.

He, a man of fashion, should have noticed. And never finding her outside of the circle, he should have guessed the night of the ball when he had been transported by Lyssa's kiss. He thought it had been the ghost playing tricks. Well, it had been in a way. Perhaps deep down, he just hadn't wanted to believe.

There was a knock on the door, and he called, "Enter."

Bevan stepped into the room. "It is almost time for dinner, my lord. As you did not ring, I thought—"

"Tell my grandmother that I will not be dining tonight. That I…am ailing."

Bevan took a step forward. "You are ailing, my lord?"

"Of course not." He waved his valet away. "Just tell my grandmother that. Truth is, I have no appetite tonight, nor the strength for idle chatter." Closing the shutters he pushed away from the window and moved to stand with his back to the fire. "Count Denero, has he gone?"

"This afternoon, my lord. He looked to pay his respects, but you could not be found."

"Unfortunate," Aidan replied dryly. "And Dr. Arlington and his new bride, have they departed for Brighten?"

"Directly after lunch, my lord."

"Good, he must have found someone else from whom to leech money. His new wife is bleeding him dry." He turned to stare absently into the flames. "Freddie and Lady Carolyn? Are they still in residence?"

"Indeed, they are, my lord."

"Pity."

"Sir?"

He shook his head. "Give my excuses and tell my cousin I will meet him at the stables for our ride at ten in the morning."

"Yes, my lord."

"And Bevan?"

"My lord?"

"That will be all."

Bevan's shoulders slumped, and he hesitated. "Perhaps a small plate, my lord. To appease your grandmother?"

Aidan almost smiled, but not quite. He nodded and heard the door close behind him as he faced the window. No doubt Lady Elizabeth would cross-examine poor Bevan until satisfied he kept no secrets from her.

****

Tom shivered and closed the gatehouse door, shutting out the bitter wind. He pulled a puppy from inside his old tweed jacket and watched it totter off toward the hearth, smiling as the puppy chased a few dry leaves that had blown in through the door. He shrugged out of his jacket and cap and, after hanging them on the coat stand, stretched and arched his back. His rheumatism was acting up. It had been a long day having to do the accounts and his lordship confronting him over Alyssa. He moved around the room, lighting the two oil lanterns.

He was still unsure of what to do. He hated keeping secrets from Alyssa. Felt somehow like he was betraying her trust. He rubbed his hands together, trying to get them warm, and looked around for the puppy, laughing out loud as it tripped itself up while chasing its tail.

He trudged across the faded rug to warm his back at

the meager fire.

The five rooms of the gatehouse weren't of a grand scale, but at least they were his while he lived. Then there was Grace. Her lily-of-the-valley fragrance lingered after all these years, and her presence lived on all around him. He remembered her placing the blue earthen vase upon the mantel where it still held a place of pride. Her lithe form standing upon the chair near the window, him steadying her with his hands about her waist as she hung the new lace curtains. She had been so proud of them. The mistress of the castle at the time had given her the cloth.

He crossed the threadbare rug to the side table and picked up the miniature of Grace and the boy. His wife's face, serene and gentle, would ever live in his heart. He'd never told her he loved her, never knew he had until she was gone, and then it had been too late. And the boy, little William, he couldn't think about that—he coughed, cleared his throat, and replaced the miniature.

Picking up the fire iron, he poked life into the few embers left at the bottom of the grate and added two pieces of precious coal and a few sticks of wood, staring into the igniting flames. It was cold nights like this he felt so alone, even with the company of the pup. Some nights, he just longed for another body to talk to.

A knock sounded at the door, and he struggled to his feet. Crossing the large red and gold rug, carrying the fire iron with him, he eased open the door a crack and peered out. The wind still bitter, the moon not yet risen, he recognized the figure of Count Landon Denero lounging nonchalantly against his door jamb from the light filtering from the oil lamps inside.

The man straightened and Tom opened the door a

farther few inches.

"Lovely evening." Denero pulled his greatcoat closer to his chest. "You will not be needing that," he commented regarding Tom's fire iron clenched firmly in his fist. "I am not here to harm you."

"Never thought you were." Tom bristled, lowering the iron.

"I need to speak with you. A private matter."

He stepped aside, allowing the man room enough to pass. "Don't know what you would be wantin' with me."

Denero glanced over his shoulder and signaled to his coachman to move on, then stepped into the room. He indicated that the count should be seated in the armchair by the fire.

"Please, do sit." Denero indicated the chair opposite. "This is your home, after all."

He perched on the edge of the overstuffed chair. The gentry always made him nervous. They never saw someone unless they wanted something. He wondered what the Italian count would need with him. Suddenly, his cozy night by the fire with the pup faded to an illusion.

He had seen the Italian up at the castle that morning, almost bumping into him as the man had stepped from the breakfast room, and again noted him that afternoon slinking around the stables.

He'd heard the master's man, Bevan, mention to Eleanor that the master was not taken with the Italian and could not wait to see the back of him, but Tom decided to see what the man had to say before laying down his own judgment. "Tea?" he asked, coming to his feet.

Denero nodded. "Might as well make ourselves comfortable. This may take a lengthy while, and my blood needs some warming."

Tom hesitated. "I 'ave a Port I've been savin'…"

Denero shook his head. "Tea will surfice."

He grunted and moved through a doorway on the other side of the room into his small kitchen.

****

Landan leaned forward and scooped up the puppy to sit on his lap. The pup had taken an uncommon interest in his boot, pawing at it, and taking small nips.

He settled back and scanned the room as he fondled the pup's ears. From what he knew about Tom Jeffreys, his wife had died over a decade ago, yet the small room in which he now sat still held the traces of a woman's touch. Jeffreys must have loved his wife dearly, not to have stamped out her presence.

When the old man greeted him at the door with the fire iron, Landan had held reservations, but from seeing his home and the care he took with preserving the smallest details of his wife's former inhabitance, he was more certain than ever Jeffreys was the man he'd been seeking. The old man seemed a stern type of character, but from all accounts, honest and loyal.

Jeffreys reentered and settled an ancient pewter tray with a pink teapot and two floral cups on the table between them. "They were my wife's," he said gruffly, noting the twitch of Landan's lips.

"And very fine they are," Landan commented, lowering the sleeping pup to the rug, and settling back in his chair.

"No. They're horrid, but they were hers, and I wouldn't be partin' with them for the last farthing in all o' Cornwall."

Landan didn't know what to answer, so he remained

silent, watching Tom pour two cups of tea, add sugar, and rest back in his chair.

"Now what would you be wantin' to speak with me about? And none of that beatin' around the bush, either. Plain speakin' is always best."

Landan picked up his cup, thankful that Jeffreys' initial fear of him had vanished. He took a mouthful of tea, burning his tongue, and cursed beneath his breath. "Plain speaking, it shall be, then." He longed for a dash of cream but decided against asking. "Your employer, the Earl of Dunmore. I believe his life to be in danger."

Jeffreys balanced his cup on his knee. His clear gray eyes held not a flicker of emotion. "I know."

It was his turn to frown. "What do you know?"

"Someone tripped 'is horse and killed it on the moors. The master had to find 'is way home in a storm. Took 'im all night. In the mornin' we found a broken rope across the road, which 'ad been stretched between a boulder an' a tree stump."

He nodded. "The magistrate in St. Agnes told me. He thought it might be the work of thieves."

"Weren't no thieves."

"What makes you say that?"

Jeffreys shook his head and glanced into his teacup. "Shouldn't be sayin' this, him bein' gentry and all, but I don't trust that cousin of 'is."

"Lord Fitzwilliam?"

Jeffreys met his gaze. "Not one bit."

He folded his hands between his knees. "That is a pretty strong accusation, Mr. Jeffreys. Have you any proof to back it up?"

"I know what I know, but I would be preferrin' not to say 'ow I know. And while we're on it, 'ow do I know

I can trust you? What 'as any of this got to do with you?"

Landan rose and stood with his back to the fire. "You're right, Mr. Jeffreys. Here I am questioning you, and I have not given you one reason to trust me." He wondered how much he could tell the old man without revealing too much of himself, and how much he could trust Jeffreys. "All I can tell you is that the people I do business with have an interest in de Morgan and would like to see him kept alive."

"The people you do business with? What kind of business?"

"You have your secrets. Allow me mine."

The two men regarded each other in silence. "Very well," said Jeffreys. "But you best be who you say you are. If one hair on the master's head should be 'armed—why are you tellin' me this, anyway?"

"I want to stay here in your home for a few days without anyone knowing. I also want you to watch for anything out of the ordinary. Especially anything pertaining to Lord Fitzwilliam and Miss Carolyn Simms."

"You think Miss Carolyn is in on this, too? We had our suspicions."

"We? You mean the Earl?"

Jeffreys shook his head and glanced away. "I meant to say I had *my* suspicions. I get a little mixed up at times. Old age creepin' up, sometimes I think my Gracy's still 'ere." He set his cup on the table and stood. "You can sleep in my son's room."

Landan frowned and rose. "I didn't know you had a son. That could change matters. I would not wish to put anyone from their room."

"He died," said Jeffreys, turning away, not

elaborating.

"I'm sorry."

"Don't be. It was a long time ago." Jeffreys led Landan across the parlor into a small hallway. "The room is up those steps." He pointed to the staircase at the end of the hall. "Don't go up there much these days, not good for me joints. The room's clean, though. Eleanor's daughter Mary comes twice a week and does a bit of dustin'. Good girl, she is."

"I'm certain she is."

"I'll tell her not to come for a few days."

Landan rounded and put his hand on Jeffreys' shoulder. "I appreciate this. As I said, my people are worried about the earl, and this is the only way I can keep tabs on the matter. I would not ask otherwise."

Jeffreys nodded. "Just catch the beggar before he harms the master."

"I will do my darndest to stop that from happening, but that is where I need your help. Now, wait here. There is something I must collect." He retraced his steps and opened the front door. Hidden within the bushes at the bottom of the steps was a small black bag. "A change of clothes," he said, turning to find Jeffreys behind him.

"You were pretty sure of yourself, weren't you? What if I'd said no?"

He grinned. "I knew you wouldn't."

****

Carolyn's maid had just finished putting the last touches to her coiffure when a light tap sounded on the door and Freddie slid into the room.

She came to her feet and dismissed her maid. "You may go now, and remember, not a word," she said, putting a finger to her lips.

Her maid curtsied, cast a shy glance at Freddie, and hurried out the door.

"I've told you not to come here. It's too dangerous. Last time you were almost caught."

Freddie smiled. "Yes. But I wasn't." He closed the gap between them, and his arms snaked around her waist, drawing her close, but she pushed him away and turned to her mirror to pat her hair into place.

"What is it you want, Freddie?"

"What is it I want?" He growled, straightening. "I want my upstart of a cousin dead. I want to be an earl, and I want his fortune. That is what I want." His jaw hardened. "He should have died on the moors. If it wasn't for his military training…"

"I thought you were leaving this to me?"

"Your way is too slow. You never crossed paths today."

She rounded. "What do you want from me? I am trying my best, but the man has grown a heart of iron. He seems immune to my charms."

"Yes, well." He looked into the mirror, and his gaze met hers. "It happens."

"What is that supposed to mean?" Her eyes darkened. "That you are tiring of me?"

"Of course not, my dear. I was merely commenting. Now be a good girl and fetch me the wolfsbane from your trunk."

"What?"

His fingers dug into her shoulders. "You heard me. The wolfsbane—monkshood—whatever you wish to call it. I know you have it. I saw it in your trunk."

"You have searched my belongings."

Freddie crossed his arms. "I was looking for

opium."

Her lips drew thin. "What made you think I have opium?"

"That's of no consequence. Do as I say."

"You go through my belongings, and it is of no consequence?" Her voice rose an octave.

"You will get the poison." His tone hardened, and the dark look in his brown eyes intensified.

She flounced to the window and stared down at the ocean lashing the needlepoint rocks below. Suicidal in extreme, she reflected, but no more suicidal than what she was about to do. Either way, she was doomed. How could she have aligned herself with Freddie? He was a wastrel and a leech, and he always would be. But not only that, he was becoming more unstable each day.

She should have noted his weak jaw and too-pale eyes, but all she had seen was the money. Now she had come too far, and she feared Freddie with his impulsiveness would be the ruin of them both. "You will not use the poison on Aidan," she said at last, still looking out the window. "I won't let you."

His fingers sank into the soft flesh of her shoulders like tiny vises, forcing her to face him. She had not even heard him approach.

"And why would that be, madam?" His words punctuated the air, hard, icy. "Could it be you still hold a fondness for my dear, soon-to-be departed cousin? You thought little of using the poison on your husband."

She pulled away and stepped back. "How dare you insinuate…Conrad died at sea."

"He breakfasted with you that same morning. It would have been quite easy…or, who was that young lieutenant you were so fond of at the time? Reynolds, wasn't it? What did you promise him, marriage, money, your favors?"

She remained silent. He'd been just a little too close to the truth.

Her thoughts flowed back several years to the young Lieutenant Reynolds—tall, blond, hard-chested, just the way she liked her men, not like the pot-bellied Dr. Crenshaw whom she'd had to lie with to get the drug. She shivered with revulsion, then smiled inwardly. Lieutenant Reynolds's lovemaking had been long, hard, and slow, and as good for her as it had been for him. Their affair had continued for some time after Conrad's death but keeping it quiet became far too difficult. She'd had to let him go, and he'd cried like a baby, poor pup. She never could stand a man who cried. Her mother had been right. Do not get involved. That way no one got hurt.

She stepped back to deliver Freddie a slap, but he caught her wrist in a vise-like grip and twisted it up behind her back, bringing her face up close to his. Why had she never noticed the sweet, sickly smell of his breath?

"A little too near to home, my dear?" He smiled cruelly, slowly. "Now, you will do exactly as you are told. Have you forgotten we are partners?"

"You are hurting me." Her teeth clenched against the pain racing up her arm, and tears welled in her eyes. "Let me go. I will do as you ask."

"Good girl," he soothed, releasing her, stroking a knuckle down her soft cheek.

She flinched away and flounced across to the far corner. Kneeling beside her black metal trunk, she threw back the heavy lid and pushed her hands into the silken undergarments at the bottom. Her hand touched something cold and hard, and for a moment she contemplated taking the poison herself. At least she would be free of Freddie.

However, she knew she was too much of a coward, and she enjoyed her pampered life too much. No, she would bide her time. Freddie's turn would come, as Conrad's had. Strengthening her resolve, she clasped the vial firmly, marched back, and pushed it into Freddie's large, soft hand, so unlike Aidan's. His were strong and lightly calloused. "Satisfied?"

"Quite."

"One question. How did you know what it was?"

Freddie's gaze glittered with malice as he stared down at the small purple vial in his hand. "Let me say that most physicians are not known for their expert card playing. There are a few whose notes I still hold."

"Blackmail?" she breathed.

His lips twisted in distaste. "Blackmail, such a disagreeable word. I would like to consider it as doing one's friend a favor."

Carolyn's lips formed a ruby line. "Aidan dines with us at lunch and dinner and has a disgusting habit of eating in the kitchen at breakfast with that wretched cook hovering over his shoulder. How will you get the poison into his food without doing away with us all?"

"That, my dear, is your concern."

"Mine?" She squeaked, the breath almost leaving her body as she stepped back. "Are you daft?"

"I heard his manservant, Bevan, tell the cook that Aidan is ailing. That he wishes only for a small plate brought to his room," he explained as if he were speaking to a small child. "You will intercept the maid and tell her you will deliver his lordship's meal. You will add the wolfsbane to his food. He will think nothing of you taking it to him. You are there to check only on his health. You care about him," he finished with a cynical smile, caressing her cheek.

She turned from him in disgust and strode to the window to gaze out over the endless moonlit sea. A seagull swooped past her window, and she wished wholeheartedly she were so free. Free from Freddie's claustrophobic presence. How had she been so foolish as to get mixed up in his reckless plans? How had she ever thought she loved him? "He may not wish to see me."

Freddie closed the gap between them, his fingers digging into the fleshy part of her arms as he forced her to face him. His usually pale countenance flushed red. "Why? What have you done?"

She winced at the pain shooting up her neck and down her arms. "Only what you told me to do. Use my wiles upon him. Try to force him into marriage." She pulled from his brutal grip and turned back to the window. "We argued."

"Then, my dearest girl, you will apologize." He swung her around and pushed the vial into her hand, curling her fingers painfully around the glass. "You better leave now if you are to intercept the maid."

"I won't forget this, Freddie."

He smiled and straightened his jacket, brushing an imaginary speck from his velvet sleeve as he moved toward the door. "Perhaps not, my sweet. But when he is dead, and I am an earl with several houses and a fortune at my disposal, your memory might certainly grow dim." He checked to see that the corridor was empty and stepped into the shadows, leaving her to stare blankly at the door.

****

Rain blew through the window, plastering Aidan's shirt to his chest, yet he barely acknowledged the cold. He ran a hand over his eyes, which felt raw and gritty. He knew he should close the shutters, but still he lingered lost in a world of melancholy, attempting to penetrate the gloom in the courtyard. It was as if the weather conspired against him seeking her out.

He had spent almost half the hour standing before the large swivel mirror in the corner, examining it for her image. He had called her name, all to no avail. Wherever she dwelt this dreadful night, it was not in this world. Tom had told him she could not enter the gatehouse, and she was not in the courtyard. What sort of world did she inhabit when she was not at the castle?

The world where mortal men could never follow, that he could never enter? Was it dark, cold, lonely, like he was now without her? How could he have been such an imbecile? What other simpleton would fall in love with a ghost? Pain shot up his arms as he thumped his fists onto the window ledge.

A light tap on the door startled him from his mournful thoughts. The knock was not Bevan's customary tap—that was usually a lot softer. He called, "Come in," and waited, only to see Carolyn slip into the room carrying a covered silver tray. He waited for her to speak.

"I hope you don't mind, my lord, but I intercepted your man and convinced him to allow me to bring up your supper. I heard you were ailing." Her gaze swept over the disheveled state of his clothing, and she hurriedly set the tray on the table. "I do hope this has nothing to do with the silly misunderstanding we shared last night. I have come just now to ask your forgiveness."

She took a small step forward. "I do hope you will forgive me. I do not know what possessed me to act in such a rash and common manner. It was just that…" She wrung her hands. "I thought the signs were there." She smiled hesitantly. "I only hope…that perhaps…you will give me the chance to mend the rift between us."

Was this another ploy by Carolyn to trap him into marriage? Aidan forced a smile. "Apology accepted, madam. We were all a little bedeviled last night. Too much good wine, I suspect." He kept his expression bland.

She gave a tiny laugh that came out like a squeak, then she seemed to relax.

"Now I must insist." She took his elbow. "That you come away from that window. You are drenched. No wonder you are unwell." Her voice softened. "Perhaps you should change your shirt."

His jaw hardened, as did his look.

Her smile weakened. "Or perhaps not." She reached past him and stretched out with both hands to close the shutters, then led him to the small table against the opposite wall. "You must try this wonderful beef stew that Eleanor prepared." She drew out the chair, forced him gently into the seat, and lifted the lid from the plate, bending swiftly to inhale the aroma. "It smells positively divine."

Aidan had to admit that it did look good, but his appetite just wasn't there. Indeed, as the savory smell reached his nose, he had to swallow the bile that formed a lump in his throat. He was about to turn away, but Carolyn grasped his arm.

"Really, darling, you must have something. I am certain once you have eaten, you will feel so much better." She reached for the silver fork resting on the tray, scooped up a small amount of the chunky beef stew, and brought it to his lips.

For a moment, he thought to refuse. Looking into her eyes, he wondered why she was so insistent he ate. But her wide-eyed gaze held the same intense innocence it always did, and there was no answer there. With a sigh of resignation, he opened his mouth and took the food she offered. The stew was rich with wine and spices and another flavor he could not identify. He forced a swallow, and the food slid like a stone to a river into the bottom of his stomach and sat there with the same heaviness.

"Now," he said, twisting his head to resist the second larger mouthful she aimed at his lips. "I have done as you asked. Surely that pleases you." He rose, took the fork from her hand, and dropped it with a clatter onto the tray.

"But Aidan, I really think—"

He took her arm in a firm, not-too-gentlemanly grip, and began leading her to the door. "I am certain all I need is a good night's rest."

"I must insist you eat some more. Your grandmother—"

"Tell my grandmother I am fine."

She tried to stop, but he forced her on. "And your supper?"

"I promise I will eat it," he said, although he knew he lied. His appetite truly had died with the realization of Alyssa's true identity. He opened the door and almost forcefully ushered Carolyn into the hallway.

She made to step back into his room, but he blocked her way with his body. “I am well, Carolyn, really.” But he felt anything but well. He was beginning to feel positively ill. Goosebumps chased themselves up his arms, then shivered down his spine and thighs. He had to be coming down with a chill. Perhaps Carolyn was right. Standing in front of the open window in only his shirt and trousers, with the wind and rain blowing in on him, could have affected his health. Though it was likely the fact that he had slept naked in the courtyard the evening before. A shocking thing in itself and a sin for which, he believed, he was about to pay.

He stifled a groan as agonizing pain ripped through his vitals and had to stop himself from doubling up. He felt the blood draining from his face even as he took Carolyn’s hand and brought it to his lips. “I will see you in the morning,” he said in a tight voice, drawing a deep but painful breath to cover his agitation. “We shall ride together.” He smiled through gritted teeth. “I trust you will extend the invitation to Freddie if Bevan has not already done so.”

“Of course I will, darling.” She gripped his arm. “But you are positively ghostly. I think perhaps you should rest and see how you feel in the morning.” The look she gave him told him she was worried for him, but all he wanted was to escape her to find the comfort of his own room. A terrible numbness replaced the shivering in his legs and was growing worse. “Would you send Bevan?” He put a hand to his temples as they began a crescendo that could rival a full broadside of a battleship. “I…I really do feel wretched.”

She opened her mouth to speak.

“Please no more, Carolyn.” He closed the door in

her face and turned slowly to stumble to his bed. Another pain clawed at his insides, his legs gave way, and he was helpless to save himself.

The blue-and-red rug rushed up to greet him and cushioned his fall, but his elbow struck agonizingly at the side table as he fell, causing a rose vase to crash to the floor to lie beside him. The water flowed toward him, but he could barely feel the dampness as his body was flooded with overwhelming heat. Sweat dampened his temples and nape even as shivers spiraled down his back and legs.

Turning his head to the side, willing his body to respond, he tried to push to his knees, but his arms and legs refused to do his bidding. Painfully, he forced his head to a more comfortable angle, and for a fleeting moment thought he saw a red-haired woman looking out at him from the swivel mirror. He could not quite make out her expression, but he could have sworn she was laughing.

Red mist overwhelmed him, and he fell into a world of darkness.

Images danced through his mind, terrible and lovely all in one. Anni's features flushed and beautiful as she had been the first time they made love. His grandfather's aged face as he begged him not to return to France. Then his grandfather, his face pale in death. Then his grandfather's blue eyes had flown open, and he was lost in their depths, sinking ever deeper. He watched Antoinette's anger and urgency as she told of another of her friends being taken by the Royalists. He envisioned her alone, defiant, her doe brown eyes meeting his through the jeering crowd in love and acceptance as she stood bravely before Madam guillotine—her father's hand restraining him. His horror and sense of failure as he turned his head, unable to watch her die. He had sworn he would never love another as he had loved her. Yet he had betrayed that memory, as he was now betrayed.

He concentrated on moving, but his body felt heavy, weighted. Was he dead? Voices drifted in and out of his consciousness, loud then soft, all incomprehensible. Alyssa's face filled his vision. She was calling to him, yet he could not hear her words. Then fire. Flames encased her face like a burning aura. She screamed, and her face melted away. He was afire. Her heat had transferred to him. The devil was inside his body, stealing him away. He struggled, but a great weight pressed down on him. The weight vanished, and he was filled with an immense fullness as if he would burst. Pain ripped through his stomach. His innards were aflame. His eyes shot open.

Saul and Tom hovered above him.

"Now!" snapped a woman's voice.

He was dragged unceremoniously from his bed, positioned on a chamber pot, and felt himself explode as the waste was expelled from his body, and the two men held him. He had no time to think of the propriety of his situation. He was lucid. He felt movement in his limbs, and he had survived another attempt on his life.

Chapter Seventeen

Midnight dark as pitch. Rain dripped from roses hugging the arch leading into the stone garden. Tom pushed his way through the foliage, dislodging even more raindrops upon his head. He swore softly and positioned the old woolen blanket he wore more securely above him in an attempt to keep the rain at bay.

"Tom." Alyssa rushed toward him out of the darkness, wringing her hands.

He jumped. "Steady there, lass. Me old 'eart can't take too many more scares."

"At last, you come." She brushed aside his words. "How is he? He must be well, for I am certain I would know if he had gone from this earth. But for some reason, the powers that be are playing tricks on me tonight. Denying me entry to his room."

"He is well, lass. No thanks to that fiend Freddie, and that scheming hussy, Miss Simms. If only I could tell 'is lordship 'oo his real enemies are. But I know it would do me no good. For 'oo am I but an old steward he 'as known for less than four months compared to Lord Fredrick, 'oo is blood kin, and 'e has known all 'is life."

"Yes." Alyssa heaved a sigh. "It is so frustrating knowing their schemes, their lies, yet being helpless to act. What are we to do? What can we do? As Alyssa, I cannot tell him, for I cannot communicate with him in my ghostly form. As Lyssa, how could I possibly know of such occurrences?" Her worry changed to anger. "I could kill those two for what they did."

"And where would it get you?" He eyed her steadily.

"At least they would be where they deserve. In the depths of hell with their own kind."

"That may be so," Tom chastened, "but it will not be your doing. You don't want to stir up that kind of trouble."

She bowed her head. "Of course not."

"Besides, the master is well. Therefore, there is no need to be doing away with anyone."

She clasped her hands. "And thank God for that." She shifted to the stone bench and perched daintily on the edge, her small feet peeping out from beneath her hem. Tom shivered at the sight but knew from long knowledge that she never got cold. Yet *he* was feeling it right enough in his bones this night, and it was not just the weather. Words were an icy hard lump in his throat. Words he could tell her about his lordship. Like Lord Aidan was aware of her true identity.

However, he had been sworn to silence, and although it tore at him, for he loved this girl as a father would a daughter, he could not betray his master. Instead, he said, "I am certain good will win out against evil in the end, lass. Why else would God, or the powers that be, as you like to call 'em, 'ave brought you and 'is lordship together? There must be more. A greater plan."

Alyssa glanced up and met his gaze as he moved closer, her pale face alight with hope. "Do you really think so, Tom? I have tried so many times to believe that there will be a happy conclusion, but I can never see it clearly."

He smiled gently, and still clutching his old woolen

blanket with one hand, patted her shoulder. "All will be well, lass. You will see." He only wished he believed his own words. "Master Freddie and Miss Carolyn failed in their attempt on 'is life a second time. That must stand for somethin'."

Alyssa nodded and smiled weakly. "I suppose that is true. Now sit and tell me how you saved his lordship." She shifted over and indicated the seat beside her.

"'Twas not really my doing, but Eleanor's," he said, settling beside her on the cold stone bench. "She is a real witch, you know. Not that black magic blah-hoo. No. She's what they call a white witch."

Alyssa nodded. "I know."

He frowned. "You know her?"

"I mean, I have seen her. She comes here quite often, seeking me."

"She has seen you?"

"No." Alyssa shook her head emphatically. "Of course not. You have cautioned me long enough on such foolishness. But I left my book of herbal remedies for her to find several weeks ago."

"Ah. That explains all. Knowledgeable with 'erbs is that woman. Even cured me gout. But that's another story." He pulled his blanket closer and wished that he'd grabbed two. The cold was gnawing through his skin. "She worked a darn miracle, she did. I thought for sure he was a goner. Eleanor was just finishin' in the kitchen when I caught 'er and explained 'is lordship had taken ill. She asked me a few questions. I told 'er what you told me.

"Well, not exactly, but I told her I thought he had been poisoned and that he couldn't move. She nodded real calmly like and told me to fetch Saul while she gathered up 'er 'erbs. She would meet us in 'is room. Luckily, we didn't run into that haughty man of 'is or there would 'ave been some questions. 'Is lordship must have given 'im the night off." Tom stopped as a shiver slithered down his spine. Soaked to the skin, he would be lucky not to be taken with the ague himself this frightful night.

"Go on," urged Alyssa. "What happened then?"

"Well, the rest ain't for delicate ears like your own. Just let me say that woman done things with whisky I ain't never seen done before. Lucky we 'ad some on 'and. And even for a man like meself who's seen a lot of things in 'is life, and 'as a stomach like cast iron, it was almost too much for me to bear. But it worked all right, what she done. Cast that poison right from 'is body. 'E's restin' easy now."

He looked up as the sky opened with a heavier deluge of rain. "Eleanor said 'e would be up and about in a few days." He dragged a large square of cloth from his pocket, blew his nose with gusto, and put it away. "Now I best be goin'," he said, pushing to his feet. "The garden in the dead of the night and pourin' rain is no place for an old body like meself."

Alyssa stood and helped to arrange the blanket over his head and shoulders. "Sorry, Tom. As I do not feel the cold, I forget others do. Yes, go, warm yourself by your hearth. I will see you on the morrow. And thank you…for everything." She bent, kissed his stubbled cheek, and drifted back into the darkness, leaving him standing alone in the garden staring at the place she'd been.

Shaking his head, he stepped onto the path that led down the side of the keep. As he hastened along, he wondered at the words he had spoken earlier. Would this story really have a happy ending as he had predicted? Or would it only be another chapter in an ill-fated tale that had started long ago in the whispers of yesterday?

****

Sunrise dawned with a harsh chill in the air.

Alyssa gave a small gasp as Aidan stepped into the stone garden.

He moved quickly to take her in his arms, knocking her hat haphazardly from her head, causing her hair to tumble down around her shoulders and face. She gave a small chuckle as he drew her close. Their lips touched, then melded—so insistent, stirring her longings, her wild hopes and dreams that had been buried an age ago. She had no idea how he had discovered her true identity. She could only imagine Tom had given in. But now he knew, she could not deny she was relieved to have her secret out in the open. And the finest thing of all was that he still cared.

"Alyssa, my beautiful, my lovely." His words were soft, sweet, and an aphrodisiac against her hungry lips. Then he took her mouth again, pressing deeper, harder, bringing her body up flush against his.

****

Aidan burned with her, for her, but he held himself in check. He had told Tom to have her here. He did not care how, and now he had his answer. She was indeed Alyssa de Morgan.

This was no sweet miss, this woman whose body throbbed against his. She knew exactly what she was doing. However, he had to be certain. He would give her a last chance. He drew back enough to whisper against her lips, "Alyssa, darling, I want—"

She did not refute the name. Instead, she put a finger to his lips and drew his mouth against her own. She did not stop him—proof of her guilt by her own actions. He pushed her to arm's length. "So, you do not deny it."

She frowned and shook her head. "Deny what?"

"That you are Alyssa de Morgan." He thrust his hands into his pockets. He did not trust himself to have them free, lest he throttle her. His legs were still shaky from his three-day sojourn in bed, but the strength of his anger drove him on.

"That Gedrych de Morgan bound you within these stones—a spirit not of this earth—a two-hundred-year-old ghost. A ghost who has tried, not once, but twice, to kill me."

****

Alyssa's eyes widened as she stared at him, aghast. She felt the blood drain from her face. She must look the very specter he accused her of being. However, she raised her chin. First and foremost, she was a Llewellyn, and a Llewellyn did not back away from a fight. "Deny who I am? Most certainly not. I am Alyssa de Morgan, cursed by Gedrych de Morgan to be locked between these stones for eternity. Cursed by my own words to await my love, Cai de Morgan, until his return to this castle." Her gaze locked onto his rigid jaw, then slid to his azure blue eyes. So like Cai's the first time she had looked into them. Now they burned like chips of sapphire without a speck of leniency. What more could she have expected? He was a de Morgan, after all, and the de Morgans had not been known for their kindness.

She knew she had lost him, but still, she fought on. "As for trying to kill you. I will deny that with every fiber of my being, for to do so would be the equivalent of driving a stake through my own heart. I am no dullard to think that you would reside in the same place as I, should you die. If it is a killer you seek, a betrayer, perhaps you should look to your own kind."

He raised his chin a notch and went very still. "What are you suggesting?"

She glanced away, willing Tom to appear. Anyone.

He grasped her elbow and swung her back to face him. "I demand an explanation, madam. A clarification for all the trickery that has been played upon me and mine. You cannot suggest such a thing and leave it hanging."

She pulled free and rubbed at the pain in her arm. "You are a fool, Aidan de Morgan. Can you not see what is beneath your nose? Upon your death, would not your cousin come into a sizeable fortune? Not to mention an earldom."

"Freddie!" Aidan laughed harshly and took a step back. "That is preposterous." His voice held an edge. "He has no need to be rid of me to gain a stipend. All he need do is ask, and my grandmother or I would never see him poor."

"Perhaps he is tired of begging."

Aidan remained silent, then shook his head. "No. I grew up with Freddie. He has his faults, but he is no murderer. You think to shift the blame and take it from yourself."

Her gaze held to his, she straightened willing away the tears that threatened her eyes. She would not cry. She would stay strong. Her whole existence depended on it. Without him, without his love, she was nothing. Her reason for being would be no more. "I love you." She breathed. "Why would I do such a thing?"

"Love." He scoffed. "Love does not trick and deceive and use people to gain its own end. Love does not try to murder the one it professes to love. You do not know the meaning of the word, madam."

As if she had been struck, she stiffened. "I told you—"

"I will listen to no more of your falsehoods. It was never really me you loved. It was a dream, a whisper of a man who died two hundred years ago. I may have his face, but I am not Cai de Morgan. I never will be Cai de Morgan and I never was."

She tilted her chin, her red-gold hair streaming down her back, her green eyes awash with unshed tears. "No. You are not Cai. He loved me, and never would he have judged me so harshly."

He did not respond. A closed expression shuttered his face, and he pushed past her to stride to the edge of the garden. "I and my party will depart from Thornwood as soon as it can be arranged." He stopped. "I will not be returning, *ever*. I do not want to see your face again between this time and that. Understand? Or I will call ten priests to cast you from this castle and not have them stop until you are gone. I swear."

She did not answer. The words lodged in her throat with those to call him back, to beg his forgiveness for her deception, her pardon for loving him and wanting him to love her. Words of a broken dream, they would not pass over the lump forming in her throat.

With her heart splitting in two, she watched the only man she would ever love step from her life for a second time. In the same instance, the darkness began to claim her, and for the first time, she did not fight it.

She waited only for its blessed release.

****

Three days since his quarrel with Alyssa and Aidan had not seen her since. She must have decided to do as he asked. He sat alone in the library with the tome of de Morgan history he had unearthed in the library, adding to it his own experiences at Thornwood, warning any future de Morgans of the beautiful ghost who inhabited the castle. Noting down *his* thoughts, *his* aspirations, and disappointments since arriving five months earlier, and his words of goodbye to his descendants. In the morning, he would leave. It was time he went home, to his real home in Northern England.

Perhaps if he thought it or said it enough times, he would believe it, but he had never really thought of Dunmore as his own. It was his grandmother's home. Indeed, he had never actually felt at home anywhere until he had won Thornwood. However, he knew he would never return. Alyssa was part of Thornwood, and he needed to distance himself from her, although it pained him to do so. He did not need her twisted kind of love, and as for himself—how could he have thought he was in love with a ghost, albeit a beautiful one? Their story could only have ended in one way—tragedy.

He took his fob watch from his pocket. It read a quarter to twelve.

Everyone was abed or should be. Bevan had been dismissed hours ago and he made to push from his seat to replace the history journal when there was a light tap on the door.

He studied his steward with surprised concern as he closed the door quietly behind him and stopped just inside the door.

"You wished to see me, Tom?" He leaned back in

his chair, watching the old man fidget with the woolen cap he had snatched from his head. He had never noted Tom so agitated. "I thought you would be in your bed at this late hour."

"Just wanted to tell you, milord, that all is in readiness for your leavin' in the mornin'. That…well…you will be sorely missed by meself and the staff." He looked down at his hands.

He refrained from answering. How could he tell Tom that leaving Thornwood would be akin to cutting off one of his limbs? That he, the staff at Thornwood, and the harsh beauty of the countryside would be forever embedded in his mind. And then there was Alyssa…but he would not think of her, not now, not ever! It was with that thought he spoke in a tone harsher than intended. "I appreciate that, Tom, but it will not alter my decision."

"That was not my intention, milord." Tom took a step forward, wringing his cap in his hand. "'Tis just that 'er ladyship—"

"My grandmother, you mean?" Aidan raised a brow, and his voice took on a hard note as he cut off the older man's words.

Tom swallowed and looked away. "No, the other one…"

There was silence for a moment, then despite himself, Aidan nodded. "Go on."

"I told 'er you wouldn't want to 'ear it. To let things be, but she's a strong-minded lass, that one. She wanted me to tell you—"

"This is from Alyssa?" He clarified, his lips thinning.

Tom nodded and rushed on, this time his pale-gray eyes meeting his. "That you didn't 'ave to worry about

’er no more. She doesn’t want you to leave. This is your ’ome.”

Aidan’s jaw tensed. “I have already decided—”

“She’s leavin’,” Tom blurted, cutting him off, his gaze dropping to the floor. “There, ’tis said.”

“Leaving?” He frowned, repeating the words. He picked up the history journal from where he had placed it on the side table and walked deliberately to the bookcase. Crouching, he placed the book on the shelf next to the Llewellyn history and stood. “Is that possible?” He turned to face Tom.

“There are ways.”

Aidan stood in silent thought. “What ways?”

Tom shuffled back toward the door. “I should be gettin’ back to the gate ’ouse, ’tis late. Ain’t no time—”

“What sort of ways, Tom?” He cut off the old man’s ranting.

Tom tightened his lips. “I promised ’er I wouldn’t say nothin’.”

He waited.

“Eleanor. There, I’ve said it. Now she’ll ’ave me guts for garters t’ be sure if she don’t turn me into a toad first.”

“Eleanor. A toad.” He closed the gap between them. “I think you better explain.”

“She’s one of them white witches, you know. Her mother was one and ’er grandmother before ’er. ’Tis common knowledge in these parts, but it was dangerous for people to know back then. Still is a tad, I guess. That’s why we don’t speak about it much. But that’s beside the point. Eleanor thinks she ’as a way.”

“A way to what?”

“T’ send Alyssa through to the Otherside, of

course."

Aidan's hand shot out to grasp Tom's shirtfront. "Otherside? How?"

The old man's eyes widened. "But I thought—she thought—"

"You don't want to see me angry. How?"

The old man hesitated, but the look in his eyes made him reconsider. "Midnight tonight, the witchin' hour. 'Tis All 'allows Eve—the night that brings the doors of the spirit world closest to the world of the livin'. Some believe on this night the doors are thrown wide open. She's goin' to send Alyssa on her way. You know…wherever people go when they're d—"

"By Jove, she will not." He shoved Tom aside. "Whatever Alyssa has done. She does not deserve that. This is her home." He dragged his fob watch from his pocket. It read ten to twelve. "Quickly. Where are they?" He was halfway to the door.

"In the stone garden. What are you going to—?"

"Stop this madness, of course. She only did what she did because she loved Cai. Because she could not let him go. I know that now."

"You're wrong. It's *you* she loves. She knows you're not Cai. She told me she appeared in a dream you 'ad. That you both traveled back. That you were both there. That could only have happened if both your souls were entwined. You and her, not Cai and her," the old man said, standing in the middle of the room. "It 'as been *you* since you entered the castle, and she had nothin' to do with the attempts on your life."

Aidan spun to study his face. He had no idea what to believe, what was truth, who was lying, and why. He only knew that Alyssa needed him, and he could not let her go. "Are you coming or not?"

"I'm with you. But she won't be 'appy. She 'as 'er mind set."

"Then she can change it because she's going nowhere without me." He set off at a run down the corridor, leaping down the winding staircase and sprinting through the foyer into the kitchen. All he could think of was Alyssa's pale, unhappy face the last time he had seen her. The desolation in her soulful green eyes when he had refused to believe in her innocence.

What had he done?

He knew now she was blameless. No one as scheming and manipulating as he had believed her to be would sacrifice herself in such a manner. He didn't know who had tried to kill him, but he knew now it was not Alyssa. Perhaps being stranded on the moors *had* been an accident. Perhaps his sickness *had* been a simple case of food poisoning. Perhaps it had all been a misunderstanding. Aidan struggled with the lock on the kitchen door and swung in frustration as Tom came up behind. "It's locked."

"Eleanor must 'ave the keys," the old man rasped.

"Then stand back." He raised his foot and kicked at the door. Twice more and the lock gave with a splintering crack and flew back on its hinges. He stepped through into the night and waited for Tom.

"You go," said Tom, pluming the frigid air with his harsh breath. "I'll only slow you down."

Aidan nodded. "Wish me luck." He thumped Tom on the shoulder and took off at a sprint down the path toward the faint light up ahead.

Tom watched with a smile on his weathered face as he clutched his heaving chest. Perhaps he would have his happy ending after all. But first he had an errand to run.

Chapter Eighteen

A full moon shone high in the sky, the night clear. A myriad of stars peppered the darkness like grains of silver scattered across black velvet. Aidan needed no man-made light to guide him this night. He rounded the corner marked by hedge groves and daisies to find Saul blocking his way into the stone garden. The roses seemed a thing alive, in the darkness more serpent than vegetation. Wreathing and curling across the ground, winding their way up around the tall standing stones, building a barricade between each and blocking all entry into the garden, except for the one entrance where Saul stood with his arms folded across his chest.

"Step aside, Saul. I do not wish to hurt you."

"Can't do that, milord." Saul's voice held a note of steel that Aidan had never heard before.

"You could lose your livelihood for this."

Saul, a big man, almost a head taller than Aidan and wider across the shoulders, raised his chin and remained steadfast. He strove to duck around him, but the groundskeeper was too fast. He frowned and straightened, then cupped his mouth. "Alyssa! Alyssa, I know you are in there. You do not have to do this!"

Only silence met his call.

"You're too late. The ritual 'as already started." Saul spoke without a spark of emotion in his dark eyes or on his rugged face.

He realized Saul was not about to budge, so stepping back, he feigned to leave, then at the last minute rounded and powered a hard right into the big man's jaw. Saul's eyes glazed over, and he dropped to his knees. Aidan stepped around him.

"Sorry, old chap, but you gave me no choice." He left Saul kneeling behind him, shaking his head, as he began his fight through the barrier of sharp prickled roses into the garden.

****

A pentagram had been scratched into the ground and enclosed in a circle. In the center of the pentagram, a fire burned. Around the circle stood twelve women Alyssa had never seen before. Dressed in long robes of white with hoods, they carried brooms fashioned from rushes. Eleanor named the women her coven and introduced them to Alyssa. They were quite in awe of her.

She heard Aidan's voice call from amidst the rose wall.

"Quickly. You must begin the ritual."

"The time is not right." Eleanor's hair shaken from its strict confines streamed down her back like a black silken veil. She wore a tight form-fitting white gown with a split in the front cut almost to her navel. Her face pale in the moonlight, her dark eyes gleaming with a fierce light of excitement. She looked a primitive goddess—a witch from the past. "I dare not proceed. There is no telling what could happen if this is not timed exactly."

"I care not. Do it! Do it now! I order you." Alyssa wrung her hands. "He's coming. I can hear him. I will not have him stopping me."

Eleanor's confidence seemed to dwindle, but only

momentarily. "Then let it be upon your head. And blame me not if things should go awry." She looked at her coven. "Ladies."

The women laid their brooms to the ground, each straw head touching the edge of the circle and spiraling out like rays of the moon. A woman stood between each to face into the circle.

"Alyssa, you stand in the pentagram with me. We then join hands over the fire. Are you in agreement with that?"

"Anything, just hurry." But even as she spoke the words, she bit back her fear. She hated fire, considered it the root of all evil, but she knew she had to comply. Fire had taken her from the world of the living and brought her to this. Now fire would help send her on her way. It was only fitting. She grimaced and took five apprehensive steps to bring her into the center, facing Eleanor.

All in place, the witch woman signaled to her coven to join hands, then began a low, keening chant.

The flames of the fire turned deep orange and leaped higher. A wind swept from the north, knocking the women's hoods from their heads. Eleanor's long, dark hair whipped about her face and shoulders like a beautiful woolen cape, and her black eyes glittered in her pale face.

Mist seeped up from the ground to writhe and swirl all around them, casting an eerie satanic light within the stone garden. Alyssa saw Aidan as he broke through the rose bower, Saul on his heels. Saul grasped his arm and hauled him back before he could reach them and was thankful to the ground's man for his help. Aidan turned angrily to Saul, but his words did not carry.

She spared a few minutes to commit his face to memory; black trousers, white linen shirt, open at the throat, a lock of raven-colored hair hanging loosely across his forehead, and a day's growth covered his normally clean-shaven jaw.

Several dark scratches marked his cheeks where the rose thorns had torn at his skin. He looked tired, worried, and never more dear.

She wanted to cry out and tell Eleanor to stop, but could not find the words. He would be better off without her. He could stay at the castle, marry, and perhaps sire children. Why did her heart weep so at the thought of another woman's child in his arms? But, no, they were not meant to be. She was convinced of that now. Had their love been right, Cai would never have perished at Marston Moor. She would never have died at Gedrych's hand. Things would have worked between her and Aidan.

No, it was better this way. She turned from his beseeching eyes and faced resolutely toward Eleanor as she opened her arms to the night sky.

The coven who had again donned their hoods wove in a complicated dance, two steps clockwise, three steps back, carefully stepping over the brooms, their hands linked securely. The circle tightening as they chanted louder.

Faintly at first, then gradually more distinctly, she felt a change in the flow of energy that swept over, around, through her. Then the relentless tide stilled. The chains of the unknown power that kept her imprisoned within the courtyard for over two hundred years relaxed. She was fading. A tightening in her chest, then a dreadful tearing as if she would be ripped asunder.

She doubled in pain, with a small sharp scream escaping her lips, then jerked upward, her body weightless her arms stretched wide. She could see her hands, but just. She struggled to peer down at her now transparent body. The solid form, which had always been hers within the circle, was no more.

She was like a wraith of old. She had always been whole within the stone circle and invisible without. Never like this. The change terrified her as nothing else had. For the first time, she truly believed she was a ghost, and it spoke to her the sense of her own mortality.

Never again would she see Aidan or Tom or sweep through the ancient halls of Thornwood. She glanced down at her hands again. She could see right through them.

Then her essence, her spirit body, floated upward to hover above the circle. Beneath, her body crumpled, and the women danced their dance and chanted, their words dissolving in a long keening wail, words lost within a chorus that blended and unified the night.

Eleanor bent and pushed her hands into the ground, the dirt around them melting like water. Then she delved into the deepest depths of the earth and drew energy into her very self. She raised her hands and a tremendous stream of white-hot energy cut through the night and poured into Alysa's chest. She screamed as it burned, and the fire below rose high, the flames flickering with an intense red and green, lighting up the whole of the circle. Still, the coven chanted.

Eleanor's voice broke through the monotone of the coven's words.

"Alyssa de Morgan!"

Losing control of her body, Alyssa jerked upward.

Her arms thrown back and wide at the command.

"Alyssa de Morgan. The way is free! Your time has come. Your path is clear, so leave this place! Seek your soul's release! Go in peace, find rest! Your path is free—so smite it now!"

"So, smite it now!" shouted the coven.

Although drawn as she was by the call in the voice, she fought it, as was her habit when the darkness attempted to claim her. Then she relaxed as Eleanor repeated the words. Suddenly, an overwhelming sense of peace and contentment encompassed her. She reached out her arms. Above her, the stars blazed hotter, as if they were tiny bonfires on a dark foreign shore. In the distance up ahead, a great shining light grew, reaching out for her.

The north wind rose to howl around the circle, enclosing the women, tearing at their clothing and hair, miraculously leaving the red and green fire ablaze. She felt nothing. Blessed. Free of form, she floated upward, weightless, as the witch woman repeated her incantation. *"Your path is free—so smite it now!"*

"So, smite it now!" moaned the other women, but their steps faltered. She felt a tremendous surge of energy, and her journey stopped. The light vanished, and the women screamed and stumbled as their feet caught in the grass, their hands tearing free of each other, the circle breaking asunder.

Hurled into a dark void Alyssa could not see her way. The peace encompassing her moments before vanished. Forever or a heartbeat she seemed to tumble, then finally she found solid ground coalescing in her prone body.

Eleanor cried out again, this time in frustration. *"So,*

smite it now!" The woman opened her eyes and stared at Alyssa, her dark eyes burning with inner energy, then she closed them again and her shoulders slumped.

The coven collapsed against each other. Their faces wet with perspiration.

"Alyssa!" Aidan cried her name.

She turned, and he was there.

"Alyssa. My beautiful girl, are you hurt?" He dropped to his knees, his arms tightening around her. He stroked her hair back from her flushed face.

She pushed him to arm's length and struggled to stand. "I…am well." She focused on Eleanor. "Why…what happened?"

The witch woman shook her head. "I do not know," she said, composing herself and coming to stand beside her.

"Why should that be? You were so certain. Perhaps we should try again."

"No," said Aidan emphatically. "I am so sorry. I have been a fool. Please…please forgive me."

She looked at him then. His eyes desolate pools of midnight blue in the firelight. Bloody scratches from the roses marred his cheeks and neck. His shirt torn in several places. She had never loved him more. He must have seen her answer in her eyes, for he took her in his arms, and his lips settled over hers. In a kiss that promised forever and always.

They heard a gentle cough and realized Eleanor still stood beside them.

****

Aidan frowned, regarding Eleanor in the flickering firelight. She was around forty, he knew, but the firelight was kind, erasing all the tiny signs of age around her eyes and mouth. She glared at him, her eyes brilliant in the firelight, her hands on her hips. If there were ever a goddess, he thought, surely she would look a lot like Eleanor Armstrong this night.

"So, what is your theory?" he asked, not that he wanted Alyssa going anywhere. He had her safe at his side. He rose and helped her to her feet, bringing her up beside him. His arm curved firmly around her waist. His question was more perfunctory than anything else.

"It could have been the timing. But I think not. Perhaps it was not meant to be." Eleanor gave Aidan and Alyssa an astute look.

The coven women lay back on the grass, passing flasks among themselves, chatting quietly with each other. Eleanor spared them a few words, then turned to Aidan to give him her answer.

"I cannot be certain." Her expression was thoughtful as she stood her ground, her glance going from one of her sisters to the next.

"I could feel the change in the energy," said one woman, looking across at Eleanor.

"So did I," chimed in another.

"Yes," said Eleanor, "we held the energy back, and I could feel the pathway opening. Her way was almost clear, then suddenly it snapped back." She gazed around the circle. The mist had settled, and the fire now burned low. She swung back to Alyssa and gave her an appraising stare, from the tips of her bare toes to her wild red hair falling in heavy waves down around her cheeks.

"Perhaps it was not your time, or maybe you have unfinished business in this world." Her look softened. "Perhaps the goddess knows something we do not." She leaned forward and held the flat of her hand to Alyssa's stomach.

Alyssa pulled back and free from Aidan's hold. "What are you doing? What are you saying? I am dead. I *have* been dead for over two hundred years. Of course, it is my time. Nothing you can do or say can change that."

To Aidan's horror, he watched Eleanor reach out and pinch Alyssa's cheek. "You do not feel dead to me." Eleanor laughed softly and turned away, and the other women echoed her as they came to their feet.

"Wait," said Alyssa, grasping her arm.

Eleanor rounded and spoke kindly. "There is nothing else I can do, my lady. The time has passed. We can try again All Hallows Eve next year."

"Next year. No, that cannot be. And what did you mean about not my time?"

Eleanor shook her head. "I meant, maybe you have issues left you need to address." She looked pointedly at Aidan. "And maybe you have to do them in this body…" She caressed Alyssa's cheek, then turned to join Saul at the edge of the circle and with a strong arm around her waist they disappeared within the archway of roses as they mysteriously parted. The rest of the coven trailed silently behind.

Aidan turned Alyssa into his arms and buried his face in her hair. "I thought I had lost you."

"I thought you did not care. That you hated me."

"I did, and then I didn't. Then nothing seemed to matter but having you in my arms and never letting you go. Never try to leave me again. I promise we will work something out, even if I have to build a house in this darn garden." He smiled and touched his lips gently to the tip of her nose, then her small, bowlike mouth. She opened it willingly.

"Now, isn't this just so cozy?"

Alyssa broke from Aidan's embrace to see Freddie burst into the garden, his face flushed and scratched. There were leaves and twigs in his hair. Carolyn stepped through after him and came up alongside him, brushing down her skirt and patting her hair. She appeared just as disheveled.

"We heard noises, and—" She stopped speaking as she saw Alyssa beside Aidan. "Oh." She took a step back.

Freddie drew a pistol from beneath his coat and leveled it at Aidan's chest.

"What are you doing? You said we were going to talk." Carolyn laid her hand on his arm.

"What I should have done a long time ago." He pulled away. "I am going to finish this. Can't you understand your plan will never work? He has *her* now. This little hussy has ruined everything. With them both dead—"

"Shut up, you idiot!" Carolyn dragged at his arm. "Put that gun down before you hurt yourself." She smiled at Aidan. "Darling—"

Freddie rounded, and a hard slap rang into the night. Carolyn staggered, her hand going to her cheek as her eyes filled with tears.

Aidan pushed Alyssa behind him. "Now look here—whatever this is. Whatever you think I have done. I am certain we can sort something out." He took a small step toward Freddie.

"*Enough.* Stay where you are, Aidan. Do not make this harder than it is. And I told you before"—Freddie glared at Carolyn— "that I will not have my future wife calling me names."

"Future wife?" Aidan slid an uneasy glance from Freddie to Carolyn. "What is going on here?"

He paused as the pointed gun finally registered. "Or…perhaps I already know."

"He made me do it. He threatened to tell everyone that I killed Conrad."

"Shut up, you crazy bitch! You know that is a lie. You gave Aidan the poison. I'm not totally at fault."

"You forced me." She glowered at Freddie as he straightened his aim at Aidan.

"You do not have the guts to pull the trigger. You know it, and I know it." Aidan edged closer, but kept twelve feet between them. "You would not join His Majesty's Service because you never had the courage to fight."

"Indeed. Or was it because I thought there were enough willing fools ready to die for the cause?" Freddie waved the gun pointedly at Aidan. "Such as your late wife. You were so happy when you told me of your marriage, I wanted to be sick."

His next words were tight, forced from his throat. "What do you know about Anni?"

"Who do you think informed on her?" He smiled and Aidan wanted to tear out his throat. "Did you believe I wanted her giving birth to some squalling brat and cutting me out of my inheritance once I had rid the world of you?"

"Why you murdering—" Aidan leaped across the clearing as Freddie's finger tightened on the trigger.

"*NO!*" Carolyn launched herself at Aidan and clutched at his shoulders as Freddie's bullet struck her in the back. He heard her grunt, saw her stiffen, and caught her in his arms before she fell.

"Now look what you made me do," Freddie growled, throwing the pistol to the ground. He stared down at it as if it were a snake gone mad and ran a tight fist through his hair. "It was supposed to be *you*. She was never supposed to get hurt."

Aidan dismissed his cousin's ramblings as he cradled Carolyn in his arms and lowered her to the grass. Her face drained of color, her pulse rate fading. However, he felt no regret. She had been the driving force behind her own demise. If it had not been Freddie, no doubt it would have been some other man who'd done her in. But he'd never suspected she would try to murder *him*.

It all made sense now. She and Freddie had tried to kill him on the moors, and when that failed, Carolyn tried to poison him. That was why she had been so insistent he eat that night. She even spoon-fed him, and he had fallen for her feigned concern. What an ego he must have to believe the woman was in love with him and allow it to almost lead to his own demise. He shot a look at Alyssa. She spoke the truth. It had been Freddie.

Carolyn gave a small cough, and her eyes fluttered open. "I…I could not let him hurt you. The poison…he made me do it." She grasped for his hand, and he turned her small one in his own. Blood dribbled in a dark stain from the corner of her lips as she forced a smile. "I…still love you…" Her head sagged to the side, and her forget-me-not eyes stared blankly as her spirit slipped into the afterlife.

Aidan closed her eyelids and laid her on the ground. He came to his feet, his fist clenching at his side as he studied his cousin. Did Carolyn's words ring true? Had she really loved him? If so, why had she tried to poison him? She must have been terrified of Freddie, and he had never known Carolyn to be afraid of anything.

Tonight, Freddie flaunted a side Aidan had not known existed. He could barely breathe for the shock and rage consuming him. Freddie, whom he had treated like a brother all his life, sought to murder him. And now Carolyn was dead. He held his anger in check. Not wanting to goad Freddie to further damage. He needed to time his actions right.

"She's dead, isn't she?" Freddie took a step back, a bubble of laughter escaping his throat. "Fool woman, as my wife, she could have had every luxury." His smile twisted as he flipped open his evening jacket. "Now you can join her. It was always you she wanted anyway." A pearl-handled pistol resided snugly in his waistband against his stomach. He drew it quickly and aimed it at Aidan's heart. "Luck has it I brought a spare. Plenty of balls and powder to go 'round. And in case I miss…" He flipped open the other side of his coat and revealed another pistol.

"You are ill, Freddie. Put the firearms away. Tomorrow we will journey back to London. Doctor Mountbatten—"

Freddie waved the pistol at Aidan. "Yes, I'm sick, but nothing a doctor can cure. Sick of waiting for you to die. I thought the moors would finish you…then the poison…but no. A matter of days. That was all. If I had been born first, I could have had it all! But no, it was you. You who does not care a fig for Dunmore!" Freddie fired, and Aidan dove, taking Alyssa with him to the ground. The ball ricocheted off the standing stone behind them and disappeared into the surrounding foliage.

Freddie made to pull the other gun, and Aidan leaped at him. The two men grappled, and the first pistol slipped from Freddie's hand.

"Get the gun, Alyssa!"

Freddie swung at Aidan and connected with his cheek as Alyssa crawled across the ground. There was a sickening crack of bone hitting bone, and a cut opened up on his cheek. Alyssa scrambled for the pistol, searching among the moonlit grass. Freddie grabbed her by the waist and hurled her with a madman's strength to the opposite side of the stones. She landed heavily and cried out as she saw Freddie wrap his arms around Aidan and ram his head into the stone bench.

****

Alyssa's head ached where she'd hit the stone, and her world tilted and spun as she staggered forward. Out of the corner of her eye, she watched Freddie pick up the pistol and hastily load it as Aidan struggled to his feet. She would not lose Aidan again, not when they had just found each other. She leaped at Freddie with renewed fury, clinging to his back, hammering her fists into his head and shoulders as he tried to dislodge her. "Run, Aidan! Get Saul. Anyone!"

He stopped to look at her, his eyes still glazed from the heavy blow to his head. He staggered, indecision marring his face.

"Go! I cannot die, remember!"

He cast her one more frantic look, then pushed his way through the roses.

Freddie flung back his elbow. A blinding pain caused her to cry out as she slid from his back to her hands and knees. His pistol had discharged and found its mark in her shoulder.

He glanced down at her as she looked up, his face full of uncertainty. Then purposely, he bent and picked up the second pistol from where it glinted in the moonlight and sprinted from the garden, calling Aidan's name.

She heard a shot, heard Aidan swear, and raced after Freddie, oblivious to the pain in her arm. She saw Aidan lying on the path up ahead, a hand clutching his hip, and Freddie looming over him with a log in his hand.

Then Saul was there. Like a fallen angel, he tackled Freddie, bringing him to the ground, punching him over and over. But with hell-bent determination, Freddie scrabbled for the log, finding purchase. He swung and struck Saul hard to the temple. The big man grunted and fell. Freddie pushed Saul to the side and came to his feet, advancing on Aidan lying helpless only feet away.

He raised the log. "At last," he ground out, even as she raced toward them, shouting Aidan's name.

A shot split the air, and Freddie's eyes widened as he dropped to his knees and toppled face forward onto Aidan's chest.

Aidan groaned as she reached his side. She dragged Freddie away and slipped her arm beneath his head to cradle it on her lap. He opened his eyes and gave her a weak smile. Then his gaze fell to the sticky red stain spreading across her shoulder and the front of her gown. "Alyssa," he managed to say. "You're bleeding."

"Ssh. 'Tis no matter." She held him close. "I can barely feel it. Your wound is worse." She released him momentarily, tore a strip of cloth from her shift, balled it, and pressed it to his hip. However, as she did so, she stilled, too afraid to move. She barely dared to breathe. She had escaped the prison of the stones that had held her for two centuries and, she was indeed, alive!

****

Aidan gritted his teeth as Alyssa tendered to his hip. Hazy, barely able to focus right, his hand went to his brow, and a new fire raced through his skull. He knew there was something he should know, something he should remember, but his memory failed him. He looked at his cousin. "What happened? Who shot Freddie?"

"That would be me." Landan Denero, hair immaculate, dressed only in an open-necked white shirt, black trousers, and bracers, stepped out of the bushes onto the path. He hastily tucked his pistol into the waistband of his pants. "You can thank your man Jeffreys. He has been hiding me up at the gatehouse since the night of the ball. He watched Fitzwilliam and his lady friend leave the house and informed me. I followed them to the garden." Denero bent to examine Freddie's body. "The bullet entered his heart, killing him instantly."

"You killed my cousin?" He frowned. "But I thought…"

"I know what you thought." Denero ran a hand over Freddie's eyelids, closing his eyes for a last time. Then stood. He drew a handkerchief from his pocket and wiped his hands. "You thought I was spying on you, perhaps even trying to kill you." He smiled and Aidan could have sworn his teeth glinted in the moonlight. "You thought I was the double agent."

He grimaced. "Well, the thought did cross my mind. You always appeared in places you had no right to be."

"Yes, well, I suppose it might have seemed that way. But I have had an eye on your cousin since that debacle in Ireland."

"You mean Freddie was in Ireland? That it was

he…"

"We are still not certain, but we had our suspicions. The agency sent me to watch him. We suspected for some time your cousin was an informant for the enemy. However, it could not be proven."

He shifted, tried to sit up, then grunted as a burning pain stabbed into his skull and traveled to his hip. "I should have been told," he ground out, his teeth clenched.

"Sorry, old man, but the agency felt you were too close. That you could not view the matter objectively, being family and all."

He shook his head and winced as the wound to his temple throbbed. "Freddie, an enemy agent? It is inconceivable."

"Even now, after he tried to kill you, and what he did to your late wife?"

Aidan's voice deepened. "You knew about that?"

"No. I heard him in the garden."

"You heard everything, yet you did nothing to intervene?"

"I could not get a clear shot without endangering you or…Miss Jeffreys, is it not?" He gifted Alyssa a studied look, making her wonder what else he had seen or heard.

"I think that is enough now," she said, signaling Saul, who had gained his feet and was now speaking quietly several feet away with Eleanor and Tom.

"We need to get his lordship up to the house and his wounds tended." She squeezed Aidan's hand and smiled up at the Count. "You can talk later. I am certain there is a lot more you wish to discuss."

"You are right, Miss Jeffreys. I bow to your better

judgment." He bent his head in respect and stepped aside as Saul approached. "I will look in on the Earl in the morning before riding for the authorities."

She nodded and watched him speak to Tom before moving off into the darkness in the direction of the guardhouse. What a strange man, she thought, so cool and mysterious. Woe to any woman who teamed up with that one. She would never know what he was thinking.

She came to her feet as Saul bent to lift Aidan gently into his powerful arms and start down the path.

Aidan had no time to protest, but just as well because as he closed his eyes, nausea from the pain in his hip threatened to overwhelm him, and blackness descended on him like a dark whirlpool. The last thing he heard was Alyssa's voice speaking his name from somewhere beside him. He knew there was something he should remember. Something that was not quite right, but he could not think of it now. Not now…

****

"I told you, you did not feel dead," Eleanor said with a gentle smile, patting Alyssa on her good shoulder and hurrying into Aidan's room after Saul and Tom. "Hot water, Tom, and plenty of it," she said, sending the old man on his way. "Saul, plug that wound in his lordship's hip more securely. He will be out for a while, and I don't want him bleeding all over the linen. I have to tend Lady Alyssa's shoulder first."

Her husband approached, and she turned to face him and gripped his jaw. "You might need a stitch in your temple, my sweet, and your lip doesn't look too grand either. Appears Mr. Fitzwilliam got one in, after all."

The big man grimaced and pulled back from his wife. "Mr. Fitzwilliam didn't touch me other than to clout me with that log. The lip's from where his lordship slugged me when he was trying to get to his lady. Lucky punch 'twas all."

She raised an arched brow.

Alyssa felt herself redden as Saul cast her a rare grin and left to do Eleanor's bidding. She sank into a high-backed chair beside Aidan's bed. "So, how do you explain this?" she asked, meeting Eleanor's eyes. "My being here, that is?"

"I told you there was something more you had to do in this body." Eleanor pulled a vial of laudanum and a small sharp knife from the satchel she wore at her waist and laid them on the table beside her. "Only be thankful that the Goddess saw fit to grant you another chance."

She breathed a heartfelt sigh. "For every day of my new life."

"Speaking about life. I think I should tell you; you are with child."

Alyssa's hand went to her abdomen. "A child." She breathed the word in reverence. "A child." Tears came to her eyes. "Mine and Aidan's?"

Eleanor raised her brows. "Unless there is someone else."

"No. Of course not, but it is such a miracle. How? Are you certain?"

"As to how…" Eleanor gave a small smile. "Most likely in the normal way. As to if I am certain…I wasn't at first. When the ceremony was taking place, just before it failed, I heard the strong rhythm of a heartbeat. It seemed to be in my head, but not."

"Why did you not tell me?"

"I wasn't certain it hadn't been my imagination, but now that this has happened and you have left the circle,

I have no doubts. It can be the only reason you are now bound to this earth. You have a life growing within you. A small miracle."

There was a light tap, and Tom entered with the hot water.

"We will speak more of this later," said Eleanor.

Tom grinned at Alyssa, seeming too shy to speak.

"'Tis all right, Tom, I am not going to bite now I have regained my life. I am still the same Alyssa you always knew. But is this not wondrous?"

The old man set the water on the table, and she stood and hugged him close with her good arm. "I am alive again! I have to keep pinching myself. I can barely believe it."

He countered gruffly. "I can believe it. Something magical happened the day his Lordship set foot in Thornwood. It could never have ended any other way. If only it could 'ave 'appened when I was young." He dipped his head. "I'll get more wood for the fire," he said hastening from the room.

Eleanor laughed softly as she picked up a clean cloth, soaked it in the water, and cleaned gently around Alyssa's wound. "Tom will soon get used to having you around. I already am. Now brace yourself, my lady, and let me have a good look at that shoulder. There is a ball in there, and it has to come out."

She acknowledged the blinding pain coming from her arm. The excitement up to now had dulled it she guessed. Two centuries since she had last felt pain, and although now with Eleanor probing at her arm, the pain turned excruciating, nothing would ever compare to the bite of the fire from Gedrych's pyre!

She closed her eyes and bit down on the cloth Eleanor passed her.

Chapter Nineteen

When Aidan awoke next morning, he found himself in his bed. A dull sun shone through the mullioned shutters, and Eleanor was bending over him checking a bandage around his head. She had reverted to her plain prim self. Her dark hair pinned back, her cook's uniform clean and neat as a pin.

As he shifted, she straightened and moved silently to join Tom, standing at the window.

Aidan made to sit up, but a fiery burning attacked his left hip and sent him a painful reminder of the night before and the events leading up to it. Everything came flowing back.

Then he saw her.

She sat beside his bed, wearing a pale pink gown, which he was certain would look garish on any other woman of her coloring, but brought out the rosiness of her cheeks. She was more beautiful than he remembered. And she was here. Really here, sitting next to him. And she was his.

He reached out and touched her arm, remembering as she half-turned that she too had suffered a wound.

Alyssa, who had been speaking quietly to Tom and Eleanor across the room started, and looked around as she felt his touch. She smiled, and it was the most wonderful thing he had ever seen. Like a brilliant sunrise lighting the morning. "You—you are here? In the flesh, in this room." He shook his head. "Really here," he repeated softly, stroking her cheek. "Does your arm hurt overmuch?"

She smiled gently and placed her hand on his. She was about to speak, but there was a crash as the door burst open.

"My God, it is true," blurted Lady Elizabeth, stopping in the doorway, her chest heaving, her inquisitive gaze alighting on Aidan, traveling to his bare chest, then moving on to Alyssa. She held a handkerchief to her nose and turned to Dora. "Quickly, woman, find my smelling salts." The long-suffering Dora turned in a flurry of petticoats and fled down the corridor.

Alyssa came to her feet. "My ladyship—"

"Grandmother," Aidan boomed. "I demand that you settle yourself. Alyssa has every right to be here, and Eleanor and Tom are chaperones enough."

Lady Elizabeth waved his words away. "Do not be ridiculous, boy. I care not a fig about the girl or the propriety of the situation, though I imagine it will not be long before you set things to right on that score." She took a small bag of smelling salts from her reticule and brought them briefly to her nose.

"I thought you had forgotten those." He arched a brow.

She arched a matching one. "You did not want Dora, sweet though she is, hanging on your every word, did you?"

He smiled. His grandmother could still surprise him.

"No, I did not think so." All levity dropped from her voice, and she raised her handkerchief to dab one eye. "It is Carolyn. I would never have believed it of her, coming from such a good family. To think she tried to poison you. Though I did have my suspicions when you were ill." She straightened when she noted Aidan's frown. "Well, it could not have been food poisoning as we all ate the same meal. It could not have been Bevan. He would never dream of tampering with your food. He's just too well-trained.

"No, Dora and I had our misgivings, especially after Bevan told Dora that young Carolyn had insisted on bringing you your supper herself that night. However, of course, there was no proof. And as for Freddie, how could my only other grandson turn out to be such a frightful scoundrel? A murderer at that." She dabbed at her eye. "How shall I ever live down the scandal?"

"With dignity, I am sure, grandmother. I assume you have seen Count Denero?"

"Of course. Delightful man. A true gentleman and so understanding. He said he would do what he could to keep the situation quiet. And how else would I know about Freddie's death and Carolyn's betrayal?" She sniffed. "Dora woke me early this morning to inform me that the count was waiting in the parlor."

"How much did he tell you?"

"I dare say as much as he wished me to know."

"And the count, is he still here?"

"Goodness gracious, Aidan. I am not a common servant to be acquainted with everyone's comings and goings. Whether the man is here or no, I care not. All I know for certain is that Freddie and Carolyn are deceased, you are injured, and a strange young woman is sitting at your bedside as if she belongs. Surely, *I* should be the one asking the questions?"

Aidan smiled reassuringly at Alyssa but remained silent. When he did not comment, Lady Elizabeth heaved a sigh. "Very well. Bevan informed me on the way up that Count Denero has ridden to St. Agnes to speak with the constable. He should return late this afternoon. I sent Saul after him to fetch back a proper physician and a priest for the burial." She looked away. For the first time, Aidan sensed she was uncomfortable, unsure of her ground. "Carolyn will be taken to her parents' estate in Hampton, but I was hoping you would allow Freddie to be buried in the de Morgan burial plot here at the castle, as we are his only living relatives."

Aidan maintained his silence. Freddie buried here, after all he had done, and all he had tried to do. His first thought was to have his conniving cousin cast into the sea, but he could tell, for all his grandmother's bravado, she was grieving. If it would set her mind at ease, he was sure he could find some small corner of Thornwood in which to drop Freddie's traitorous body. He nodded. "It will be done. Now about that physician. You needn't have bothered. I will have no butcher sucking me dry with leeches. I have lost enough blood. Eleanor's doctoring is good enough for me."

Lady Elizabeth raised her quizzing glass and observed her grandson's face. "Yes, well, you do look well for your ordeal, except for that bandage decorating your skull. The woman must know something of healing." She pinned Eleanor with her gaze. "And about a lot of other things, from what I have heard. We must speak sometime, madam. I have a terrible cough no doddering physician seems able to treat."

Eleanor gave a small curtsy. "I would be pleased to be of assistance, Your Ladyship."

"Yes, well, you would be, would you not?" Lady Elizabeth nodded and came to her feet as a tap sounded on the door. Dora popped her head around the edge. "A minute, Dora." She waved the other woman away. "Wait for me in the hall." She paused and waited as Dora disappeared.

"And as for you, young lady," she said, rounding on Alyssa, who had been standing at Aidan's bedside all the while, holding his hand. "I think there is a lot more to *your* story than meets the eye." Her gaze slid over Alyssa's shoulder to the large gold-framed painting hanging above the bed. "A lot more indeed, and I look forward to the telling."

She turned back to Aidan. "I suspect you might be well enough to eat dinner downstairs if Saul carries you. Then perhaps you could formally introduce me to your friend, who I will also expect to attend." She gave Aidan a pointed look, then turned back to Alyssa.

Alyssa gave a small bob. "I will look forward to it, my lady."

"Good." With a twinkle in her violet eyes, Lady Elizabeth pivoted sprightly on her heel and exited the room.

Tom excused himself and hastened after her. "Got to see about the milkin'," he said as he reached the door. "Some things must stay the same."

Aidan watched them go, giving Alyssa's hand a gentle squeeze as she settled at his side. "Do you think my grandmother knows?"

"I think she will have many questions. You better look behind you."

Aidan twisted the best he could without causing himself more injury and glanced up. The wedding portrait from William and Jane's hidden abode—the portrait of Alyssa and Cai—hung behind him. "How did that—?"

Alyssa rested her hand over his. "Tom brought it up early this morning. He hoped you would not be mad."

"How could I? When I have known Cai, been in his body, and loved you in that lifetime as well as this one? I understand now the pain he must have suffered knowing you were going to be parted. I went through it myself as I watched Eleanor perform the ritual that could very well have taken you from me." He looked to the witch woman across the room. "How do you think this miracle came about?"

Eleanor turned from her vigil at the window and shrugged. "The Druid Stones, perhaps. Who can say what energy those ancient monoliths harbor? The ritual itself or the fact that we did not perform the ceremony exactly at midnight. Perhaps a combination of all. Or maybe it was plain and simply love. What is that old proverb? *Love conquers all.*" She smiled knowingly at Alyssa and turned to look out the window, then swung around, meaning to say more but realized that the two young lovers were not really listening. They were gazing into each other's eyes, speaking soft words, thinking about the days and years to come. Not so unlike the young couple in the portrait above their head—a portrait that once held whispers of yesterday and now promised of tomorrow.

She crept silently from the room.

Chapter Twenty

Present Day

Jeannie Jeffreys stretched her legs and arms out in front of her. "So there ends the story of Alyssa and Aidan de Morgan."

Cole sat silently. What could he say? He had hung on her every word. The old lady had a way of telling a story that made each detail come to life. "You really should write that down," he said. "It would be a shame if it were lost. Maybe you could have it published as a novel." He laughed softly. "It certainly sounds like a work of fiction."

Jeannie frowned. "You don't believe me, after everything I—"

Cole held up his hand. "I didn't say that. Of course, I believe you. I have seen her. However, one question? If she became a living being again, how did I see her in the rain tonight? How is it she still looks so young? Didn't she and Aidan marry? Did she die again almost immediately?"

It was Jeannie's turn to hold up a hand. "One thing at a time, lad. I am an old woman, you know." She leaned forward to pour a cup of cold tea, took a sip, and sat back in her chair. "Yes, she married Aidan, and they shared their lives between Dunmore and Thornwood castles. I learned they lived happily to a ripe old age. Alyssa passed away first, and after her death, Aidan lost all will to live. He slipped away quietly in his sleep three weeks later. As to how Alyssa is still here, I cannot explain. My grandfather had a theory that it was the stones that held her. That the ritual Eleanor performed was only temporary. When Alyssa died, the curse again came into being." She shook her head. "A sad business indeed."

Cole rose and knelt to kindle the ashes in the hearth, adding more wood. "Then there is the matter of the will. Why do you think he worded it the way he did? Do you think he saw her again after she died?"

"He must have. It was told he called for his man of business and changed the will the day before he passed away."

"And as for her being at the gate. You said in your story, she could only appear in the courtyard and was invisible in the castle except in a looking glass. How was it she was at the gate when I arrived?"

Jeannie shook her head. "It was All Hallows Eve. That is all the explanation I can give." She stopped and frowned, as if deep in thought. "She told me she would appear again when *he* returned." Jeannie seemed to age before his eyes. "And now it looks like I have missed her again, and it is too late." She stared down at the cold tea in her cup.

"Too late," he said frowning. "What aren't you telling me?"

She shook her head as if coming from a trance. "Nothing." She smiled. "Just an old woman's ramblings." She glanced at her watch and came to her feet. "It's three in the morning and time we sought our beds. I don't know about you, but I need as much beauty sleep as I can get."

He opened his mouth, but Jeannie held up her hand. "No false compliments, please. I know how many wrinkles line this old face."

Cole yawned and stretched his arms. He had to admit he was tired, but he had to know one more thing. "The baby, was it born? Was Eleanor, right?"

Jeannie had moved toward the door, but she stopped. At first, he thought she wouldn't answer. Then as she reached for the handle, she spoke. "Yes. The baby was a girl. Catherine. There is a portrait in the picture gallery. I will show you in the morning. She married a young earl from London and later sailed to the Americas not long after. She corresponded with her parents for a while, then they received word she had died of tuberculosis. Broke their hearts."

"What of a son? Did Aidan have an heir?"

"Unfortunately, no. There were no more children. I have no idea if Catherine had any children. Her husband cut contact after her death. And I have told you what Aidan stated in his will about Thornwood. Now, to your room." With that, she opened the door and walked through. He had little choice but to follow.

She led him up the grand staircase and along a dimly lit hall, stopping outside an oak door on the left. "This was Aidan and Alyssa's room," she said, taking a key and fitting it to the keyhole.

The room was large. However, the first thing he noticed was the portrait above the bed. It was the wedding portrait, and this was the bed Cai and Aidan had both shared with Alyssa. He took a step backward, almost colliding with Jeannie. "I don't think I can sleep here."

"But you must," she stated matter-of-factly. "It is a

stipulation of the will."

He laughed shortly. "There seem to be an awful lot of stipulations I didn't know about."

She gave a small laugh of her own. "There is, isn't there. But I am certain all is for a reason."

He regarded her through narrowed eyes. "Very well, but in the morning, I think I'd like to see this mysterious will."

"As you wish. In the morning." She stood watching him, and he had little option but to step back into the room.

She closed the door, and he heard her soft footsteps move away. What an unusual old woman, and cunning. She had gotten him here, and here he was, in the room of a ghost. Not at all what he expected. Then again, he had never frequented a haunted house. Indeed, he had never believed in the paranormal until his arrival at Thornwood. He scanned the room.

Two Oriental rugs added shades of red and blue to the color scheme, while the whitewashed walls above the wainscoting were decorated with a delicate artwork of realistic green vines and pale pink blossoms. A small table and chair stood against the far wall, probably the same table at which Aidan had sat when Carolyn had attempted to poison him. The oval mirror in which Alyssa had first appeared to his ancestor stood a little way to the right. And a chunky dark dresser and Louis XV desk added a touch of old-world charm.

Funny, he had not noticed on entering that there was a fire in the black marble fireplace which afforded the room a certain coziness. He crossed to the fire and placed several more logs on the already roaring blaze, then strolled to the window and pushed open the shutters. The wind blew in a deluge of rain, which had him quickly closing the window again. He would have to see the standing stones in the morning. He faced into the room. It was still hard to believe that this was the same room Jeannie had spoken about in her story. So filled with history, pain, and love.

He strode to the end of the bed to look up at the portrait. His likeness to the man in the painting was uncanny. The hair was longer, of course. Cai's hair hung almost to his waist, and the clothes were those typical of a sixteenth-century gentleman. He wore a doublet of embossed cream satin and held a plumed hat of like color. And beside him stood Alyssa. She almost took his breath away. No wonder Cai fought so hard with his father to stop being separated from her. No wonder Gedrych coveted her, and Aidan wanted her. He had never seen a more beautiful woman. Oh, there was beauty, and there was *beauty*, but this was an old-world, ethereal loveliness that seeped into his bones with every look and robbed him of his breath. Not the cold, hard, diamond beauty of women such as Janna. He had once thought his ex-fiancée beautiful, but he had not known the true meaning of the word. Hers had been a selfish beauty used to gain her own end.

Had Alyssa really been his in another lifetime? He groaned in frustration and the unfairness of it all and flopped back on the bed. Pulling off his boots, wool shirt, and jeans, he drew the comforter to his chin and for a small moment thought he smelled roses. He smiled. If she was in his room, he knew instinctively she wouldn't hurt him. She had brought him here for a reason, and he doubted it was to harm him. He sniffed again, exhaled a satisfied breath, and closed his eyes, drifting into a deep soundless sleep.

He was floating. Three men in armor sat on large warhorses below him. Before them, overlooking the ocean, was a squat castle of blue-gray stone. Part of the wall had collapsed where it had been hit by a giant catapult. A battering ram lay discarded beside the gate. Bodies littered the ground. Women were weaving in and out of the battlefield, tending to the wounded and rifling through the dead. Most likely stealing anything of value.

The castle portcullis was raised. Two men and two women rode through the gates. The elder of the men bore a white flag.

Cole remained as he was, watching, those below oblivious to his presence. One of the men turned. His features were strong, his eyes deep brown, his hair long and blond, and he had a moustache of the same color. The second man swung to speak to him. Cole put the man's age at around forty-five. His ebony hair, sprinkled with silver, hung past his shoulders. He had a black, pointed beard and cruel, dark eyes. His ebony tunic bore the crest of a golden lion and a red rose. Cole dated the armor as that of the mid-sixteenth century.

A second man turned and spoke to the first, but his words failed to register, as Cole's gaze was riveted on his face—around twenty-five, dark hair that waved and curled over his shoulders, and deep blue eyes—his own.

He plunged out of control into the body of the man. But he did not hit him. Somehow, their two bodies merged. He was the man. And his name was Cai de Morgan.

"Well," he heard the second man say. A man he knew now by the name of Gedrych de Morgan, his father. "Shall we accept Llewellyn's terms?"

The two men and women had stopped roughly eight feet away and sat on their horses, facing them. The younger of the two men had a face with the stamp of a hawk, strong, ruthless. Hate burned in his amber eyes. The older man appeared tired—beaten.

"A heretic," de Morgan said with a cruel twist of his lips. "But Llewellyn's promised five thousand in gold and sworn his men to me for battle should the need arise. What do you say, boy?" He slapped Cai on the back. "Speak up." The man's words were rough and loud. "Has your tongue frozen on seeing the wench? Has she bewitched you already?" Gedrych and the blond man gave a bark of laughter.

Cai could not take his gaze from the woman.

She stared back at him defiantly.

He urged his mount closer, but the young man from the castle rode to block his path. Cai's hand flashed to his sword and his jaw hardened.

"Let him go, Cullum," the older Llewellyn ordered, riding up alongside his son.

Cullum reined his horse around and moved back several feet, but the look he rested on Cai was deadly.

He ignored him, pulled in alongside the woman, and ran his gaze insolently down her length. Fine tendrils had escaped to lie softly against her pale cheeks. But it was her eyes—they burned with an emerald brilliance unlike any he had ever known. They spoke of strong passion. Her full lips pulled tight with displeasure and looked in need of plundering, something he would take his time in doing. Her breasts were high and firm, her waist thin, and her hips well-rounded. He memorized every curve, and with every newfound asset, his body responded more.

"Let the deed be done," he said, but as he was about to turn, he looked into her eyes again and saw something else. A softness, a yearning, a vague familiarity.

Then he saw more.

He saw Alyssa and himself on their wedding day. He saw them dance. He felt their love and embraced her smile. He saw them make love, and Gedrych ordering him to war. Then him being struck by a broadsword in the back and falling face-first into the mud as he stepped in to defend his prince. He saw Gedrych striking Alyssa and her losing their baby. Gedrych condemning Alyssa to death. He saw her curse Gedrych. Aidan de Morgan watching on as Eleanor performed her ceremony. Then an aged Aidan de Morgan lying abed as Alyssa watched on from the confines of a large looking glass.

"Help me," she mouthed.

And in that instant, he knew, and everything came crashing to the fore. He was not Cai de Morgan. He was Cole de Morgan, forensic scientist. He had seen what Aidan must have missed when he'd had the same vision, and he knew what had to be done. What Aidan de Morgan had not been able to do because he had not had the knowledge of the tragic events ahead. He drew his dagger, swung his horse, charged across the space separating him from Gedrych, and drove his dagger into the older man's heart.

Gedrych's face mirrored shock and pained surprise. "Why?" he whispered as his hand closed around the hand still grasping the dagger in his chest. He looked into the eyes of the man he thought his son.

"I could not let you destroy so many innocent lives."

Gedrych's eyes widened. "You are not my son."

"You are right." He pulled back, and Gedrych

toppled from his horse. For a moment only, a sense of remorse washed over him; then it was gone as he swung and looked into the shining eyes of Alyssa de Morgan and saw gratitude.

Still, he had a part to play.

He snatched the reins from her hand. "I will send my man to collect the bride price come morning," he said to Herbert Llewellyn, who sat with a puzzled expression without moving a muscle.

"I shall have her wed properly," the old man growled.

"She will be wed properly," he answered. "And happier than you would ever think," he mouthed softly for his own ears. He dragged his mare around and pointed her north with the woman in tow. "Bring my father's body, William."

Cole sprang up in bed. He was sweating. He glanced down at his hands. They shook. But moreover, one hand still wore the blood-covered black leather glove belonging to Cai de Morgan. He tore it from his hand, clambered from the bed, and flung it into the fire as he strode to the window. Pushing open the shutters, a cleansing cool breeze washed over him. It was near morning and pastels of sunrise painted the small courtyard with their pale hues.

Closing his eyes, he breathed deeply, attempting to cleanse the thoughts of last night from his mind. He had done what needed to be done and felt no guilt. Not after what he knew of Gedrych de Morgan.

He opened his eyes and shifted his gaze, and an iciness like no other crept down his back.

The standing stones were gone.

Gone!

He shook his head and spun. The faintest shades of dawn and a low-burning fire lit the room.

Clothed only in his boxer shorts, a frigid breeze blew through the window, but he was sweating.

It had been a dream…then it hadn't.

He ran a hand through his damp, disheveled hair, trying to reconcile himself with the belief he had been in Cai's body, looking out. Transported there by only the gods knew how. He had seen what the other man had seen, mirrored his actions, knew his thoughts.

A spectator in another time. Though fantastic as it seemed, he'd accomplished what he now believed had been his destiny. Stop Gedrych de Morgan from murdering Alyssa Llewellyn.

He didn't know what history he'd changed with the acts of last night. Mayhap there would be a lot more de Morgans and de Braceys roaming the earth. He laughed out loud. A good thing or bad, he wasn't certain. All he knew was he'd saved Alyssa and Cai, and that was enough.

Switching on the low-wattage bed lamp, he crossed to stand before the freestanding mirror in the corner. Was Alyssa in the room watching him? Was the smell of roses only a figment of his confused mind? Had she already passed over?

He searched the mirror, but there was no sign of her. Then his gaze went to his own image, and the hair on the back of his neck prickled. A shiver washed down his back. Was it his imagination, or was there the slightest hint of another image superimposed over his own? Did the face look more angular, the jaw harder? He slanted the mirror to a different angle.

The black hair on the man in the mirror waved and

hung past his shoulders and there, standing at a distance behind him, was a woman. He went very still. A woman with a riot of long red curls, deep emerald eyes, full lips, and fine brows—a woman with the face of an angel—Alyssa de Morgan. His tongue stuck to the roof of his mouth, and his throat seized up. All he could do was stare into those wide green eyes.

She no longer wore the yellow gown and headdress she had in his dream, but the white shift she had worn the first night he had seen her clutching the gate in the rain.

Their gazes held in the reflection.

He swallowed, trying to free up his throat. Trying to say words that refused to form. He watched her drift closer, yet no step could he detect on the polished floorboards.

He swung around. She was gone. He flung back. She stood behind him with reproach painted across her face. It was as if he was a moth and her gaze the flame. "Sorry. I should have remembered." He spoke quietly, afraid to raise his voice lest she disappear. "I thought you would be gone. I didn't know…" He touched the looking glass where her image stood. "Was it real?" he asked. "Or was it all a dream? Did I really kill Gedrych de Morgan last night?"

She drifted closer, and the heat of her body reached out to him in the reflection. She raised her arms, encircled his waist, and leaned her soft cheek against his shoulder.

His mouth dried again, and he couldn't swallow.

"Thank you," she whispered.

He had always thought a ghost would be cold, but he had never felt such heat as that which now infused his body and raced to pool in his loins at the caress of her silken hair and soft hands on his body. He hardened with desire, and she tilted her head to the side, watching him in the mirror through sooty lashes, her eyes dark and intense with wanting. Then she stepped back, and everything happened at once.

The roof vanished, exposing pure blue sky with one perfect white cloud. White light streamed from the cloud to encompass Alyssa's body.

He swung and tried to seize her, but his hands passed through her spirit as she ascended through an almost blinding light.

"Wait," he cried. "There are so many questions—I wanted to get to know you."

Her smile was radiant as she hovered above him, just out of reach. "You *have* known me, Cole de Morgan. You have known me better than any. You have known me in two lifetimes, and you *will* know me again. I promise." Then she faded from sight.

The roof closed over. He felt alone and bereft. Then he smiled. What a fool. He should have known he could never capture something as elusive as an angel.

He pulled on a pair of blue jeans and a clean white shirt from the case which someone must have popped into his room overnight, moved to the door, and stepped out into the hall.

Chapter Twenty-One

Still half dazed, Cole wandered down the steps and into the foyer. It was early; he surmised Jeannie was still in bed. He cut through the kitchen and followed the partly overgrown path that once led to the stone garden. The large standing stones were gone, of course, but the garden stood still intact and surrounded by a high green trellis, as he'd seen from his window.

Wondering if the stone bench on which Alyssa once sat to await Aidan survived, he fought his way through an arch of white banksia covering the entrance. A red rose caught at his jeans, and he bent to brush it aside, pricking his finger painfully in the process. Sucking the blood from the small wound, he continued on.

The garden held more plants than he imagined: hollyhocks, bluebells, violets, daisies, and roses. It was a veritable hothouse; even a small kumquat tree resided at its center.

Suddenly he stilled as a sound came to him on the breeze, and he strained to listen.

The soft gentle tune of a bygone era, the tinkling strands of a music box—*Greensleeves*. Around six feet ahead stood the ancient stone bench with a lion and a rose carved into the sides, and on the bench sat a young woman with deep red hair. She glanced up and eyes the color of brilliant emeralds sparkled. She came to her feet, and he could only open his mouth and stare.

"I think you better shut that, or you might catch a bug." She laughed. A soft, happy sound. "There are varied species roaming this garden, from what I've studied. But the beauty of the place far outweighs the disadvantages, don't you think?" The young woman cocked her head to the side in the same manner Alyssa had used in the mirror, not an hour before. However, Cole was certain Alyssa had never worn cut-off denim shorts that showed legs that stretched all the way to heaven and more. Or had she?

He lifted his gaze from her legs and closed the gap between them to look down at the music box. It was exquisite and very old, decorated with precious gems and embossed with an *A*. "Alyssa?" The name was released on a heavy breath. "Where did you get this?"

"Jeannie gave it to me, and yes, Alyssa." The young woman laughed again softly. "Not the one about which you would be thinking, though. However, I have been told I resemble our notorious ghost."

"You know of her? You have seen her?"

The girl picked up the music box and handed it to him to inspect. "Careful, it's very fragile, and yes, of course, everyone around here knows the story, but I have never seen her myself except in the painting with Aidan de Morgan in Jeannie's parlor. So tragic and romantic, don't you think?" She went quiet, studying him. "You know, you look a bit like him. Except for the hair, of course."

He smiled. "You think so?"

"I know so. I have stared at that painting so many times, wondering what those days must have been like. Very hard, from what Jeannie has told me."

"I've heard one tale, but I'm not sure if it's the same

one you mention. Could you tell me *your* version?" He wondered if it had changed. Then realized it must have.

She looked a little uncertain. After all, he was a stranger.

"If…you like." Her answer came hesitantly. She stood for a moment more, then indicated the stone bench. "Do you think we could sit first?" Her tone lightened, and she smiled.

He nodded, and she settled onto the bench and waited until he took the place beside her. "I'm sure it's probably the same story." She glanced down at her folded hands.

"I've heard only one. You know? How Alyssa, being a trophy of war, fell in love with Cai de Morgan. How the King summoned Cai to fight at Marston Moor and he lost his life while saving Prince Rupert. How Alyssa swore on his grave that she would haunt the castle until he returned to her, and the next morning they found her body at the bottom of the cliffs."

Cole stared down at the music box, his hands tightening till they hurt, his insides suddenly cold, his mood dispirited. So, for all he'd been through, this is how he'd changed history. All had been for naught. That in the great scheme of things, the first Alyssa had been *meant* to die. History had been altered, yes. But he hadn't saved her at all. It had all been about Cai and Alyssa's love. A love that could not perish. A love that would stretch throughout eternity and through all the phases of history. And fortunately, or unfortunately, he just happened to be one of those phases.

He tried to hide his dismay. "Then how did Alyssa come to be in the painting with Aidan?" he asked, now curious to know the rest of the story.

"It is claimed Aidan was Cai de Morgan's reincarnated soul if you believe in such things." She looked at him as if waiting for him to speak, and then when he didn't, she went on. "It is told that after a quarrel with Aidan, a witch named Eleanor performed a pagan ritual to send Alyssa to the afterlife, but instead it restored her to life. It's rather hard to believe, and creepy really when you think about it, yet somehow still romantic." She held out her hand. "I am Alyssa Llewellyn, her namesake. I feel my parents had a warped sense of humor the day they named me."

He took Alyssa Llewellyn's small hand in his larger one and didn't release it as he set the music box on the stone bench. The workmanship and condition of the box was impeccable, but he was more interested now in the warm-blooded woman beside him. Her hand was soft and thankfully belonged to someone very much alive. Involuntarily, he stroked a knuckle down the curve of her cheek. "The resemblance, it's uncanny. Where did you come from?"

She frowned and pulled away just a little, and his hand dropped to his knee.

"From my mother, I hope. My father, Ted, is the groundskeeper here. I teach in St. Agnes and visit on weekends. They have a cottage down back of the property."

"I will look forward to the weekends and getting to know you better. I hope you don't mind me saying that." He released her hand and stood, not wishing to seem overly familiar. "St. Agnes," he said, looking over her shoulder. "Charming village. I stopped there last night. Met a man called Fergus Dane. Do you know him?" He looked back at her.

She laughed. “My uncle. You will find if you are staying around here for a time many people in these parts are related.” She viewed him almost shyly, then glanced away. “You *are* staying?”

“I have just found out I’ve inherited the castle. I was wondering what there was to keep me here.” He smiled. “Now I know. The prospect has suddenly grown more appealing with the sunrise.”

She laughed and peered up at him from beneath her lashes. “And what would that be now?”

“Why, meeting all your relations, of course.”

She gave another small laugh. “I think, Cole de Morgan, you are a man I will have to watch.”

He raised a brow. “I hope so.” He reached for her hand. “I was wondering if…” He paused, not wanting to frighten her overmuch but unable to contain himself. “If perhaps we could share breakfast and you tell me a few more stories? If there are any to tell.”

She looked away, then back again. He sensed her hesitation and didn’t blame her; after all, he was pushing his luck. “We could go back to the keep. I don’t know if Mary is awake, but I’m certain I could rustle up some cheese and eggs for an omelet. Or we could drive to St. Agnes. I still have the hire car from last night.”

She wavered only fractionally. “I do know a tale of a seventeenth-century countess who once met a tragic end. Will that do?”

“Was her name Meredith, by any chance?”

“You already know the story?” The light died from her eyes.

“Not all of it, no.”

“Good.” She brightened. “Then I shall tell you all I know.” She linked her arm through his, but as he turned her away, she hung back. "Better still, would you care to join *me* for breakfast down at the gatehouse? I could cook you some of my famous French toast."

"The gatehouse? He frowned. I thought you lived with your parents."

She raised a fine brow. "Did I actually say that? No. Jeanie allows me the use of the gatehouse on weekends."

He nodded. He could see *this* Alyssa, like her predecessor, was a woman to keep him guessing. "You mentioned famous French toast. Why famous?"

"The recipe belonged to Tom Jeffreys, the old steward, no less."

"You have heard of Tom Jeffreys?" His tone was incredulous.

She smiled and shook her hair back from her face, peering up at him through sparkling green eyes. "Of course. No self-respecting ghost story would be without an old steward, would it?" She laughed merrily and took his arm, and they chatted quietly as they strolled toward the postern gate. Although he listened to the clear dulcet tones of her soft voice, his thoughts were already drifting to another red-haired woman from a time long ago. A time when his name was Cai de Morgan and he had first looked into the bright emerald eyes of a woman called Alyssa and knew that he loved her and would love her through all eternity.

He turned and glanced over his shoulder as an odd sensation prickled his neck, compelling him to do so.

Beside the music box, wet with dew, lay a blood-red rose.

THE END

A word about the author…

Hello, and thanks for reading my book. I grew up in North East Victoria Australia, and live with my two spoiled Oriental cats, Keila and Sarsha. In my early days I enjoyed reading the likes of Lord of the Rings, Once and Future King, and every fairy tale I could get my hands on.

Later on, I fell in love with the works of David Gemmell, Terry Brooks, Johanna Lindsey, Rosemary Rodgers, and Barbara Cartland. My love of both Fantasy and the Romance genres prompted me to try my hand at my own novel and I began writing in 1995.

My first release, Time of the Wolf, was published in 999 and went on to win the 1999 Dorothy Parker RIO Award for Women's fantasy fiction. The book also placed as a runner-up in the Australian RWA Ruby Award, the USA PEARL AWARD, and the SAPPHIRE AWARD.

I am delighted to say The Wild Rose Press re-released Time of the Wolf in 2019. It went on to garner 5-star reviews from all reviewers who read it and won the Crowned Heart Award from InD'tale Magazine.

My hobbies include reading and listening to audiobooks, gardening, PlayStation games, and traveling. I have visited the UK, Thailand, and many European countries, and hope to one day visit the U.S.

Thank you for purchasing
this publication of The Wild Rose Press, Inc.

For questions or more information
contact us at
info@thewildrosepress.com.

The Wild Rose Press, Inc.
www.thewildrosepress.com

www.ingramcontent.com/pod-product-compliance
Lightning Source LLC
LaVergne TN
LVHW020533100826
845148LV00010B/1447

* 9 7 8 1 5 0 9 2 5 2 8 5 5 *